In the Company of Like-Minded Women

A Novel By
Elaine Russell

Belle Histoires
2743 14th Street
Sacramento, California 95818
www.elainerussell.info

Publisher's Note: This is a work of fiction. Names and characters, places, and incidents are a product of the author's imagination. Locales and public names are sometimes used for atmospheric purposes. Any resemblance to actual people, living or dead, or to businesses, companies, events, institutions, or locales is completely coincidental.

Cover Design: My Custom Book Cover

Book Layout © 2017 BookDesignTemplates.com

In the Company of Like-Minded Women/Elaine Russell. -- 1st ed.
ISBN 978-1-7324994-0-9

For my great-grandmother Dr. Elizabeth (Lida) B. Russell, an early advocate for women.

To throw obstacles in the way of a complete education is like putting out the eyes.

Elizabeth Cady Stanton

I think the girl who is able to earn her own living and pay her own way should be as happy as anybody on earth. The sense of independence and security is very sweet.

Susan B. Anthony

In the adjustment of the new order of things, we women demand an equal voice; we shall accept nothing less.

Carrie Chapman Catt

Contents

On Small Miracles

T he assembled crowd on platform two exuded a touch of trepidation, which sparked the air like fireflies glowing on a hot summer night. This Saturday morning, June 22,1901, we waited for the Union Pacific train due into Denver at six o'clock, but it was already twenty-three minutes late.

Mama fussed with her auburn hair and checked Papa's gold pocket watch, which she'd worn pinned to her waist since he'd passed two years before. "Where can they be, Sara Jane?" she asked in a voice riddled with worry.

"I'm sure it will be here any minute." I tried to sound confident, although unease niggled at my middle. At fifteen years old, I was unaccustomed to being the one to offer reassurance.

At long last, the planks beneath our feet began to tremble, and a great roar, like a fierce windstorm sweeping through the Rocky Mountains Fremont Pass, rolled across the station. A charcoal plume rose from around the bend as the clacking of wheels grew louder. The black nose of a steam engine barreled into the station, sending a collective *aah* through the anxious throng. I covered my ears to soften the piercing screech of locking brakes and metal wheels scraping on the tracks. The train lurched to a stop and belched a final blast of smoke and cinders.

Mama took a deep breath and grabbed the hand of my five-year-old brother, Cole. The imminent arrival of her two sisters, Mildred and Evangeline, or Eva, as she was called, from Lawrence, Kansas, had set her aflutter in a way foreign to her nature. It left me feeling untethered. My self-assured and resolute mother, always ready with a warm smile and encouraging words, had momentarily gone missing. Where was the bold woman who marched for women's rights and battled the multitudes of injustices burdening our world, the woman who had persevered through four years of medical school despite the daunting odds? I needed her comfort once more. True, we had not seen my aunts since my family's unhappy trip to Lawrence eleven years before, when I was not quite five years of age. Clearly a deep uncertainty caused Mama's disquiet this day.

My aunts' arrival seemed nothing short of a small miracle to me, although I doubted grumpy old Sister Agnes at Catechism class would agree. No one from Mama's family had ever come to visit us. All she would say on the subject was that, with the exception of Aunt Eva, she didn't "get on" with her family. She always added that speaking ill of others served no purpose. So it came as a strike of lightning, perhaps a message from a higher power, when Aunt Mildred's letter had arrived two weeks earlier announcing their trip. She and Aunt Eva planned to stay six weeks with us, the better part of summer.

I whispered a quick prayer of thanks to Saint Christopher, the patron saint of travelers, that my aunts had not met with an accident, train robbers, or an attack by a band of Indians—all still possibilities. Being new to saints, after our recent conversion to the Catholic faith, I felt uncertain of their powers. Did these holy spirits listen to the pleas of someone like me, who had yet to take communion?

Conductors emerged from the train cars in unison, like the two carved cuckoos that popped out of our grandfather clock each hour in the entry hall at home. They placed stairs on the platform and assisted ladies stepping down. A regiment of porters with trolleys waited to collect luggage.

Cole glanced up at Mama, his sleepy blue eyes filled with worry. "Will they like me?"

A smile touched Mama's lips for the first time that day. "Of course they will." She placed a damp hand beneath my elbow and edged us forward little by little, scanning the weary travelers descending from the train. Her fingers pressed tighter around me. "Do you see them?" A note close to panic tinged her voice.

I doubted I would recognize my aunts, as I remembered little of our meeting when I was young. My knowledge of their faces came from a sepia photograph sitting on the bookshelf in our library. It had been taken six years earlier in front of a big house with my grandmother and assorted aunts, uncles, and cousins standing on the lawn. Sometimes I stared at the barely discernable faces trying to remember if I had met them. Had I played with any of the children? I asked Mama questions, and occasionally she explained their relationship to us. Now I searched to find a flicker of familiarity among the multitude of people streaming down the platform.

"Mildred, over here." Mama's arm flew up in the air as she rushed off, leaving Cole and me behind.

Aunt Mildred stepped from the Pullman car onto the platform, securing a stray wisp of graying hair under a simple black straw hat. Her beige poplin traveling suit and white blouse made her pale skin look sallow. If it had been up to me, I would have dressed her in a soft green with a more flattering cut to the suit. Her plain face was broad in the forehead with narrow eyes set close together and a chin that disappeared into the multiple folds of her neck. Yet with her hefty figure drawn up straight and her shoulders arched back, she had a commanding presence. A great sigh escaped her lips as she raised a hand of recognition.

Mama, always quick with a loving embrace, threw her arms around Aunt Mildred and kissed her cheek. Aunt Mildred stiffened, and her eyes went wide. Her arms hung at her sides as if she had no recollection of how to hug someone back. She stepped away, clutching her reticule.

My breath caught in my throat. Standing on the step behind Mama and Aunt Mildred, smiling down like a benevolent spirit, was one of the loveliest women I had ever seen. Aunt Eva was twenty-five years old, fifteen years younger than Mama. The photograph at home completely failed to capture the delicate features of her oval face: the small, straight nose, and shapely lips. She glanced at me with large, intelligent eyes the brilliant blue of a Colorado sky on a clear day. Her silk voile traveling suit, a shade darker than her eyes, had a rounded bolero jacket with a large collar. Decorative tucks adorned the collar, sleeves, and waist. It looked exactly like the sketch of a French design I had cut out of the March issue of the *Ladies' Home Journal*. I knew immediately we would share a common interest in fashion and design. Her wide-brimmed gray hat, decorated with blue silk ribbons and two ostrich feathers, tipped to one side above a cloud of silver-white hair. She had warned us in a letter that the scarlet fever, which nearly took her life the previous October, had sapped the color from her normally brunette hair. She appeared thin and frail, reminding me of the baby bluebird Cole had found in the backyard under the oak tree a few weeks before, almost fully formed yet not quite strong enough to fly away.

Despite the age difference and miles separating their lives, Aunt Eva and Mama cherished their relationship. They wrote to each other every week without fail. How Mama loved coming home after a long day to find a thick envelope filled with Aunt Eva's blue scented paper. After dinner we sat in the parlor while she read me the letter. The fine, even script held a treasure of stories with the latest news and gossip about family and friends in Lawrence. Her writing entranced me: witty and clever, sometimes a bit sly, but never mean. It was my favorite part of the week. Often the news set Mama to reminiscing, recounting tales of her girlhood, a dreamy time in a different world. I always wanted to know more.

That previous October a week had passed, then two and three, without a letter from Aunt Eva. Mama grew distraught and sent a wire to Aunt Mildred. Three days later a wire arrived back: *Eva ill with scarlet fever. Past worst. Recovering. Mildred.*

"I can't believe they didn't let me know sooner," Mama muttered. An anger I had never seen before erupted like a shower of sparks from an imploding fireplace log. She bit her lip and marched off to the library. Cole and I tiptoed after her, hovering by the nearly closed door. She paced across the carpet and ranted to the bookshelves. "What mean-spirited people, impervious to my feelings, finding yet another opportunity to punish me for marrying William and leaving home." She spread her arms in mock grandiosity. "Mother, Her Royal Highness, sitting on her throne, judging me, trying to rule everyone's lives. How could she keep this from me?"

Cole let out a nervous giggle, undoubtedly baffled—as was I—by Mama's strange behavior. Mama rushed to open the door and found us. "Oh, my dears," she gasped, "those rash words were never meant for your ears. Promise me you'll never repeat them." Cole and I solemnly swore ourselves to silence.

"I'm just so worried about Aunt Eva," she said, hugging us close and bursting into tears.

Almost a month had passed before Aunt Eva was able to write us. Her shaky scrawl promised she was feeling stronger at last and would send more news soon. Mama had written letter after letter begging her to visit us. Colorado was renowned for its restorative dry, clean air and temperate climate. Large sanatoriums in Denver and surrounding areas drew patients with tuberculosis and other ailments from around the country for treatment.

Aunt Eva regretted that no one could accompany her, and she felt too weak to make the trip alone. She said my grandmother's arthritis and nerves prohibited her from traveling, which prompted Mama to mumble, "Thank the lord for that." Aunt Mildred claimed she couldn't possibly leave her husband, my uncle Franklin, for such a long period.

Then Aunt Mildred's note had suddenly appeared in the mail at the start of June without explanation, announcing their arrival. A curious turn of events.

Aunt Mildred stepped aside and snapped her fingers for a porter. Aunt Eva descended the last step and fell into Mama's waiting arms. They hugged and kissed as tears spilled down their cheeks.

"Oh, Lida," Aunt Eva cried, stepping back at last and dabbing her eyes with a lace handkerchief. "You are a sight for sore eyes. And the children." She touched Cole's cheek. "What a fine boy. The spitting image of his father."

Cole stared up at her, his mouth agape. "Are you an angel?"

Eva tilted her head back, releasing a soft chime of laughter. "No, my darling; far from it, I'm afraid." She turned to me. "And, Sara Jane, you've grown into a young lady, a beauty like your mother."

Aunt Mildred studied me with a deep frown. I felt self-conscious that my white cotton dress, not yet three months old, reached an inch above my ankles. I'd grown nearly two inches since my last birthday the previous August. "Tall for her age," she said. "What are you now, fourteen?"

"I'll be sixteen in August, Aunt Mildred. We're ever so pleased to have you visit." Awkward and uncertain under her appraising gaze, I dipped in a small curtsy.

Cole glanced at me with a puzzled expression. With great ceremony, he bowed to Mildred and said, "Your Highness."

Mildred startled. "You say the oddest things, child."

"But Mama," Cole began before I put my hand over his mouth and whispered in his ear I would explain later.

"This is your aunt Mildred," Mama said quickly, "and this is Aunt Eva."

"Horrible trip. I have a splitting headache," Aunt Mildred said, mopping her brow with a cotton handkerchief.

"I know you're exhausted. We'll find a cart to deliver the trunks and valises and get a carriage home," Mama said as passengers continued to pour past us. Large immigrant families and modestly clad farmers, carrying bundles wrapped in paper and string, worked their way down the platform from the third-class cars at the far end of the train.

Mama placed a hand under Aunt Mildred's elbow, leading our small contingent through the Union Station lobby. Our footsteps echoed on the marble floors of the cavernous hall as travelers bustled to and fro. I held onto Cole, and Aunt Eva slipped a hand through my arm and squeezed it gently.

"The soot and smoke were unbearable. Almost twenty hours on that infernal train, and I never slept a wink," Aunt Mildred complained to Mama.

Aunt Eva smiled at me. "I was too excited to sleep much, either, but it wasn't so bad. The meals in the dining car were delicious, and we chatted with a lovely couple headed for Los Angeles.

I gazed shyly at Aunt Eva as fleeting images of our trip to Kansas returned to me. What I recalled most clearly was the thrill of riding the train to a faraway place. While Mama held my brother Peter, two and a half, I perched on Papa's lap and watched the flat barren landscape fly by outside the window. Papa and I made a game of spotting distant farmhouses, cattle, or bunnies hopping among the sagebrush—any sign of life. Soon my excitement turned to boredom on the seemingly endless ride. Papa invented funny stories about other passengers and where they were traveling, relating them in his deep voice, until I drifted off to sleep. The biggest treat was eating dinner in the dining car. We sat at a table with a white linen tablecloth while they served our food on china plates.

The waiter brought me a cup of hot chocolate and two butter cookies for dessert.

"You've been a proper young lady," he said. "So grown-up and polite." Even little Peter had behaved himself.

The details of our time in Lawrence remained hazy in my mind, but now flashes came to me of a picnic on the Kansas River, a Fourth of July parade, and an argument between Mama and my grandmother that sent us packing home. I never understood what caused the trouble. Whenever I asked, Mama said it was best forgotten. Aunt Eva, fourteen at the time, had doted on Peter and me. She insisted on giving me one of her beautiful porcelain dolls. I played with it for hours on the train as we retraced our path across the plains amid a somber silence and Mama's occasional tears. I treasured the doll and still kept it by my bed.

Out in front of the train station, Mama found a man with a flatbed cart to deliver the luggage, then we stood in line for a carriage.

Aunt Mildred stared down Seventeenth Street, which was quiet at this hour of the morning. Only a scattering of people dotted the sidewalks. One of our brightly painted red-and-yellow streetcars rolled down the tracks, clanging its bell. "I can't imagine why you continue to live in this place," she said after a moment.

Mama's mouth flew open, but she held her tongue.

Aunt Eva put a hand on Mama's arm. "How wonderful you have electric trams."

Mama relaxed. "We're very up-to-date."

"I ride the tram with Sara Jane," Cole boasted.

Aunt Eva leaned down to his level. "Maybe you'll take me for a ride one day."

Cole beamed. "Yes, ma'am." He reached up and took her hand.

Aunt Eva nodded toward the white-capped mountain peaks visible beyond the tops of city buildings. "The mountains look like an artist painted them as a backdrop for a theater. I shall take long walks and breathe in the delightful, clean air." She grinned at Mama. "And we'll have all the time in the world to catch up."

"Slow down, Eva," Aunt Mildred said, reminding me of stern, uncompromising Sister Agnes. "You're still recovering from the scarlet fever."

My eyes darted between my aunts, as different in appearance and temperament as one could imagine, the essence of winter and spring. Their visit promised changes that I could not begin to anticipate. Whatever happened, I felt sure it would not be a boring summer.

Chapter 2   **LIDA**

More than Meets the Eye

I sat next to Eva in the carriage, clutching her arm to reassure myself my dear sister was truly there in flesh and blood. Her presence calmed me like a soothing balm. Wise beyond her age, Eva understood me better than any person next to my beloved William. We had forged a bond not in childhood—for she was only three when I left for college, and I married right after graduating—but through our correspondence over subsequent years. For the pleasure of Eva's company, I could endure Mildred's unpleasant temperament. I would put aside my anger with Mildred for siding with Mother in rejecting my marriage to William and the unforgiveable words she spoke at our last meeting. In my heart, I hoped we might find a way to mend the rift and start anew.

Eva appeared terribly thin and delicate, like a sapling barely able to withstand a strong wind. I feared the raging fevers that had racked her body had left her more damaged than she would admit. After Mildred's wire arrived, I read every medical book and journal article on scarlet fever I could locate. Little was known of the long term effects for patients who survived severe fevers, other than anecdotal accounts.

In November I wrote Dr. Bartley, the family's longtime physician in Lawrence, explaining how I would be graduating from medical school in five months. I asked as one doctor to another for his diagnosis of Eva—the extent of her illness and fevers, how he had treated her, and the prognosis for her future. He responded with a terse note informing me that I had no standing to question him or ask for such information. He took the opportunity to advise me to find another profession. In his opinion women were unfit in mind and body to endure the rigors of practicing medicine. Did I not understand the female brain was smaller than men's and less capable of complex reasoning? That I should even consider taking the well-being and health of others into my hands was indefensible and close to criminal. This infuriated me beyond words, of course, but it was hardly the first or last time a male colleague would insult me or degrade my abilities as a physician.

I had completed my medical degree that April at the Denver Homeopathy Medical College, one of four medical schools in the Denver area. The colleges all welcomed women applicants because of the intense competition to attract the few students interested in pursuing a medical career. I shared the philosophy of the homeopathy school, which strove to meld modern science with less invasive natural treatments. I assumed the school staff and students would be more open-minded toward women joining the profession. While true of some, the progressive attitude did not extend to all. Most of my teachers were male, and only one other woman student joined me in our class of twenty-six. My female compatriot did nothing to help our cause when she quit after the first year to marry and move to Montana. I endured four years of male doctors and students treating me with disdain and belittling my intellect. Somehow I persisted and graduated first in our class. My revenge. I had the advantage of being older and clearly focused on my purpose of helping others.

"Normally I work on Saturdays, but a friend is filling in for me today. What a treat to have two free days to welcome you here." I squeezed Eva's arm. "How are you feeling?"

"I'm fine." Eva tossed her head as if the question no longer needed consideration.

"She tires easily," Mildred said, "and you can see she hasn't regained her appetite. You look a bit peaked yourself. Too thin, the both of you."

"What with finishing school and beginning work...it's been busy." I didn't know why I felt compelled to respond to Mildred's comment. Certainly it was none of her business.

I had the carriage driver turn down Sixteenth Street so I could point out the Tabor Opera House, one of the grandest buildings in Denver. "All the best touring companies perform here," I said. "The interior is beautiful."

"Mama took me there to see my first opera in March, *El Capitan*," Sara Jane said. "It was thrilling."

"I bought tickets for a performance of Gilbert and Sullivan's *The Mikado* in a few weeks," I added.

"How wonderful!" Eva exclaimed.

Mildred stared out the window. "The building looks more like a dry-goods store with all those businesses on the ground floor."

I studied my elder sister, awash with unkind thoughts that sapped my good intentions to get along with her. While not quite four years my senior, her silver-streaked hair and wide girth made her appear at least ten years older. She had gained a great deal of weight since our last meeting eleven years before. Her jacket and skirt strained at the seams, and her wedding ring cut into her pudgy finger. She looked not only unbecoming but uncomfortable. I had noticed her struggle while climbing into the carriage, complaining of arthritis in her knees. Her chest rose and fell with labored, wheezy breaths, perhaps a reaction to the altitude. She had turned into an old woman, taking on the demeanor of our mother.

Although never what one would call pretty in a classic sense, as a young woman Mildred had been witty and full of spirit, cutting an appealing figure that attracted many suitors. Back then we were close, laughing and sharing confidences about boys as we emerged from childhood to become young women. I wondered what had happened to my fun-loving sister.

The driver turned onto Colfax and continued past the State Capitol with its imposing dome. He pulled in the horses to a slower clip, taking us down Pennsylvania Street then Logan Avenue, as if he wanted to show off the elegant mansions of Denver's wealthiest residents that lined the streets. Mildred stared out the window, allowing several low murmurs of approval to escape her lips.

"This area is called Capitol Hill. You can't imagine how the city has grown since William and I first arrived in '84." Pride swelled in my voice for this former Wild West mining town that had transformed itself into a thriving metropolis, with all the amenities of the modern age. I couldn't help boasting. I suppose part of me still needed to justify my life, to prove to Mildred and, in turn, my mother, that I had made the right choice. It irked me considerably that I could not let go of this infantile need for approval.

"We're almost there," Cole said, bouncing off his seat.

"We live in the more modest part of the neighborhood, but a pleasant street nonetheless," I said.

Our carriage veered onto Seventh Avenue then turned down Pearl Street and halted in front of our two-story Queen Anne home. Dark-brown trim and patterned shingles beneath the gables set off the white clapboard walls. If one looked closely, it became apparent that the front porch sagged slightly on the right side and the paint had cracked around the window sills and door jambs. I hoped the profusion of lilacs, roses, and daisies filling the front yard with color and an enticing scent would distract from our home's flaws.

After Mildred's letter arrived, I had done what I could to make things more presentable, hiring a temporary day woman to help our housekeeper, Katherine, scrub the house from top to bottom. Sara Jane carried excess clutter from the spare bedrooms to the attic and planted fiery red geraniums in the front porch window boxes. I replaced the parlor curtains and bought new linens for my sisters. A handyman fixed the drip in the faucet in the upstairs bathroom and replaced the cracked windowpane in the dining room (the result of one of Cole's misguided tosses of his red rubber ball). But many other details still needed attention.

The driver helped Mildred down as the rest of us climbed out the other side. Mildred insisted on paying the fare.

"It looks exactly like the photograph you sent," Eva said, "only it's even prettier in person."

I pointed to the new addition on the left side of the house. "This is my medical office. The builders finished it right before..." I stopped, a hard lump forming in my throat. I found it impossible to speak of William's death as merely a sidenote to a story, referenced in the most inconsequential way. The grief I kept locked away sprang up when least expected. It caught me unaware when someone made a comment, which might be totally unrelated to William but somehow evoked a memory. Or when I glimpsed a picture or an object he had given me and recalled our happy times together.

Cole clamored up the front steps then turned around. "Aunt Eva, I'll show you my bug collection."

"Oh, Cole, no one wants to see your silly bugs," Sara Jane said, affecting her most grown-up tone to place herself squarely among the adults.

"You're wrong, my dear. I'm very interested," Eva said. "I majored in biology in college, so I learned a great deal about insects."

Mildred held onto the railing, pulling herself up the porch steps with some effort. Sara Jane took an elbow to help her, but Mildred shook her off. "I don't need assistance, for heaven's sake." Her tone was sharp yet carried a trace of embarrassment.

Cole threw open the front door and pounded through the hall, his new leather shoes clacking on the wooden floors. "Katherine, we're here," he cried out.

As we crowded into the entry near the stairway, Katherine emerged from the kitchen and hurried through the dining room, wiping her hands on her apron. "My lord, such a racket ye make," she said, ruffling Cole's hair. Wisps of red tresses escaped the tight bun on top of her head and circled her freckled cheeks and brow like puffs from a cottonwood tree riding the wind. Her green eyes nearly disappeared in a broad grin. The deep wrinkles lining her face, born of the unfathomable loss of her family, aged her beyond her thirty-nine years.

"Katherine McClellan, these are my sisters Mrs. Bolton and Miss Delacroix." I turned to my sisters. "Katherine is our housekeeper and lives in the apartment over the carriage house. We couldn't have survived these past years without her."

"Thank ye, Dr. Clayton." Katherine's cheek's bloomed pink splotches as she curtsied. "And welcome ye are. Once ye settle in, I'll have breakfast and a pot of hot coffee ready."

"That sounds heavenly," Eva said. "I must wash up. After all those hours on the train, I feel gritty."

Cole led the way to the second floor, an excited jack rabbit hopping on the newly polished steps. Our enormous orange tiger cat sat at the top of stairs, licking a paw and warily watching the group ascend. Cole gathered her into his arms. "This is Buttercup."

"You'll have to put that creature outside," Mildred said, stepping as far away as possible on the landing. "I dislike cats. They shed hair everywhere."

"Sara Jane, take her out to the yard when you come down," I said.

Buttercup jumped from Cole's arms and pattered down the hall toward the back of the house, indifferent to the fuss.

Sara Jane showed Eva to the guest room across from my bedroom, while I steered Mildred to the front room next to mine.

Mildred removed her hat and jacket, placing them on the caned rocking chair. She collapsed on the bed with a heavy sigh and sagging shoulders. "I believe I shall have a nap. We had a sleeper car, but I never found a moment's rest the entire way. So much noise and the constant rocking back and forth."

"Of course. Katherine will keep something warm for you."

She gently touched the quilt embroidered with lilac violets. A soft breeze drifted through the open window rustling the white organdy curtains and carrying the sweetness of the climbing roses into the room. A cream-colored afghan lay across the bottom of the bed, which Aunt Effie, our favorite aunt, had crocheted for me when I married William. Katherine had placed a vase filled with sweet peas and coral bells from the backyard on the dresser and a pitcher of water and a glass on the nightstand.

"The room is very pleasant. Thank you." Mildred's eyes met mine, looking softer now. Perhaps she meant to call a truce, to find a way back from the deep chasm between us.

"Of course. Get some rest now." I hurried out of the room and softly closed the door.

Eva joined Sara Jane and me in the family parlor thirty minutes later, where I'd asked Katherine to serve us cinnamon rolls and coffee so we could be more relaxed. Eva, washed and refreshed, looked the picture of summer in a pale coral linen blouse with a straight collar, ruffled at the top, and the new puffy bishop sleeves. Feather stitching in a deeper shade of coral ran down the front, along the sleeves, and around the neck. It was tucked into a white linen gored skirt that flared into soft folds around her feet. Her white hair was gathered in a loose pompadour. I envied her natural affinity for stylish, youthful fashions that suited her so well.

"Look out for Cole's box," I warned as she stepped near his bug collection, which lay in the middle of the floor. The wooden apple box, lined with an old tea towel and white gauze, contained a cricket, an assortment of black beetles, a slightly shriveled, furry caterpillar, a yellow spotted butterfly with half a wing missing, and four pill bugs in various stages of curling into a ball.

Eva picked up the box and studied the contents for a moment. "It's quite nice. Where is Cole?"

Sara Jane sighed. "He's gone out back to find something new to add. I hope he doesn't dig up any flowers the way he did last week when he was trying to catch a worm."

I smiled. "We mustn't squelch the budding scientist, dear. Katherine will keep an eye if he attempts anything naughty."

Eva placed the collection to the side of the fireplace and sank onto the settee next to me. "I have to pinch myself that I'm really here."

She gazed around the room as if savoring the details of our home, most of which I had probably described at some point in one or another of my letters. Her eyes stopped on the silver-framed photograph sitting on the rosewood side table next to her. She picked up the formal family portrait taken five years before on William's thirty-eighth birthday. I was perched in a straight-backed wooden chair holding three-month-old Cole in my lap. William stood behind me, his hand on my shoulder, attempting to look dignified and serious in his dark suit and stiff, starched shirt, with his unruly sandy-blond hair slicked into place. But as always, a hint of mischief worked at the edges of his generous mouth. Sara Jane, ten years old at the time, had tightly braided pigtails the color of ripened wheat. She leaned her head on my right shoulder and peeked up shyly at the camera. And our dear Peter, seven years old, stood on my other side, white-gold curls tumbling down his

19

forehead, his hands hanging at his sides with fingers still in motion, barely containing his excitement. The image did not capture his sparkling blue eyes or his laughter that floated in the air like the happy trill of a meadowlark. God had lifted his soul from this world two months later, the result of an outbreak of typhoid fever. Now only our memories of Peter lived on.

"It was the last picture of all of us together," I whispered.

Eva squeezed my hand as her eyes grew misty. "Such terrible losses."

Sara Jane leaned forward with an anxious expression. I knew it pained her to see me so sad and stirred her own grief.

Thankfully, Katherine bustled into the room with the breakfast tray. "I made a fresh pot of coffee for ye and my special cinnamon rolls, don't ye know," she said.

"They look delicious. I'm ravenous," Eva said.

Katherine beamed. "Can I bring ye some eggs and bacon?"

Eva smiled. "Oh, no thank you."

"Well, I have a lovely roast beef for the luncheon," Katherine said as she headed back to the kitchen.

I poured coffee and handed out plates of rolls as Eva related the latest news from our cousin Lois and her husband, George. They had recently moved with their five children from Lawrence to Richmond, Virginia. "Lois says George is getting involved in politics and hopes to run for office soon."

"Who would have imagined that the shy young man who came courting Lois would grow into such a confident, successful lawyer?" I drifted off for a moment, feeling wistful for those innocent days long ago when we had discovered boys and the future's possibilities. "As I get older time passes too quickly," I said with a sigh. "But you're still young and have everything before you."

"Ha! Everyone in Lawrence thinks I'm a hopeless old maid! Imagine, twenty-five and not married," Eva said with mock horror.

I laughed. "What nonsense."

"They are right, I suppose. All my friends in Lawrence and from college are married now, and many have children," Eva said. "But I don't care a whit what anyone thinks. Anyway, I may surprise them yet, if I can only break free of mother."

"How is Mother faring?" I asked, working to keep my tone neutral.

"The same as always." Eva's lips twisted into a wry smile. "Every time I speak of going back to finish college, she relapses and takes to her bed. Dr. Bartley gives her laudanum and sherry."

"Oh dear, laudanum is very addictive."

"Don't worry. Once I agree to remain at home awhile longer, she has a miraculous recovery and gives it up."

Eva had followed in my footsteps by continuing her education on the East Coast, attending Bryn Mawr College in Pennsylvania. I had encouraged her to escape the small-minded attitudes of Lawrence and explore broader horizons. Mother was apoplectic over the decision, blaming me for putting foolish notions in Eva's head. My decision in 1879 to go to Smith College in Northampton, Massachusetts, had created a deep divide in our already testy relationship. I attributed much of her anger to the fact that Father had given me his blessing without first consulting her.

Eva persevered in the face of Mother's opposition and spent three years studying at Bryn Mawr, dutifully returning home each Christmas and summer. She hoped to become one of the rare women to go on for a postgraduate degree and a career teaching at a college. Shortly after Eva left for her final year, Mother suffered the first of her "spells." I never understood why it took Mother so long to devise this scheme, but naturally nothing would satisfy her except Eva return home to care for her. Eva complied, thinking it a brief interruption, a mere pause in her studies. Instead, Mother had manipulated her for three long years, feigning illness every time Eva mentioned leaving again for Bryn Mawr. Mother was particularly skilled at leveling heavy doses of guilt.

Dr. Bartley had diagnosed Mother's condition as a case of nervous prostration and hysteria. It didn't fool me. I knew she had the resilience and constitution of an ox. If anything ailed her, it was boredom, loneliness, and a lack of intellectual purpose in her life—not to mention a loss of control over her youngest child. She took to her bed for weeks on end, complaining of headaches and weakness, keeping poor Eva at her beck and call. She was unconscionably selfish to hold Eva hostage in this manner.

I wrote to Eva on several occasions, pressing her not to allow Mother to dictate her future out of some misguided sense of duty. She must get on with her own life, I urged. Given Eva's sweet nature, I withheld my most negative opinions regarding Mother. She wrote back explaining that Mother depended on her presence. She didn't have the courage to leave again and risk mother's demise. I sensed she also feared causing a permanent break and being exiled from the family as I had been.

"It is remarkable that she didn't come down with scarlet fever after tending to you, considering her delicate health." I could not keep the sarcasm from my voice.

Eva played with the remaining bite of her cinnamon roll. "She was very devoted, Lida. She stayed by my side the entire time. As did Mildred."

"Of course. That was unkind of me." I felt ashamed for being so petty, and in front of Sara Jane.

Eva put down her plate and took a deep breath. "I have something most urgent to tell you before Mildred comes down."

My pulse quickened at the ominous words. Was she feeling unwell? Or Mildred? What kind of calamity might be brewing?

Sara Jane, sitting erect and attempting to remain ladylike as she nibbled on her roll, peered over with interest.

Eva glanced at her uncertainly, then looked at me. "Perhaps I should wait until later."

Sara Jane's face fell.

Whatever Eva had to say, it wouldn't be anything untoward that Sara Jane could not hear. She was a mature and thoughtful girl by necessity, given how our lives had unfolded. "You may tell Sara Jane, if you're comfortable doing so."

"I promise not to tell anyone," Sara Jane said.

Eva smiled. "Of course, you're nearly grown."

The color in Eva's cheeks heightened as she stared at her hands. "I've met a gentleman, a lovely person. I mentioned him in several letters to you." Her words spilled out, gaining momentum like rain pouring off the eaves of the house. "I first made his acquaintance last August at a dinner given by my dear friends, Sylvia and James. He's an attorney from Boston who came to Lawrence to settle a property claim for a client. He had an introduction to James's law firm to make use of their offices while he stayed. We attended a second dinner together, then he called on me one afternoon at home to meet Mother. She acted horrid, barely responding to his questions, remaining dour and silent. After ten minutes, she claimed a headache and asked him to leave. Her rudeness stunned us both. I wept all evening."

She shook her head. "When he returned to Boston, we began corresponding. Mother made it clear she didn't approve of my acquaintance with him, claiming we knew nothing of his background and family. She warned me that there was no point in forming an attachment to someone in Boston whom I would likely never see again. When his letters arrived, she became sullen for days. I had him write to Sylvia's house instead.

"He came back to Lawrence for a few weeks the end of September before I took ill. We had dinner one night and tea another day at Sylvia's. I only mentioned it to Mother after he returned to Boston again."

Sara Jane's eyes sparkled with excitement, as—most likely—did mine. I remembered Eva mentioning a charming man several times, but nothing more seemed to transpire. Eva's remarkable beauty and sweet disposition had attracted dozens of suitors over the years in Lawrence and Pennsylvania. Yet no man had managed to capture her affections. She wrote of meeting boys who were too immature or frivolous or overbearing, always flawed in some fatal way.

"What is his name?" Sara Jane asked.

"Mr. Bertram Dearman." Eva's hand fluttered to her chest. "He is the kindest, most intelligent man I've ever met. We share the same ideals and interests in education and the many injustices plaguing society. He supports the women's vote, of course, or I could not possibly consider him worthy."

She smiled shyly. "I might add, he's extremely handsome. We are...most in love. I wanted to write more about him to you, but then I became ill and feared Mother or Mildred might intercept my letters." Her face crumpled with distress as she grabbed my hand. "I can't tell you how difficult it's been. They've conspired against us from the beginning.

"After I recovered from my illness, Mr. Dearman returned to Lawrence in March. Mother found out he was in town and forbade me to see him. The worst of it is Mildred sided with her. This cut me to the quick, as we've become quite close these past years." Eva's eyes sparkled with defiant tears and her chin trembled. "Mr. Dearman and I met in secret at Sylvia's several times, anyway."

"What happened next?" Sara Jane asked, leaning forward in her chair until she almost fell off.

"Mr. Dearman returned once more earlier this month, determined to find a way to win over Mother and Mildred. When Mother found out he was in town and wanted to talk with her, she flew into a rage. Her heart began palpitating, and Dr. Bartley warned me she must avoid all excitement."

My long-held anger and resentment flared up. "Now I understand why Mildred brought you here. To take you away from your young man."

"But how did Grandmother and Aunt Mildred find out?" Sara Jane asked.

Eva pulled a handkerchief from her pocket to wipe her eyes. "Sylvia's sister revealed our secret to a friend, and given the way people gossip in Lawrence, it wasn't long until Mother and Mildred heard. That's when Mildred bought our train tickets for Denver." She dabbed her wet cheeks. She looked up, alarmed. "Please don't think I didn't want to come. It means everything to me to be here with you. But I must find a way to be with Mr. Dearman as well."

"Whatever are their objections?" I asked.

"They invent endless arguments asserting that he's not suitable because they don't know anything about his past or his character. It happened too quickly, and he can't be trusted." She looked down once more. "Dr. Bartley told them my illness has left me too weak for marriage...and the possibility of bearing children." Her voice choked on these last words.

"That old goat," I grumbled. "Once you have settled in, I would like to examine you. There are a number of promising homeopathic treatments you could try to rebuild your constitution."

"I'm sure you'll find me perfectly healthy." Eva gave a vehement shake of her head. "Really, this is all about Mother. She wants to keep me at home forever, caring for her until I shrivel up into a bitter old woman as miserable as she has been her whole life. I know that is a most vile thing to say about my own mother, but I can't...c-can't stand it." Her voice dissolved into soft sobs, shaking her delicate shoulders.

"I'll help sort this out," I insisted, although I hadn't the slightest idea how to right this dreadful situation.

Eva lifted her head, struggling to catch her breath. "Mr. Dearman says he won't give up until he finds a way to win my family's approval." She blinked several times. "If he is unable to do so, I cannot say what I shall resort to."

Being Privy to a Romantic Intrigue

I could barely contain my excitement. Aunt Eva's predicament called to mind the dime novels that my best friend, Rose O'Malley, and I had taken to secretly reading after she found a stash hidden in the armoire in her mother's sewing room. The romantic novels told complicated sagas of hopeless liaisons filled with improbable plots and unbelievable coincidences. We had found several rather sensational and shocking. Only Aunt Eva's story wasn't cheap or unsavory like those books. Her tale was more like a Jane Austen novel of thwarted romance and secret rendezvous, certainly nothing illicit.

The thrill of being privy to Aunt Eva's intrigue offered an escape from my sheltered world and the dull, monotonous routines and sorrows of the past few years. My aunt had taken me into her confidence, and I could not disappoint her. I thought of Saint John, the patron saint of discretion, whom I had read about the previous week. He had died at the hand of King Wenceslas IV of Bohemia rather than divulge the confession of the king's wife, Queen Sophie. Such loyalty was to be admired. I would pray to Saint John to help me keep Aunt Eva's secret.

Mama bit her lip before speaking. "I can talk with Mildred on your behalf."

Aunt Eva grabbed Mama's hands. "I don't want to burden you, but you're my last hope. You must meet Mr. Dearman first, so you can argue in earnest on his behalf. If we can only convince Mildred to give him a chance. She's never even talked with him."

Mama blinked several times. "But how will I meet him?"

"I'm expecting a letter…" Aunt Eva began, but she halted at the sound of heavy, uneven footsteps descending the stairs. She wiped away her tears and took a ragged breath.

Aunt Mildred loomed in the doorway. "What is going on? Eva, have you been crying?"

"It's only a cinder from the train in my eye. I'll run some water over it." Eva bolted from her seat and brushed pass Mildred.

"What has she been telling you?" Aunt Mildred's tone implied wrongdoing on Eva's part and perhaps on my and Mama's as well.

I gave Aunt Mildred my most serious look, frowning slightly. "She was talking about her illness." This was mostly true. Eva had mentioned concerns over her health.

"Did you sleep?" Mama asked calmly. "Come have some coffee and a roll."

Aunt Mildred blinked several times. "I didn't sleep at all. That dreadful feline of yours is somewhere upstairs mewling like a hungry calf."

I cringed. "I'm sorry, Aunt Mildred. She must have gotten locked in Cole's room."

Cole clattered from the kitchen across the dining room and front hall, sliding to a halt next to Aunt Mildred. He lifted his clasped hands toward her face. "Look, Aunt Mildred! I found a frog in the bucket by the water tap outside."

Aunt Mildred gave a short yelp and clutched her chest with one hand. "Get it away from me. Right *now*." She stumbled forward and collapsed onto the green velvet armchair, causing it to shudder with a worrying groan.

Mama jumped up. "Cole, take that back outside."

"But, Mama, I want to keep him. Just look." He scooted forward and tripped over the edge of the Persian carpet. His arms flew out as he hit the rug, and the frog sailed through the air. "Jesusmaryandjoseph!" The words slipped out as one from Cole's lips.

The poor creature landed on the fireplace hearth and remained still as if stunned by its sudden freedom. It was only three inches long at most, a rubbery, gray-green blob with bulging black eyes. Harmless looking, really. I felt rather sorry for it. Cole lunged for the frog, but it hopped across the carpet and under Aunt Mildred's chair.

Aunt Mildred leaped up, emitting staccato shrieks while shaking out her skirt and lifting her feet as if dancing one of Katherine's Irish jigs. The frog proceeded to hop into the entry and down the hall toward the library. Cole sprang up and down in hot pursuit, always a moment too late.

There were murmurs and a scuffle. Eva appeared around the doorway with a bemused expression brightening her face. She gently held the frog in her hands. "We'll be back soon. Cole is going to show me his yard."

"Mercy," Aunt Mildred cried, struggling to regain her composure. Her cheeks looked like someone had splattered

red paint across them, and the bun at the nape of her neck hung askew. Her breathing came fast. "Whatever possesses that child?" She flopped down on the green chair once more, provoking an even louder groan from the wooden frame. "It's clear he's had no discipline while you were in medical school, Lida. And now, with you working at those frightful Catholic homes…"

"Cole is a normal five-year-old, interested in all the things small boys find fascinating," Mama said with surprising composure as she handed a cup of coffee to Aunt Mildred.

"And the sacrilege. Where did he ever learn to utter such a thing?"

"That's from Katherine," I said, chuckling. "She says it when she gets excited."

Aunt Mildred glared at me. "Such impertinence. It is not in the least amusing, young lady." She turned back to Mama. "You've hired an uneducated Irish Catholic immigrant with no sense of propriety to care for your children. Really, Lida, what could you be thinking?"

Mama bristled. "Katherine is wonderful with Cole and Sara Jane, and we all love her like family. She may have a few rough edges, but I trust her implicitly." Her clipped words barely suppressed her anger. "What would you know about raising children?"

A shadow darkened Aunt Mildred's face, and her mouth settled into a grimace. I knew she and Uncle Franklin had been unable to have children. The depth of sadness in Aunt Mildred's eyes caught me off guard. It was out of character for Mama to say hurtful things to others. I had never known her to disagree so openly and fervently with anyone before. Aunt Mildred seemed to have a knack for stripping Mama's emotions bare. Perhaps what Aunt Eva had just told us played into her anger.

Silence hung in the air for an excruciatingly long time. "I do know that small children must be taught appropriate behavior and manners," Aunt Mildred said at last, her voice icy. "What will people think?"

Mama stared back, more constrained in her response. "I care for my family the best I can. It hasn't been easy to keep a roof over our heads and food on our table since William passed. It was only thanks to Uncle Clyde's inheritance that I was able to get by." Uncle Clyde was my Great Aunt Effie's husband, who had passed away six months before Papa. Since they had no children of their own, he had left Mama and her sisters a generous amount of money.

In October it would be two years since Papa had been killed in an accident at the Cherry Creek Mine. As the company engineer, several miners had come to him complaining that the latest blasting had left the supporting timbers unstable. He had followed the men into the deepest shafts to inspect the damage and determine how best to reinforce it. But he never made it out. The walls collapsed, killing twelve men, including Papa. It was Mr. Gordon, the owner of the mine, with his wife alongside him, who knocked on our front door that evening. I could still hear Mr. Gordon's gravelly voice murmuring how sorry he was. Mama crumpled onto the floor, calling out Papa's name over and over. Mrs. Gordon had knelt and put her arms about Mama's shoulders, crooning words of sympathy, while I stood by, numb and mute.

Aunt Mildred glanced at Mama now with a great deal of discomfort. "I know it's been difficult, Lida. We're all very

33

sorry for your losses. Mother offered for you to move home to Lawrence with her so the family could help you. I don't know why you insisted on staying here."

Mama took a deep breath. "Our home is in Denver. Now that I've finished medical school and begun working, we're fine."

Aunt Mildred's lips puckered up as if she had tasted an unripe plum. "Why didn't you stick with teaching? As Dr. Bartlett said to me, practicing medicine is unnatural and unbecoming for a woman."

"Many places won't hire married or widowed women to teach. I was only offered a position in Leadville, because of the difficulty of recruiting single women to the mining town. Besides, it hardly pays enough to buy food, let alone keep up a house." Mama shook her head and sighed. "I became a doctor to save lives. After losing Peter, I had to answer my calling. No one should suffer the death of a child as we did. I assure you I'm just as capable as any man."

Aunt Mildred seemed to stop herself from responding and instead sipped her coffee and fussed with the folds of her skirt.

Mother stood. "I thought we might have a short walk around the neighborhood before our luncheon. I know you and Eva are tired and will want to rest this afternoon." The discussion was over.

The day passed quietly. After a hearty lunch, Aunt Mildred retreated to her room for a nap. Buttercup had been banished to the yard.

Following a short rest of her own, Eva joined us out back in the gazebo to enjoy the warm sunshine. "Oh, your flowers are exquisite!" she exclaimed. "I've never seen such gorgeous peonies."

"Mama loves to garden, and I love to draw all her pretty flowers," I said, holding up my sketch pad. I had begun a drawing of Aunt Eva sitting in the wicker chair.

Cole raced up. "Look what I found, Aunt Eva." He proudly showed us a small black beetle crawling up his arm and then raced off again.

"What a dear boy," Aunt Eva said. "He looks so much like William. The same hair and eyes."

"And Peter," Mama added. "He's very like him in many ways."

Her comment caused a small ache in my heart. It often felt to me as if I were watching Peter grow up again. Like the brother he had never really known, Cole embraced the world with equal parts delight and surprise, eager to learn and test out every moving thing he encountered. Although Peter had been a great deal less likely to cause havoc in the process. Because Peter was delicate and often sick, Mama didn't allow him to run loose with the neighborhood boys. He had to be content playing with me, enduring tea parties with my dolls and his stuffed bear. I read him countless books and drew pictures of funny animals to make him laugh. Like all siblings, we argued, but it never lasted long. He was as dear to me as my own life. I lost part of my soul when he passed.

"I want to warn you that I'll be receiving a letter from Mr. Dearman soon," Aunt Eva said, lowering her voice. "He's sending it to Sylvia, and she'll forward it on. I await his plans for traveling to Denver."

"How exciting," I said. "Tell us more about him."

Aunt Eva grew giddy as she described her afternoon teas with Mr. Dearman at Sylvia's house. "He brought large bunches of flowers each time, which Sylvia enjoyed, since I couldn't bring them home to Mother's. We are of like minds on almost every subject and engage in such interesting conversations. We debated the presidential election at length. He voted for William Jennings Bryan, of course."

Mama sighed. "It was a shame that Mr. Bryan lost again, while McKinley and the Republicans prevailed with all their wealth and connections. I feel Mr. Bryan never effectively communicated his message. The people couldn't see how much better off the country would be with him."

"President McKinley's campaign touted four years of an improving economy," Aunt Eva said, "and his success in China, which bought him a great deal of favor."

Mama clucked her tongue. "And then McKinley went against all the United States' principals by waging war on Spain and taking over Cuba and the Philippines, led by that horrid man Roosevelt. We've lost our moral compass. Now our nation is no better than the European countries we so often criticize for colonialism. The worst of it is the American people seem to support this imperialism. I'm appalled that Roosevelt is our Vice President now. It's a sorry state of affairs that leaves me disheartened for our future."

"That's exactly how Mr. Dearman and I feel," Eva said, leaning in to speak in a low voice. "I wouldn't say this in front of Mildred, but we felt Bryan should never have emphasized the temperance issue as prominently as he did in his campaign."

"You're right. While I support temperance in theory, trying to ban liquor entirely alienates the majority of men,"

Mama said. "It has certainly hurt in the push for women's suffrage. We were lucky in Colorado, as the liquor lobby remained complacent. They didn't bother to put up a fight against the women's vote, thinking it would never pass. But they're more vigilant now in other states where similar initiatives have been proposed."

Aunt Eva sighed. "How well I know from our defeats in Kansas."

"Miss Anthony is wise to keep the National Suffrage Association neutral on the temperance fight. We can't mix the two issues," Mama said.

Aunt Eva shrugged her shoulders. "I can't believe my good fortune in meeting someone as estimable as Mr. Dearman, who shares my deepest-held ideals." She smiled shyly. "He says he admires my mind as much as my beauty."

Mama patted Aunt Eva's hand. "And well he should. Tell us of his background."

Aunt Eva explained that Mr. Dearman was the only son in his family. His three older sisters and mother were committed to women's suffrage and other progressive ideas. "He says he wouldn't dare to cross them. They have demonstrated to him the importance of women assuming fulfilling lives and sharing an equal voice."

I'd never heard a story so romantic, at least not from a person I knew rather than a character in a novel. I tried to imagine the deep emotions Aunt Eva must feel for Mr. Dearman, the spark of longing to be with another person that inevitably possesses young women and men. The possibility both enthralled and terrified me. I could only compare it to the disquieting pleasure I felt on seeing the handsome young ticket taker on the tram. Sean, as his nametag proclaimed, greeted Rose and me each morning on our way to work. He had warm, deep brown eyes, black hair that fell in waves down his forehead, and a smile to brighten the dreariest day. "How're ye two lovely lasses farin' this beautiful mornin'?" he always asked in an Irish brogue that put Katherine's to shame. My heart fluttered every time his gaze landed on me, but I was too shy to respond with more than a smile.

Perhaps one day someone would capture my heart as Mr. Dearman had captured Aunt Eva's. But Rose and I had vowed we would go to college or art school first and embark on our careers before succumbing to the responsibilities of married life. Mama counseled me to wait for marriage and children until I defined my place in the world. I knew she had struggled to complete her training as a doctor while raising children under a cloud of grief over losing Peter and then Papa.

At six in the evening, we sat down to a light supper. Cole was on his best behavior as he stared at Aunt Eva like an adoring puppy. The conversation stayed on safe subjects: the weather, the latest news on acquaintances in Lawrence, the places in and around Denver we would like to take my aunts during their visit.

"How is Franklin doing?" Mama asked when the conversation lagged.

"Perhaps Eva wrote you. He was promoted to bank president two years ago," Aunt Mildred said.

"You must be very proud."

Aunt Mildred nodded. "No one deserves it more. However, it means he has many late nights at the bank."

"And how do you fill your time?" Mama asked.

Aunt Mildred lifted her head. "I volunteer with the Lady's Benevolent Society of Lawrence. We raise funds for the orphanage and try to assist needy women. And I joined the Women's Christian Temperance Union some time back. So many social ills are rooted in alcohol as men become slaves to drink. It's a sorry state of affairs."

Mama nodded. "That's most admirable, Mildred. It's true that many men have fallen prey to drink and, sadly, many women, too. It's always been a problem here in Colorado, especially in the mining towns. There are too many men without wives who have nowhere to go but the saloons."

Mildred stared at Mama. "When I think of our father in his youth and the damage drink did to our family, I feel obligated to remedy this curse on our society."

Mama avoided Aunt Mildred's piercing eyes and passed her the bowl of potatoes. "Please have some more."

"Mama and I are going to march for women's suffrage in the Fourth of July parade," I announced. "Will you join us?" It would be my first time to participate in one of the suffrage activities. I was terribly excited.

"Gladly!" Aunt Eva said.

"Mercy. I most certainly will not." Aunt Mildred looked askance at Mama. "I should have known you'd be involved in this nonsense, Lida."

"Doesn't the Temperance Union support a woman's right to vote?" I asked.

"The national committee adopted a platform in favor, but not all members agree," Aunt Mildred answered tartly. "As Franklin says, it's not necessary for women to vote in order to make lawmakers see reason. Eventually, Congress will outlaw liquor to restore a civil society." She pushed her dessert plate away. "Why are you marching? Colorado already passed the women's vote."

I could see Mama struggling to remain neutral. "We believe every woman deserves the same rights and we must continue the fight for our sisters throughout the country. As Miss Susan B. Anthony so eloquently said, 'There never will be complete equality until women themselves help to make laws and elect lawmakers.'"

"Franklin argues women aren't capable of understanding the complexity of the decisions our government leaders make. They haven't the education and experience. And how are women to hold office with children to raise and a home to run? Why..."

"For heaven's sake, Mildred," Aunt Eva interrupted, her tone one of exasperation, "women deserve equal rights. It's taken decades of lobbying to pass laws in the states allowing women to own property and keep their own wages, not to mention getting custody of their children following a divorce." She pounded her first on the table. "It's outrageous that women have to fight so hard to control their fate. We simply must have the vote."

Aunt Mildred folded her napkin and placed it on the table. "Franklin insists women are quite capable of convincing their husbands to vote for reforms, eliminating the need for them to vote directly."

I took a deep breath and asked, "But, Aunt Mildred, what do *you* think?"

"Really," Aunt Mildred huffed. "I think you need to learn when to hold your tongue, young lady." She stood up and glared at Mama. "I am retiring. I assume we'll go to church tomorrow?"

40

Mama paused, licking her lips. "Of course. I'm sure you'll enjoy the Capital Hill Baptist Church. It's only a few blocks away."

I realized then that Mama had not yet told Aunt Mildred of our recent conversion to the Catholic faith. Sparks would surely fly in the morning.

Chapter 4

LIDA

Examining the Patient

The first few days flew by as Eva and I planted ourselves in the parlor or backyard gazebo, talking of everything and nothing, trying to recapture our years apart. I wanted to understand the finer nuances of her life, the details not conveyed in letters. She had a talent for recreating the flat twang and vernacular of Lawrence residents as she painted the events of daily life—the gossip, misunderstandings, achievements, and petty squabbles—rendered entertaining without being unkind. Her stories left me laughing until tears filled my eyes, and they even drew smiles from Mildred.

She spoke of friends from college who wrote faithfully and kept her connected to the larger world and important events across the country. "Miraculously, I've found a group of other ladies in Lawrence, mostly from the university, who share progressive ideas and support women's suffrage. I fear we are the fringe of Lawrence society," she reported, chuckling.

"You're simply young and naive," Mildred commented.

Our conversations, while lively and enjoyable, and occasionally sad, occurred primarily in the presence of Mildred. This forced us to be guarded in our remarks, to censor our comments and avoid subjects fraught with conflict.

Clearly Mr. Dearman and the difficult nature of our mother remained off-limits. After a rocky start, I had pledged to myself not to argue with Mildred and to keep the visit as pleasant as possible.

I was anxious to understand the consequences of Eva's illness, in hopes of refuting Dr. Bartley's claims of her fragile condition, which I found most worrying. As we finished luncheon on Monday, I asked her, "Might I examine you in my office this afternoon?"

"Of course," she responded without pause. "Who can I trust more in this world than my dear sister?"

"Humph," Mildred muttered, rising from the dining table. "I shall be in the gazebo writing letters."

Eva and I escaped to my doctor's office, where I had yet to see an actual patient. The closest I had come was Cole's little friend, Bobby, who limped in one day with a badly scraped knee as I was arranging my supplies. I cleaned and bandaged his wound with an appropriate air of gravity, wiped a few tears from his cheeks, and sent him on his way. I hoped one day to tend to a steady stream of patients, but the large number of physicians in Denver—not to mention the bias against women—made it unlikely that this would occur anytime soon.

Although a door in the library connected the house to the examination room, I took Eva outside to the street entrance, wanting to give her the full effect. The small plaque by the front door read "Doctor Elizabeth B. Clayton, General Practice." Eva touched the plaque with an air of reverence. "Imagine, my sister a doctor."

We entered the small waiting room with its desk, where hopefully someday an assistant would sit, a filing cabinet, two chairs, and a side table. A watercolor painting of a meadow filled with wildflowers and a river meandering through the Rocky Mountains by Sara Jane hung on the wall.

"This is wonderful," Eva said. "It makes me feel welcome and safe."

I led her through to the airy examination room, two and a half times larger than the waiting room. It was bright with light from a bank of windows across the back, which caught the afternoon sun. I had painted the walls a calming pale blue and proudly hung my medical degree and Colorado State Examining Board registration for all to see. A desk and three chairs filled the far left corner. I had an examination table and shelves stocked with basic equipment and materials needed for checking patients and administering minor treatments—medical books, stethoscopes, hypodermic needles, disinfectant, bandages, tongue depressors, medicines, tonics, and herbal cures. But there my unused supplies sat, neatly lined up in the gleaming glass cabinets, like toy soldiers waiting to be marched into battle.

"Sometimes I slip in here for a moment of peace and quiet," I said. "I daydream of having a thriving practice and saving countless lives." I didn't add that those first few months as a full-fledged physician, I'd felt like a child playing at being a doctor, wallowing in self-doubt. I knew experience would build my confidence, but as yet I had little to claim.

"It will come soon enough, as caring and capable as you are," Eva reassured me.

"Several friends and acquaintances have talked to me of becoming patients, but I suggested we wait until I'm better established in my current job." I didn't add that I wanted to wait until I had more experience and felt more confident.

"I'm still in awe that you finished school despite all the obstacles."

"I tread a difficult path, but I stayed focused on why I had started in the first place. You can't imagine the suffering I witnessed during our early years in Colorado. I never wrote to anyone at home about it; I didn't want to give Mother any more fuel for criticizing my marriage. Between the bitter cold winters and the ubiquitous saloons and other unsavory businesses, Leadville was nearly unfit for living. The gold and silver mines attracted the desperately poor and a collection of misfits, all hoping to strike it rich. I might not have survived, if William and I hadn't been so in love."

"You never told me."

"You were still a small child at the time. Later I saw no point in complaining about the past. The constant loss of life—men killed in mining accidents, shootouts over silver claims, wives lost in childbirth, and adults and children taken to early graves by outbreaks of infectious diseases—led me to train as a doctor. So many residents lacked proper shelter and food, which weakened their bodies and made them more susceptible. Our closest friends, Harriette and Martin, lost their new baby to diphtheria. And our Katherine lived in Leadville at the time as well. She lost her husband to a mining accident and all three of her children to smallpox in the course of two years. It's beyond comprehension."

Eva put a hand to her mouth. "Oh, the poor soul. Yet she goes on and cares for your family as if you were her own."

"You see why she is so dear to us."

"I felt helpless in Leadville, unable to do anything to aid others. Once we moved to Denver, I proposed to William that I enroll in medical school. He supported me but asked if I

46

would wait until the children were older; Peter was but six months and Sara Jane only three then." Tears welled in my eyes. "After we lost Peter, I insisted on beginning my training even though Cole was still a baby. My desire to help others consumed me. William acceded to my wishes, hoping it would ease my grief."

Eva put her arms around me and gave me a gentle hug. "Life is so tenuous. My illness certainly brought that realization to me."

I stepped back and wiped a few stray tears from my cheeks. "The decision to go to school was the easy part. Then I had to deal with the male teachers and students who were not inclined to welcome women into the profession. There we were, approaching the start of the twentieth century, and you can't imagine the things some of them said to me. Women are unfit to practice medicine because we are ruled by hormones and emotions that impair our mental capabilities. Or women haven't the stamina and strength to treat the seriously ill or injured, as if we will wilt like flowers at the sight of blood and mangled limbs.

"Several doctors belittled me in front of the male students or refused to call on me when I raised my hand to answer a question. Sometimes they 'forgot' to give me an assignment the others knew about or graded my papers and tests with a standard far surpassing that for the male students. I had to hold my tongue and maintain my dignity around those idiots for four years. I dispelled many of their notions about women in medicine. And I daresay I won over a few supporters."

Eva chuckled. "I'm sure you did. Pity the poor fool who attempts to stand in the way of my brave sister."

"William was indignant at the insults, but he helped me see the humorous side of those 'nincompoops,' as he called them. After he was gone, I might not have survived without Sara Jane. Young as she was, she helped me make light of the situation. We started keeping a list of all the derogatory things men said and the slights I endured. We turned it into a game, rating them on a scale of one to ten and thinking of funny responses I could have given. Laughter is always the best cure for whatever ails you."

"This makes me even more proud of you."

"The fairer sex shall prevail in the end," I said, smiling. "Now, let me examine you."

"I am much in need of your opinion and support."

"I wish I had all the answers. As a medical student, I soon realized how inadequate our knowledge of most diseases remains. It appalls me that, in 1901, meaningful medical advances still elude our profession in America. Researchers in Europe are making far more progress, but the results are slow to be accepted here among our insular medical community."

I hated to tell Eva how poorly trained most American physicians were, relying on antiquated practices and information, filled more with bluster and hunches than knowledge or competence. I found most diagnoses and treatments appeared akin to a parlor guessing game. Our instructors at medical school constantly contradicted one another. Who were we to believe? One of the doctors who trained us in proper surgical procedures, hygiene, and care had been perpetually tipsy during classes, reeking of whisky. His pronouncements made little sense and often went against the tide of recent findings in the medical journals, which I had read. Clearly I had to keep my wits about me and trust my own research and instincts rather than rely on the so-called experts.

"Let's sit down over here." I indicated the chairs by my desk.

Eva turned her right side toward me. "I'm afraid I can't hear as well in my left ear now. Dr. Bartley said the eardrum was damaged by the fevers. Do you think it will come back?"

"It's doubtful. But you seem to manage well enough." I took out a small notebook and pen. "Let's start at the beginning. Do you have any idea who exposed you to the illness?"

"I'm fairly certain it was Rebecca Shearing's son, Charlie. I ran into them at the library right before he came down with it. I sat with little Charlie and leafed through the book he had picked out. Two other children in his class were infected as well. Fortunately, we all recovered."

"Tell me everything you remember, from onset to recovery, in as much detail as you can remember."

Eva thought for a moment, squinting her eyes in concentration. "I woke the first morning a bit tired and achy. I had planned to go to the literary club meeting with Sylvia after lunch, but a chill set in by late morning. Mother insisted I go to bed."

"Lucky for the other ladies."

"I would have felt terrible if I'd infected anyone. It progressed quickly. By evening I had a high fever, and Mother gave me some Bayer's aspirin. The next morning, the fever spiked, and my throat felt terribly raw. Mother called Dr. Bartley. At first he wasn't sure if it was scarlet fever, but ordered that no one else be allowed in the house just in case."

I jotted down details in my notebook. "What was your temperature?"

"It had reached 104 degrees, so Dr. Bartley gave me more aspirin. He told Mother to keep the room ventilated and place cold compresses on my forehead. In the early evening, he returned. By then I was burning up and felt quite distant from the world. I could hardly focus. A rash had bloomed on my cheeks, and my tongue turned bright red and bumpy. I remember the odd feeling of it on the roof of my mouth."

"He confirmed it was scarlet fever?"

"Yes. The house was quarantined. He ordered Mother to take the clothes I had worn during the previous days and other personal items to wash in hot water. He gave me something mixed with Epsom salts."

I nodded. "Perhaps podophyllin. Some recommend it to clear bile."

"He left another tonic to be given every few hours that tasted bitter and awful. By then I felt sick to my stomach."

"Most likely carbonite of ammonia and potassium nitrate, or possibly belladonna drops. I'm not convinced any of them are effective, and they can be toxic if too much is taken. Even though it's been close to twenty years since researchers tied strep throat infections to the onset of scarlet fever, there is little new in the way of treatment." I didn't add that remedies remained primitive and speculative, some doing more harm than good. I had no idea how Dr. Bartley had treated Eva, but thank heavens she had survived.

Eva let out a long sigh. "After that it became a blur, people coming and going, the quiet murmur of voices. I could hardly open my eyes, and if I did, all I saw were indistinct shadows. It felt like I was fighting my way up from the depths of a lake, struggling through the water to reach the surface. At one point, Dr. Bartley decided to bleed me. I recall the pain as he cut my arm."

I shook my head in disbelief. "Bleeding is foolishness. All it does is weaken you further. It seems the good doctor remains stuck in his antiquated practices."

"Do you remember when I wrote to you of the article I read in the *Saturday Evening Post*?" Eva asked. "Something about people having different blood types. It seemed very important."

"Yes. A critical breakthrough by Dr. Landsteiner in Vienna. Now we can give people lifesaving blood transfusions as long as it's the same type. I'm afraid early experiments with incompatible blood types killed many poor souls."

"Oh dear," Eva said and shook her head. "The worst indignity of this illness was when they shaved my hair off. However, Dr. Bartley told me it would have fallen out anyway when my skin peeled from the rash. I knew I should be grateful to be alive, but vanity got the best of me." She touched her silver-white hair, pinned up in a pompadour, and chuckled. "When my hair began growing in, I looked like some sort of deranged old person with white tufts sticking out in all directions. I wore a wig for months. Finally, it was long enough to pin up on my head, so I could use a switch. I don't even mind the color as long as I have real hair."

"You look beautiful. Go on."

"Dr. Bartley brushed the ulcers at the back of my throat with some foul concoction that made me gag. It was horrible."

"Probably nitrate of silver."

"I believe the fever broke the third or fourth night, but returned every day for over a week as strong as ever in the afternoons. Mother and Mildred gave me cool sponge baths and different tinctures. The rash on my face spread all over my body. My skin itched something fierce, but I was too weak to even lift my hands to scratch it. I couldn't distinguish waking and sleeping. It felt like a never-ending nightmare."

"They may have given you opium to keep you calm. How long before the fevers stopped completely?"

"They gradually decreased by the second week, and I grew more aware of my surroundings. They fed me broth, toast, and fruit. I wasn't allowed any meat for several more weeks." She shook her head. "And I had to take quinine. They were always forcing some awful-tasting potion down me. Then the skin over much of my body peeled. I looked like a plucked chicken, red and wrinkled. I had to remain in bed until a new layer grew in. Thank heavens Bertram couldn't see me."

I looked up from my notes. "Did he know about your illness?"

"Sylvia wrote to him in Boston. He wired her that he would come at once. But she wired back and convinced him there was nothing he could do, and he might only make matters worse with my family. The poor dear suffered greatly. When I was better, Sylvia delivered a pile of letters to me, filled with his devotion." Her expression turned dreamy for a moment. "Such lovely words. He has the soul of a poet."

"There were moments, Lida," she said as her voice quivered, "when I believed I was dying. At one point a strong breeze blew in the window and wrapped around me. I felt sure angels had arrived to carry away my spirit. All I could think was that I would never see you or Bertram again, never be able to tell either of you goodbye and how much I loved you."

I put a hand over hers as my eyes filled with tears once more. "I couldn't have borne losing you, too."

"But I am well now. And happy."

"Thank heavens." I stood and drew the blinds in the back. "Let me examine you. Please take off your outer clothes and sit on the table for me."

She removed her pale blue blouse, navy skirt, and tightly laced corset, sitting primly on the edge of the table in her chemise and drawers, looking like a shy child.

"First of all, you *must* stop wearing that terrible corset. It squeezes and damages your organs, particularly the kidneys and liver, which are surely sensitive after your illness." Eva opened her mouth to protest, but I held a hand up. "You don't need one, as slender as you are. Since I abandoned my corset several years ago, I feel a wonderful sense of freedom."

"Well, perhaps I could lace it more loosely."

"That's not good enough, Eva dear. Women have become victims of unrealistic ideals for their shape. These fashions threaten their health and comfort. The new straight-front corset introduced this year is an abomination. It forces your body into an unnatural S-curve, cinching in the waist and arching the back." I walked behind her and felt the length of her spine, which remained straight and uncompromised for now.

She sighed. "I admit my lower back is often sore after a long day. But what about with evening wear for the theater or a dance? I should feel naked without a corset."

"Wear one only on special occasions, if you must, and only if you lace it very loosely."

I tapped her knees to test her reflexes and bent her arm back and forth at the elbow. Then I placed my stethoscope on her chest and listened to her heart, relieved to find she had a strong, steady beat with no indication of a heart murmur or other irregularity. "Do you ever feel heart palpitations or a skipped beat?" She assured me she didn't.

I listened to her lungs in front and back, asking her to breathe deeply. Everything sounded normal without any buildup of fluid. "Now lie down and let me examine your stomach and abdomen." I poked around her kidneys, liver, intestines, and lymph nodes without finding any swelling or bumps. "Do you ever feel pains or discomfort in your abdomen?"

"No. I'm fine," she said, but added, "On occasion after a large meal I have a few pains here." She held her hand over the area of her liver.

"Do you ever feel numbness in your legs or arms or face?"

She hesitated a moment. "My joints are a bit stiff sometimes, but nothing that hampers me."

"And your movements are regular every day?" I asked. She nodded once, blushing. "Tomorrow I'd like you to give me a urine sample taken first thing in the morning, which I can send to a lab. Are you menstruating regularly?"

A soft smile touched her lips as she sat up again. "My monthlies stopped after the illness but began again in March and are regular. I do hope Bertram and I can have children."

"I see no reason why you shouldn't. As far as I can tell, you're fully recovered, although I want you to gain a bit of weight and continue exercising to build up your strength." I took her cool thin hand. "I will report my findings to Mildred.

They cannot rely on Dr. Bartley's misdiagnosis to oppose a marriage."

She stood and reached for her blouse, slowly buttoning it. "This illness changed me, Lida. I refuse to live my life to please Mother or anyone else. It's the twentieth century, and I'm a grown woman. If I can't even stand up to my family and choose my own future, how can I demand the right to vote for who will run our country?" She took her skirt off the chair. "My first resolution is to go back for my last year at Bryn Mawr. I've written to admissions to see if I might start this September. This time I won't let mother's histrionics stop me."

"I wholeheartedly support you. I think there is nothing more important than a woman receiving an education and following her calling. No matter what course your life takes, the ability to earn an income removes uncertainty and dependence on others." I paused a moment. "What does Mr. Dearman think of your plan?"

"I haven't mentioned it to him as yet."

"Are you worried he might object?"

"I expect him to support me, but I thought I'd wait to hear back from the college before raising the issue."

She smoothed the front of her skirt. "I've also decided if Mother and Mildred continue to oppose this match, I will marry Mr. Dearman without their blessings." She smiled. "After I've finished school."

"I hope it doesn't come to that. You would think after forcing me to such a decision, they would reconsider their stance. Surely they do not want to risk losing you as well." I didn't tell her how the alienation from my family had remained a thorn in my happiness, an irritation that wore me down and provoked a sadness that was never completely dispelled. I did not wish for her to live with that loss.

"It surprises me Mildred has so little sympathy for your situation. Surely she remembers how she felt about Franklin before they married."

Eva tilted her head to one side. "Do you suppose she and Franklin were ever really in love?"

"I know they were. Maybe they shared a more subdued romance. But I saw the love in their eyes when they courted and married."

"I'm afraid there is little of that now. They hardly talk to each other these days. She is preoccupied with the temperance union and her charities and clubs. And Franklin works all the time."

"I'm sorry to hear that. She strikes me as terribly unhappy, so different from when she was a young woman and full of fun. You probably don't remember, as you were small."

"How did she end up marrying Franklin? He is certainly a good person, but so dour and stodgy. I can't imagine their private life."

My thoughts turned to another era. "There was another young man, Carlton Sanger, who wooed Mildred. He was a darling among the girls, lively and charming. He made Mildred blush and laugh until tears ran down her cheeks. They courted for several months, then she met Franklin and broke it off with Carlton. But Franklin was different back then, too. While always shy and quiet, he had a good sense of humor and kept Mildred on her toes. Anyone could see he adored her." I shook my head slowly. "I'm sure the disappointment of not having children has clouded their lives.

It's such a shame. After you were born, all she talked about was having a child of her own."

"I worry about her," Eva said. "Despite her sharp words, underneath I know there is pain and loneliness."

"We must try to lighten her mood and show her how to enjoy life again."

Her face brightened. "I hope to hear from Mr. Dearman any day as to when he'll arrive in Denver."

"I look forward to meeting this remarkable man. And I shall do everything in my power to help."

"If only we can convince Mildred to give him a chance."

Chapter 5   **MILDRED**

Unhappy News

Monday, June 24, 1901

Dear Mother,

I have much to report about our first days here in Denver, most of it distressing. I hope you are doing well with Aunt Effie checking in from time to time. Please call on Franklin if you need anything.

Our train arrived Saturday almost half an hour late after an unbearably long and uncomfortable ride. That was to be expected I suppose. The landscape across eastern Colorado continues as in Kansas, offering no respite from endless vistas of flat, open land, sparsely populated by farmers and herds of cattle. The people toil against the laws of God and nature, eking out a living. With a great deal of relief, we found Lida and the children waiting for us at the station. It was necessary to take a hired carriage to the house as Lida gave up her horse to reduce expenses after William's passing. She assures me they have not been in dire need, yet it is clear the past few years have brought numerous sacrifices to their standard of living. Clearly, she lacked an adequate income to maintain the basic niceties of life while finishing medical school.

Yet despite her recent struggles, the house is quite large, with five bedrooms, a bathroom, and two toilet closets in addition to a large parlor, library, and dining room. It is located on the edge of the Capital Hill neighborhood, an area filled with the stately mansions of Denver society. Lida and William bought the house seven years ago from his employer, Mr. Robert Gordon, who owns gold mines and other interests throughout the Rocky Mountains. Lida explained, without a trace of embarrassment, they would not have been able to afford such a fine home had Mr. Gordon not reduced the price by more than half. It seems William's engineering skills and instincts allowed Mr. Gordon to strike a previously untapped vein of gold near Leadville at a time when the silver mines had run their course. The Gordons have built a grand house more than twice the size of Lida's not half a dozen blocks away.

After William's death, Mr. Gordon forgave the remaining mortgage. Lida considered selling the house at the time, but she didn't want to uproot the children from their home after losing their father. And the real estate market had not recovered fully after the financial debacle of '93. She said the economic depression left a string of foreclosure signs throughout her neighborhood, and several of her friends were reduced to near poverty. Her openness about personal financial matters is typical, of course.

The house is in need of a great many repairs and painting, again the result of Lida's reduced means. Lida and William built an addition three years ago to serve as her medical office for when she might start a private practice. However, she's discovered it's extremely difficult to attract patients. Personally, I cannot imagine who would want to entrust their health, or that of their family, to a woman doctor. But I have shown the utmost restraint and kept this to myself. She tells me there are over four hundred doctors practicing in Denver at present so competition is great. (One would think she might have investigated her prospects for success before starting medical school.) She assures me her situation is more secure since being hired as a physician for the House of the Good Shepherd—some sort of refuge for needy women—and the Mount Saint Vincent's Orphan Asylum (both run by Catholic sisters as you might guess from the names).

Lida is examining Eva in her office at this moment while I write, as if she might have greater insight into her health than our trusted Dr. Bartley. She certainly has a great deal of confidence in herself.

The children are comely enough with William's fair coloring. Sara Jane, almost sixteen, is at that awkward stage as she transforms from child to adult. Her legs and arms appear too long and gangly to coordinate, like a newborn foal. She constantly slouches as if uncomfortable with her increasing height. But she favors her mother's features and is becoming quite handsome. She comports herself with a maturity admirable for her age, yet often oversteps her place by offering opinions she should keep to herself. We saw the seeds of this when she was a small child visiting Lawrence.

I found the news that Sara Jane has a summer job at a millinery store most appalling. Imagine Lida letting her daughter work as a shop girl! Apparently the owner, Mrs. O'Malley, is the mother of Sara Jane's best friend Rose, who works there as well. One might ask why Lida allows her daughter to become friends with someone from this background.

61

Sara Jane is not accomplished in embroidery, her piano playing is abysmal, and her voice even worse. But she has a keen mind and reads extensively, which is a good foundation in life. She possesses some measure of artistic talent, spending much of her free time sketching dresses, hats, and such, as well as portraits and lovely scenes of the gardens and mountains. She announced to me that she plans to become a fashion designer in New York or Paris one day. Wherever she got such a notion at her age is beyond me. Naturally, Eva encourages her in this nonsense. You should hear the two of them as they pour over the latest Harper's Bazar and the Ladies' Home Journal. They critique various fashions and ogle the Gibson Girl drawings. Lida pointedly told me that she will support her children in whatever future path they choose.

Why can't women be content as good wives and mothers without pursuing men's careers? As Franklin says, the art of keeping an efficient and happy household has lost all value among this era of radical firebrands, the so-called New Women.

Cole is an unruly, troublesome imp who says the most outlandish things. I sometimes think he is possessed by the devil. No one has taught him the most basic manners or the old adage that children should be seen and not heard. Lida claims that she wants to encourage his inquisitive and cheerful nature. She'll soon see the error of such permissiveness.

Cole has taken a shine to Eva and follows her everywhere. She indulges him by displaying an interest in his bug collection and reading books aloud at bedtime. He is constantly in trouble with the housekeeper Katherine for his naughtiness, but he remains devoted, hugging her tightly as he comes and goes. I attribute his errant behavior to a lack of supervision and discipline on Lida's part. She was hardly home these past four years while attending medical school. I recognize that losing his father so young is a factor in Cole's wildness. He needs a strong hand. I also fault Lida's judgment in entrusting his care to an Irish Catholic woman of the lowest breeding with an excitable temperament and no sense of decorum. I might add, Lida treats Katherine more like a dear friend than a servant who should know her place. The household is run in a most peculiar manner.

On the positive side, Eva appears happy and content here. She and Lida sit for hours chatting about the most inconsequential things, simply delighted to be in each other's company. They hardly notice my presence. Not that I care. I'm unsure what Eva has revealed to Lida about her misguided acquaintance with Mr. Dearman, but at least she is safely away from his presence.

Lida and I have exchanged words over a number of topics as you might expect. I find her as intractable as ever and beyond listening to reason. Franklin has often commented that it is hard to fathom we came from the same parents and upbringing.

We are invited by Lida's closest friend, Miss Ellis Meredith, to a tea Thursday afternoon to welcome Eva and me to Denver. It is considerate of her friend, but I'm not sure how comfortable I shall feel among the women attending. To start with, Miss Meredith (formerly Mrs. Stansbury) is newly divorced. Imagine! She is a journalist with the Rocky Mountain News and a leader in the suffrage movement. It seems Miss Meredith played a major role in passing the

Elaine Russell

constitutional amendment for the women's vote in Colorado eight years ago. Lida and Miss Meredith belong to a number of women's clubs with other supporters. Eva, as you might guess, is most enthusiastic about meeting the women involved in these endeavors and can hardly talk of anything else. This will only foster her own misguided support for the cause, but at least it occupies her thoughts and helps her forget about Mr. Dearman.

As for the city of Denver, it is more modern than I imagined; it is filled with tall office buildings, several elegant hotels, and a grand opera house. The streets downtown are quite wide, and electric trams run throughout the city. I must say, the setting is dramatic with the vast, snow-capped mountains visible in the distance. However, the air can be smoky at times due to numerous smelting factories and other industries. I find it difficult to catch my breath at times, and my heart beats too fast when I walk any distance. Lida says it is most likely the altitude, over a mile high, but I should adjust and feel better soon. I certainly hope so.

There is a roughness to the Denver population given the large number of nearby mining camps. This so-called Queen of the Prairie is frequented by an array of unruly types: ragged-looking miners who ventured west to make their fortune and now find themselves with nothing, cowboys in big hats and leather chaps brandishing their holsters and guns, immigrants from the far reaches of the globe, and all ilk of heathens from Chinamen to Indians. Lida admits there are too many saloons, gambling houses, and other unsavory establishments in the city. The Women's Christian Temperance Union has its work cut out in this den of iniquity. Out of curiosity and to report back to the Lawrence

64

temperance chapter, I searched the Ballenger & Richards Denver City Directory this morning. I found close to four hundred saloons, liquor stores, and spirit manufacturers listed for a population of just 134,000 people. Can you imagine! Kansas City, with 164,000 residents, has less than a hundred such establishments.

I don't know how any lady can feel safe walking down the streets without an escort. Yet Lida takes the electric tram, or worse, she rides her bicycle about the city without the slightest care. Sara Jane is allowed the same freedom. Most unseemly. But as you know, Lida has never conformed to society's conventions of decent behavior.

Lida is up at dawn to be at her work by seven o'clock, so Eva and I are left to our own devices in the mornings. She stays until half past one in the afternoon, six days a week, with only Sundays free. However, it allows her to be back for lunch and afternoon excursions. Sara Jane works from nine to twelve-thirty Monday through Friday. If there is anything good to say about it, I suppose the job teaches her discipline and responsibility.

Eva took a walk in the neighborhood after breakfast this morning, as Lida is encouraging her to exercise to build up her strength. Cole accompanied her on his tricycle. I spent my free time reading and writing in my journal. I find it pleasant to sit in the backyard gazebo. Despite how busy her life has been, Lida is an avid gardener, and her flowers are prolific. (Perhaps she should be devoting equal time and attention to her children.) She says the garden is her one refuge where she can relax. Among her flowers she feels closer to William, as he always enjoyed her efforts. I'm afraid she still grieves

65

deeply for him. Whatever we may have thought of the match, they seem to have been most devoted and happy together.

I have debated if I should tell you the most shocking piece of news. But it will come back to you one way or another if I delay. Please brace yourself and make sure you are sitting down. Yesterday morning as we set out for church, Lida informed me she and the children have converted to Catholicism! I believe Eva was already aware of this state of affairs but did not warn me. While Eva and I attended services at the Capitol Hill Baptist Church, Lida and the children went off to the Catholic cathedral downtown. Lida explained, somewhat defensively, that she was forced to convert in order to get her job as physician for the Catholic homes, the only work readily available to her. It is beyond belief that she could make such a dreadful and desperate decision, forcing her children into this unacceptable religion. Her pronouncements left me all at once quite speechless. As part of Lida's remuneration, Sara Jane has a scholarship to St. Mary's Academy, a Catholic college preparatory school that is well respected and, at least, provides a proper level of discipline.

I made Eva promise she will not reveal this news to anyone in Lawrence. If people found out, how could we hold up our heads? I implore you not to tell your friends, or even Aunt Effie (you know how she lets secrets slip). The less you say about our visit here in general, the better.

I will write again soon. My first thoughts and purpose remain in keeping Eva safe from Mr. Dearman.

With deepest regards
Your devoted daughter, Mildred

Seeds of Doubt

Rose and I breezed down Larimer Street arm in arm on Wednesday, beckoned by the warm sun to explore the summer afternoon. Mama and my aunts were relaxing at home, leaving me free to spend time with my best friend. We loved nothing better than gazing in shop windows and dreaming of owning things we could never afford on our paltry wages of ten cents an hour. The trolley car rattled by, ringing its bells, and horse-drawn carriages rolled past. People hurried along, toting packages, but we had all the time in the world.

Rose had been my closest friend since third grade when my family moved to Pearl Street, and I transferred to Corona Elementary School. That first day of school, I had sat on the side of the playground, feeling shy and uncertain. Rose flashed a big smile and drew me into a game of hopscotch. She lived with her parents, three sisters, two brothers, and grandmother in a three-story brownstone four blocks from our new home. We became inseparable, sharing secrets and dreams and a fair number of misguided escapades over the years. When we were ten, we thought it would be nice to paint flowers on the side of Mr. Hopper's carriage house to cheer him up after a long illness. Another time we swiped Henry

Martin's fireworks at the Fourth of July picnic and set them off on the school playground. It seemed only fair after he had stolen Rose's straw hat the week before and stuffed it in a trash bin. Our parents and the school principal didn't agree. Rose had a lot of what she called "brilliant ideas," most of which got us into a great deal of trouble. But then, I had always been a willing accomplice.

After Mama graduated from medical school and was hired by the nuns to her new position, she told me I would be attending St. Mary's Academy, come September, for my last two years of high school. I was lucky to have this wonderful opportunity, she insisted. But it didn't feel lucky to me, if it meant leaving Rose behind. Fortunately, Rose's Catholic parents jumped at the chance to transfer her. They had always wanted to send her to St. Mary's, but she had convinced them to let her attend East High School with me. Despite a mixed academic record, the sisters accepted her application. Mama said her chances were greatly improved by a generous donation from Mr. O'Malley, who owned a successful construction company. He had prospered from Denver's rapidly expanding development. Now my best friend and I would venture forth together in a new arena.

I doubted Mr. Hartman, the principal at East High, was sorry to see Rose go. He called her an excitable girl who needed to control her impulses. This was after the incident with the stray dog during our freshman year. Rose had found the brown-and-white mutt shivering in front of the school on a snowy February day. She brought him inside, where he promptly got loose, romping through the corridors and several classrooms and relieving himself in every corner before the janitor finally caught up. Of course, there were other mishaps that brought her within a hair's breadth of being expelled. One day she tripped and spilled her lunch tray on the floor of the cafeteria. She discovered that spilled peas and milk provided an excellent surface for sliding across the floor. Soon a half a dozen girls and boys were competing to see who could go the farthest, leading to a number of alarming falls. Meanwhile, the cafeteria cook ran to alert Mr. Hartman, who soon put a stop to the fun. Once in physical education, when the gym teacher reprimanded Rose for talking too much, she threw a basketball so hard it broke the gas light on the wall behind the hoop and started a small fire.

Rose believed we must cultivate a flair for life and distinguish ourselves as out of the ordinary. She planned to be a novelist, but for the time being was writing short stories with heroines who strongly resembled herself or sometimes me. I often helped her develop the plots and settings, drawing sketches of the scenes. Rose said it was good practice for when we moved to New York City, where she would write plays, and I would create the scenery. She mailed her stories off to *Century*, *Harper's*, and *Atlantic Monthly*—the magazines that published famous authors like Mark Twain, Henry James, and Arthur Conan Doyle. Although none of her writing had been accepted as yet, she had received several encouraging notes from the editors. Our English teacher, Mrs. Bartlett, told Rose she had a wonderfully vivid imagination but must work on her grammar and sentence structure.

Mama described my best friend as exuberant, enthusiastic, and full of surprises. What I liked best about Rose was her ability to laugh off any difficulty. She confided in me that growing up with five siblings provided constant lessons in forgiveness, or otherwise she'd be a crazy person, unhappy all the time.

Rose had carried me through the darkest days of my grief over Peter and Papa. I'm not sure how I would have endured life without her and her big, boisterous family to ease my sorrow.

As we dawdled along, my thoughts returned time and again to the predicament of Aunt Eva and Mr. Dearman. Rose would be enthralled by the real-life drama unfolding in my house. If I could only tell her. The story swirled in my mind like a gathering tornado, longing to be unleashed. But I was sworn to secrecy.

"I like the sky-blue one," I said, peering in the window of the May Shoe & Clothing Company with its display of cotton shirtwaist dresses in summer pastels. "The design is simple and clean. But eight dollars is more than I can ever hope to save." I turned to Rose. "My aunt Eva knows everything about fashion and is an excellent seamstress. She's going to help me lengthen my new white dress. She's so much fun to be with."

"What about your aunt Mildred?" Rose asked.

"She's completely different from Aunt Eva." I scrunched up my nose. "A bit prickly and difficult. She seems unhappy, as if there is something important missing in her life."

"That's too bad. Oh, look at these shoes." Rose pointed to a pair of low heels with pointed toes and a strap across the top with two buttons. They were made from soft, kid leather the color of whipped butter. "Mama would never let me pay four dollars for a pair of shoes. Besides, where would I wear them?" She shrugged. "For now, I suppose I'll have to settle for some new books."

Our window shopping always ended at Western Book & Stationery. We often spent a good part of our weekly earnings there, buying books and magazines, or I would replenish my supply of sketching paper. We retraced our steps down Sixteenth Street to the familiar shop. The little bell above the door tinkled as we entered.

"How are you ladies today?" asked Mr. Samuel, the young clerk who knew us well. "When I fin...finish ringing up this sale, I want to sh...show you some books that came in this week."

He couldn't have been more than twenty-one or two. He had a spare frame and barely reached my height. His big brown eyes looked like an owl's beneath the thick lenses of his gold-rimmed glasses. He patted the hopeless cowlick sticking up from the top of his head. I felt sure he was sweet on Rose, the way he always hovered near her and stammered when he spoke. Rose and I appreciated that he called us ladies and not girls.

We nodded our thanks and waited near the front. The shop felt cool and welcoming. I loved browsing among the shelves, opening new novels to savor the smell of fresh ink and the crackle of crisp pages. I often discovered art books with color plates of famous paintings, which I liked to study, trying to decipher the artists' techniques.

Alice of Old Vincennes by Maurice Thompson was still in the center of the table of best-selling books in America, where it had remained for more than a year. Next to this, I found *Up from Slavery,* the autobiography of Booker T. Washington. "I must buy a copy for Mama. We read the first chapters published last year in the *Outlook*." I sighed. "It made me cry. Mama says everyone should read it to better understand how cruel and terrible slavery was and that more must be done to help the Negroes today."

Rose nodded and held up *The Helmet of Navarre* by Bertha Runkle. "I saw an article in the *Bookman* about Miss Runkle. She was only twenty-one when the *Century* magazine ran her novel as a serial last year. Her mother is part of the literary circle of New York, so of course her daughter's work was published. It's hardly fair."

"When you are discovered, dear Rose, you'll know it's because your writing is wonderful and not because your mother knows the publisher."

"I guess, but I hope it's soon, before I get terribly old and wither away."

I laughed. "I think you have time."

I pointed to *To Have and To Hold* by Mary Johnston. "Aunt Mildred is reading this. She says it's a silly romance. But I like silly romances sometimes."

"Especially Laura Jean Libbey's novels," Rose agreed. "Even if they aren't *lit-er-a-ture*." She drew the word out in a haughty voice with her nose in the air. The Libbey books were part of her mother's collection of romantic dime novels. We loved talking endlessly of the stories. Many readers viewed them with disdain, thinking them poorly written, offering only unoriginal and sensational plots. Then we discovered *Julie Le Roy* and *The Midnight Lamp,* scandalous, cautionary tales about young women who were seduced by dastardly men with promises of marriage only to be abandoned and ruined. They were tantalizing and disconcerting at the same time. Rose and I promised each other never to be so naive as to let a man lead us astray. Since I hardly ever spoke to anyone of the opposite sex, besides Cole or Rose's younger brothers, I was hardly at risk at present.

Rose gave me a mischievous smile. "I have a secret to tell you. I'm writing a romance novel to send to the New Eagle Series. I'm sure I can write a plot as exciting and complicated as Laura Jean Libbey. How hard can it be? I'll use a pen name in case they decide to publish it. I couldn't let my parents find out."

"May I read it?"

"Of course. I have only two chapters so far. I need you to help me work out what's going to happen next. It's about a young woman in Denver from a wealthy family who's in love with a poor young clerk at the stationary store and..." She paused as Mr. Samuel walked up. He motioned for us to follow him to the display of newly arrived books.

"I thought you might appreciate this new...new collection of Louisa May Alcott books," he said. "It includes *Little Women, Little Men,* and *Jo's Boys,* each...each filled with lovely color plates. Her books are...are still very popular after all these years," he continued, gazing at Rose as a pink tinge colored his cheeks. I thought how shocked he would be to learn of our extracurricular reading activities, a far cry from these sweet narratives of virtuous young women.

"Thank you, Mr. Samuel," Rose said, smiling sweetly at him.

He lifted another book from the table. "And here's a new book, *The Wizard of Oz,* which is al...already selling quite well." He turned as a man nearby beckoned to him. "Excuse me, I must go."

Rose held the Oz book in her hand. "Maybe I'll get this for Michael. Mostly he reads his *Horseless Age* magazines. He's totally obsessed with the new vehicles. But he's becoming interested in books as well."

I felt a pang of envy and sadness. Rose's brother, Michael, was two years younger than us, almost the same age as my dear Peter. How Peter had loved a good adventure, especially if I read it aloud to him. I lifted *Little Women* from the set. "This was always my favorite. Jo made me think of you, Rose."

"And Amy reminded me of you. Of course, you're not as vain as she was. We should read it again together."

"I fear it might bring back too many memories." I opened the first pages of the book to an illustration of the four March sisters sitting peacefully before a fire. "I was reading this at the time of Papa's accident." I paused a moment, remembering. "When Beth died in the story, it only compounded my grief. Yet another loss." I looked over at Rose. "I feel more than ever how precious life is. To think Aunt Eva almost died this past October when I've just come to love her so. What would I do if something happened to Cole or Mama? Or you?"

Rose took my hand. "You mustn't think such terrible thoughts. Enjoy every day and be happy. As much as you miss your brother and father, remember you will meet them in heaven one day."

"If only I was sure." The teachings of the Catholic faith and the church's demand for total devotion to a mysterious set of practices and beliefs unsettled me. I found it hard to comprehend and embrace the complicated rules about who would be admitted to heaven. The week before, I had asked Sister Agnes about Peter and Papa. Her stern and harsh responses festered inside me, filling me with dread. But I would not voice my fears and doubts to Rose. For her, being Catholic was as natural as saying her name. She never questioned anything. When I raised uncertainties, she brushed them off with simple assurances: (1) sins could be washed away by making confessions and doing penance, and (2) someday we would all be happily together in heaven. She said there was little else I needed to know. But it seemed considerably more complex to me. I needed Mama's advice.

Rose's voice brightened. "Why don't we pay for our books and get an ice cream on the way home?" She peeked out the window. "We'll have to start back before long. Those clouds over the mountains promise showers later."

As we stepped outside and started down the street, the loud *toot toot* of a horn sounded behind us. Rose turned around, and a broad smile illuminated her face. "Oh, Sara Jane, have a look."

Two young men, wearing suits with bow ties and golf caps at rakish angles, drove down the street in one of the new horseless carriages, which had just started appearing on the streets of Denver. I thought this one a strange-looking contraption, rather like a hay wagon resting on a frame with four wheels. The open car held two double benches positioned back to back. A loud put-puttering noise rose from the engine up front, which was the size of our bread box at home.

The driver moved a metal stick that came up out of the floor to turn the wheels, and the carriage veered toward us. "Good afternoon, girls," he called out gaily.

"That's Jimmy Harrison and Fred Cassidy from school," Rose whispered, waving and flashing her most alluring smile.

Jimmy brought the strange machine to a halt next to us. "How about a ride? It's great fun," he yelled above the sputtering motor. The boys were a year older than us and ran with the popular crowd. Jimmy had a handsome face, blond hair, and big blue eyes, while Fred could have blended in anywhere with average features and unruly brown curls that fell down his forehead.

"We're going to Barr City Creamery. Can you take us?" Rose asked.

"Sure," Jimmy answered. "We'll give you a short tour and drop you off."

"Rose!" I hissed, pulling her back. "What would our mothers say if they saw us getting into this thing with two boys we hardly know?"

"Don't be such a prude," she said, laughing. "How will they know if we don't tell them?"

"It's not proper," I added in defeat.

Fred jumped down, offering a hand to help us climb up to the second bench, where we sat facing the back of the car. I held my breath and glanced around for anyone who might recognize us. My heart pounded as Jimmy pulled out into the street, skirting a horse and carriage. The tufted leather bench held the warmth of the sun, and a breeze swept my hair up behind me, creating a pleasant sensation. The vehicle bounced along, passing a rider on horseback who cast a wary eye.

"My brother Michael will be so jealous that he missed seeing your car," Rose called over her shoulder.

"It's a Remington Runabout," Jimmy said. "My father had it shipped all the way from Utica, New York. Tell your brother to come by the house anytime and take a look."

We circled several blocks in the wrong direction, causing me to fear the boys might be kidnapping us. But soon Jimmy turned down Nineteenth Street and pulled alongside the Barr City Creamery.

"Do you want to have an ice cream with us?" Rose asked after we jumped down and stepped onto the sidewalk. My legs felt weak and wobbly.

"Thanks, but I'm worried about those clouds. I have to get the car home and in the carriage house before it rains," Jimmy said. He gave Rose a big smile. "Next time, though."

I thought Rose would swoon and collapse right there. She waved enthusiastically as Jimmy and Fred drove off. "I have a terrible crush on Jimmy," she said. "I've never noticed his eyes are the color of bluebells."

We had to walk around a woman talking with two men to reach the door of the ice cream parlor. The older gentleman had gray hair and long sideburns that looked like exclamation marks drawn on his ruddy cheeks. His blue silk vest strained over an immense stomach. But it was the second, much younger man who captured my attention and caused me to take a deep breath. He was a foot taller than both his companions. His tailored gray suit emphasized a lanky frame. Beneath a silk derby hat, he had neatly trimmed, almost black hair. His fine features formed a face of great perfection like the sketches of men I'd admired in magazine advertisements. He stepped out of our way, nodding politely at Rose and me. I wondered if he had noticed us getting out of Jimmy's car.

"Sara Jane, are you listening to me?" Rose asked as she led me inside and to a wrought iron table by the front window. "Do you think Jimmy wants to take me for ice cream?"

"Probably," I murmured.

"What are you staring at?"

"That man." I nodded toward the group outside the window. "I've never seen anyone so handsome and elegant in Denver."

She glanced over. "Yes, I see. I wonder who that woman is? She's wearing an expensive silk suit, but that bright yellow hair can only come from a bottle." She studied her for a moment. "She doesn't seem...proper, like she belongs with those gentlemen."

It was difficult to discern the woman's age, but she had long passed her youth. Her brash blonde curls struck me as incongruous with her fashionable afternoon suit, which clung to her ample figure. She raised her hand as if in protest at something the older man said then turned to the younger man, leaning in and smiling like a coy ingenue. He stiffened and took a step backward.

"He's very refined. Maybe he's from New York or even Paris," Rose said. "But he's too old for us."

I smiled. "I know, but I hope one day I meet someone like him."

Rose prattled away about Jimmy on the tram ride home and how she might add a character like him to her new story. A bolt of lightning flashed across the sky not far away followed by a rumble of thunder. My thoughts returned to Sister Agnes's disturbing pronouncements about Peter and Papa. I needed Mama's reassurance regarding my doubts over our new religion.

I arrived home at four, shortly before torrents of water broke free from the clouds. Katherine said Mama was in the library, and I hurried to find her. I put aside my guilt about going for a ride with Jimmy and Fred. If she asked me about it, I would never lie. But perhaps Rose was right that we didn't need to volunteer the information. I had more important things to discuss.

In mid-April Mama and I began worshiping at St. Mary's Cathedral downtown, while Cole attended the Sunday school. She asked me to accept the change for our family's sake and try to adjust as best I could. The Latin mass with its rituals of kneeling, crossing, and taking communion offered a stark contrast to the simple Baptist services we had formerly attended. Even Mama seemed unsure what to do at times, carefully watching the movements of others and following their lead. The grandeur of the cathedral's stone pillars, stained-glass windows, and wooden carvings filled me with a state of awe. I studied the oil paintings of the Virgin Mary, the baby Jesus, and a host of angels along with works depicting the lives of Saint Francis of Assisi and Saint Sebastian. Marble statues of other saints adorned the side altars in recesses barely visible in the flickering candlelight. A booklet on the saints I had received in catechism class detailed the histories of these sanctified beings. I read the stories of their sacrifices with equal parts wonder and circumspection. How did they fit into my life?

Mama looked up as I opened the door. She sat at the desk sorting through correspondence and bills. "I'm glad you made it home before you got drenched. How was your afternoon with Rose?"

"Fun. I brought you a present." I pulled *Up from Slavery* from my bag.

She beamed. "How thoughtful. I've been meaning to get a copy." She glanced at the first pages then placed it on the desk. "We must finish reading Mr. Washington's story and talk about it. I'd like to tell you more about when I was a little girl and lived in Tennessee. We don't have time today, but soon."

I shifted from one foot to the other. "Could I ask you something?"

"Of course. What is it, dear?"

I sat on the cane-backed chair next to the desk. "I have questions about our new religion. I'm not sure how to reconcile what I used to know about God with what I'm learning in catechism class. The Baptist Sunday school never mentioned praying to saints or confessing sins. Or the trinity of the Holy Ghost. How do we know which faith is right?"

Mama sat back, biting her lower lip. "I realize this has been a huge and confusing change for you. For me as well, in truth. But we must do our best to accept the Catholic church for now. All religions—Protestants, Catholics, Jews, and Muslims—have different practices and beliefs. Yet it's the same God listening, no matter which path we take to worship Him. Try not to worry too much over the details. I ask only that you do your best to learn the catechism and receive your first communion."

"Do you like the Catholic church?"

She hesitated. "To be honest, I prefer the Baptist church. But I had to make accommodations to get this job and support our family. It was a pragmatic choice, but I'm sure God understands my decision."

I tried to think of something positive to say about the religion. "The stories of the saints' struggles and sacrifices inspire me. Do you think they're true?"

"Well, I believe many of the stories are mostly true. Others may have been embellished over time or created to teach a lesson to remind us to be good to others."

"I find comfort in praying to them."

"Yes, I like that as well." She smiled gently. "What beliefs are hardest for you?"

"I'm worried about dying."

She startled. "Goodness, how so?"

"Sister Agnes says if we don't follow the Catholic doctrine exactly, our souls won't be saved and we'll never go to heaven."

"But you and Cole are baptized now," Mama said, seemingly unsure how to respond.

My first day in catechism class, Sister Agnes was horrified to learn neither Cole nor I had been baptized. The Baptist church only baptized adults who understood and accepted the faith. Sister Agnes explained how the Catholic church performed the sacrament on newborns to remove their original sin and save their souls. The sister quickly reported our breach to the priest, and an embarrassed Mama delivered us to the cathedral the next afternoon for the Father to perform the rite.

"But what about Peter? He was never baptized." I recounted my conversation with Sister Agnes the week before. "She says since Peter was young and probably didn't commit any personal sins, his soul is in a state of limbo. But what is limbo, and how long will he have to stay there?" My throat drew tight as tears swam in my eyes.

Mama's lips trembled. "In this case, I strongly disagree with Sister Agnes," she said. "I know our Peter is already an angel in heaven."

"And Sister Agnes says even though Papa was baptized, he's in purgatory...until his sins...are burned away." I broke into sobs. "After that he may enter a state of...grace and be received into heaven. Papa never did anything...to deserve going to purgatory. I don't want him to burn."

Mama folded me in her arms. Her shoulders shook as her tears dripped down my neck. "You mustn't worry, my darling. Sister Agnes takes the teachings of the church quite literally. I can't accept such ideas." She sat back again. "And you don't have to either."

"Do you think Peter and Papa will be in heaven when we get there one day?" I asked, wiping my tears on the sleeve of my blouse.

"Of course. They were the dearest, loveliest people. Their souls are with God, not in limbo or purgatory." She sighed. "I greatly regret putting you through this. I've leaned on you too much through our hard times, and I know it's been difficult. You must tell me anytime you are troubled."

"I feel better talking with you." Her words had lifted a great burden. Then a new thought struck me. "When I go to confession, must I tell them I don't believe these things?"

She shook her head slowly. "No. It is not a sin to follow your heart and think for yourself. Faith is very personal. We each decide what beliefs bring comfort to our souls. Take from the Catholic church what is helpful for you and ignore the rest. God will love and care for us no matter what spiritual path we choose."

A whoosh of air passed from my lips. "Oh good."

"When you reach your eighteenth birthday, I will understand if you change back to the Baptist church, or whatever church speaks the truth to you."

I rose, clutching my shopping bag, and smiled. "I think I shall found the church of books when I am older."

Mama laughed. "Bravo." Then she added, "Sara Jane, let's not mention our conversation to anyone else. I've already had one difficult discussion with Mildred this afternoon."

I kissed her cheek, feeling greatly relieved. I could always count on Mama to understand my fears. I stifled my guilt over our secret car ride with Jimmy and Fred, and nearly skipped from the room.

Sins of the Father

W ednesday afternoon while Sara Jane went off with Rose, and Eva and Cole left on a walk around the neighborhood, I took the opportunity to discuss Eva's situation with Mildred. I told myself to be brave and not let her intimidate me, but my stomach quivered at the prospect. I found her reading in the parlor. Her eyes drooped with a torpor that threatened to envelope her at any moment.

She glanced up. "Lida."

I pulled a loose thread from the cuff of my blouse. "What are you reading?"

"*To Have and To Hold.* Sometimes my literary club selects the most banal novels." She placed a marker in between the pages and set the book on the side table. She waited expectantly as I struggled for words. "I would guess that's not what you came to talk about," she said at last.

"No. I'd like a private word. Shall we go to the library?" I didn't want Katherine to overhear us in case the conversation became heated, which seemed a likely possibility.

She tipped her head as if puzzled, then heaved herself off the settee and followed me to the back room.

I closed the door behind us and suggested she sit in one of the mahogany-colored leather chairs on the far side of the room. Dappled sunlight filtered through the abundant trumpet vine outside the window, dancing across the wooden floor and carpet like butterflies fluttering past. I often retreated to the library to pay my bills, write correspondence, or read quietly, but mostly to think. Here, memories of William surrounded me. It had been his office, where he worked and dreamed and sipped a late-night whiskey to relax after a long day of work. The room's contents conjured his masculine presence. Engineering books neatly lined the shelves; rolls of sketches and calculations were filed in a specially built cabinet with deep cubbyholes; pens, an inkwell, and blotter remained on the big oak desk; and the spicy scent of his pipe tobacco still imbued the room. I'd never had the heart to change anything.

Mildred glanced at the copy of Sigmund Freud's new book, *The Interpretation of Dreams,* sitting on the small table between the chairs. She blanched. "Mercy, Lida, are you reading this scandalous book?"

I regretted that I had not thought to put it away but couldn't help smiling inside at her reaction. Nonetheless, I felt a touch embarrassed, as if I'd been caught in some illicit activity. "I just finished reading it. As a doctor I try to keep up to date on new ideas about the human condition, both physical and mental. I don't agree with all his theories, but they're thought-provoking." The book had stirred heated debate and controversy with its frank discussions of women's dreams and sexual fantasies, along with his concept of the "Oedipus Complex," averring that children at a young age felt sexually attracted to their parent of the opposite sex. Certainly, these ideas were far too radical for the likes of Mildred.

She shook her head. "It should be banned."

After a stretch of silence in which I struggled over how to begin, she asked, somewhat impatiently, "What did you wish to talk about?"

I raised my eyes to meet hers, feeling the dread of a young child called by the school principal to be reprimanded for a misdeed. I took a deep breath. "It's about Eva...and Mr. Dearman."

"I expected she'd tell you, but there is nothing to discuss when it comes to that man." She leaned back so her face was lost in the shadows of the wingback chair, her disapproval and anger cascading over me.

"Try to be receptive and hear me out." Irritation seeped into my voice despite my best intentions. "As you well know, they are desperately in love and desire to marry. I cannot fathom why you and Mother want to stand in their way. Mother has maintained her grasp on poor Eva for three years now. From what I gather, she is quite capable of getting along on her own. It's unconscionable to keep Eva at home simply to be her companion."

"Is this what Eva would have you believe? That's nonsense." She fingered the brass brads along the chair's curving arm. "Our primary concern is for Eva's health."

"Mother expressed her disapproval of Mr. Dearman from the beginning, but she knows nothing about him. It's clear she doesn't care about Eva's happiness, only her own selfish needs." I knew these sentiments did nothing to further Eva's cause, but I couldn't seem to keep the words from tumbling out.

"That's a terrible thing to say about your own mother. Dr. Bartley told us Eva's heart and other organs are damaged from the scarlet fever. He feels the demands of marriage and childbearing would be too much for her physically."

"That's only a convenient excuse, since Mother objected long before Eva got sick. Besides, you should consider that Dr. Bartley is close to seventy by now, and his medical training over forty years out of date. It's a miracle Eva survived under his care. She told me he bled her, for heaven's sake, which medical science has proven useless and often damaging. I did a thorough examination yesterday and found her perfectly healthy. She simply needs to build up her stamina and gain some weight. I see no reason why she shouldn't have children."

"You're entitled to your opinion, but there is no need to disparage Dr. Bartlett. Even assuming Eva is well enough to marry, it doesn't change the fact that Mr. Dearman is completely unsuitable. We have no idea about his people or his character. He comes waltzing into Lawrence every few months for a week or two, captivating Eva's heart. She is barely acquainted with the man."

"You and Mother hardly helped in that regard by forbidding her to see him." I shook my head in exasperation. "Does Mother find it so objectionable that he's a Northerner? Does she reject him for this alone, as she did my William? Is she still harboring her unrelenting resentment for the South's defeat? She has never condemned slavery as the reprehensible, degenerate system it was or recognized the suffering and pain caused by white landowners, our family included, by *owning* other human beings." My voice grew louder and louder with long-held indignation and anger bred from years of arguing with Mother when I was young. I could never let go of the tremendous shame I felt over my family's past. "Imagine her saying to me that slavery was a 'regrettable but necessary evil.' Please don't tell me she's brought you around to her way of thinking?"

Mildred put a hand up in protest. "Please, Lida, calm yourself. You know I feel the same way as you about this horrible stain on our country and our family's history. But, unlike you, I never saw the point in engaging in endless confrontations with Mother. It serves no purpose. And while it may be a factor in Mother's attitude toward Mr. Dearman, that is not her greatest concern."

I took a moment to compose myself. "What is it then? Eva tells me he's from an old and distinguished Boston family. He's a well-respected attorney who can provide a good life for her. And he's a handsome, charming gentleman with exemplary manners. What more could you ask for?"

Mildred sat forward, her mouth pinched. "Such a strikingly good-looking man is used to having his way. Most likely he was spoiled and pampered from a young age and allowed a free reign. Who knows where his fancy may wander, leaving Eva heartbroken. I might remind you our father was handsome and charming, and he made Mother miserable their entire marriage."

A flush of outrage burned my face. "That has nothing to do with Mr. Dearman. The circumstances are completely different." I wanted to add that Mother had succeeded in making Father miserable as well, but in the interest of Eva's cause, I held back.

Mildred narrowed her eyes, taking on the harsh, unbending demeanor she had developed over the years. "You were too young to remember our life in Tennessee and what happened."

91

"Perhaps," I allowed, "but you were only eight when we left. How much can you recall?"

"I heard the arguments and Mother's tears."

"I'm well aware of Father's…weaknesses, but I also know he wasn't the only one to blame. When we moved to Lawrence after the war, he devoted himself to Mother and our family. She refused to forgive him and reconcile. More often than naught she spurned his affections and kindness."

"I cannot listen to this distortion of the truth. Father blinded you with his charms, as he did everyone else in the family."

"Whatever you believe about Father, you cannot condemn Mr. Dearman based on your unfounded assumption that he will be the same. It's ludicrous."

"There is a certain type of man who cannot be trusted." She pushed herself up from the chair. "There is no point in continuing this conversation. It will be a great folly if Eva marries Mr. Dearman, something she would regret the rest of her life. I won't discuss it further." She strode across the room and closed the door behind her with a bang.

I remained in my chair, closing my eyes. A great lethargy sapped the energy from my limbs. I could find no way to reason with Mildred when her opinion was firmly entrenched. It made me furious that she would defend Mother and blame all the discontent of our parents' marriage on Father. I knew the truth.

Growing up, Mother and Father occasionally shared memories from their life in Tennessee, but these stories rarely revealed the conflict that had followed them from their younger years to a new start in Kansas. I gleaned more from the comments my aunts and Mother's cousins let slip at times.

My parent's union was an unhappy story of two people never suited for each other, a marriage of convenience, not of love.

Both Mother and Father were born in southern Tennessee, not twenty miles apart, to families who raised thoroughbred horses. Their parents were neighbors and close friends, members of the social fabric of wealthy landowners who lived in an insular world dependent on the ungodly institution of slavery.

Mother's grandparents, the Kendricks, arrived in America from England in 1796 as young newlyweds. They settled first in Virginia then moved to Tennessee several years later. Great-grandfather bred regal lines of English horses, which became much sought after, and the family prospered. My grandfather, James Kendrick, the oldest son, inherited the farm and married a local girl, Sarah Rousseau. They raised a large and active family of five girls and three boys. My mother, Carolina Kendrick, was born in 1839, the youngest child and prettiest of the daughters. She grew up the pampered family pet.

When my sister and I were small, we gathered around Mother in the evenings to hear her reminisce about the handsome young gentlemen who pursued her before she married and the Civil War began. Beaus from as far away as three counties fawned over her at balls, desperate to get on her dance card, hoping they might be the one to capture her heart. Her face transformed with a rapt expression as she retreated into another era, a time that had long ago disappeared and existed only in the ethereal spaces of her mind. A sigh always ended her reveries with the unspoken words: if only she could go back and choose again.

On Father's side, my grandfather Delacroix left France in 1828 at the age of twenty-five with hardly enough money to pay his passage. He landed first in New Orleans where he worked for a horse breeder. Five years later he had saved enough money to buy a small piece of property in Tennessee and start a horse farm of his own. He married my grandmother, Adele Bourdon. They had one son, my father, Gerard Delacroix, in 1835, and a daughter who died before she turned two.

As the business grew, Grandfather bought more and more land and expanded his breeds. But in 1851, at the age of forty-seven, an outbreak of smallpox ended his life. Father, sixteen at the time, had hoped to attend the College of William and Mary in Virginia, followed by travel abroad, before settling down. But duty forced him to take over the farm. He soon discovered my grandfather had overextended his finances. It took all of Father's cunning to keep the farm afloat in the following years; he was always on the edge of losing everything. He managed to keep his struggles from his mother and other families in their circle as worry consumed him.

Shortly after Father turned twenty-one, his two best sires and three mares died of a virus that had spread throughout the countryside. It was a devastating blow. He recognized his only hope was to marry into a family with the resources to make his business solvent once more. He saw no need to search further than his neighbors and close family friends, the Kendricks. He married mother a year later.

Once, when I was seventeen and furious with Mother after arguing about my plans to attend college in Massachusetts, I rushed to Father for comfort. He soothed me in his usual calm and reasonable manner, assuring me he would bring her around to the idea. He reminded me how Mother's quick temper often flared but soon subsided. He began to reminisce about their stormy courtship as young people. "Your mother was always hard to handle. I should have seen it more clearly when I began to call on her. Her beauty and flirtatious nature drew me in, but she was so young and spoiled. I believed once we wedded she would settle down. As you've observed, our marriage never attained an even keel." He chuckled. "I won her heart by feigning indifference, a sharp contrast to the constant flattery of her other suitors. I challenged her vanity."

My aunts and Mother's cousins said Father had been the handsomest man in the county, with a quick wit and intelligence. Young women found him irresistible with his dimples and big brown eyes. Used to getting her own way and the best of everything, Mother was determined to conquer him. After six months of fitful courting, Father asked Mother to marry him. Their parents were delighted. The Kendricks put on a grand wedding, drawing over three hundred relatives and friends from near and far.

According to Aunt Effie, my parents got along well enough the first few years, as Mother had Mildred to care for and parties and balls to attend. Then the Civil War intervened and tore apart their world.

Sympathies in Tennessee were split between remaining in the Union or joining the Confederates. But after the Union army attacked Fort Sumter in Charleston, Tennessee's residents voted to secede with the other Southern states. Father signed up with the First Tennessee Infantry Regiment in July of 1861. Then the trouble began at home.

A year into the war, Father was shot in the right shoulder at the Battle of Shiloh, causing permanent damage to his bone and muscles. He no longer had the strength to fire a rifle or raise his saber. He was reassigned to requisitioning supplies for the army. He traveled throughout the Southern states and war zones, making New Orleans his headquarters. Burdened by guilt, believing he had somehow failed his regiment, he turned to drink and other diversions.

"The war stripped bare all sense of gentility," he once told me. "Most of the men in my regiment died in the battles at Shiloh or Stone River. I never understood why I was spared."

Mother's family gave varying accounts of those years as they reminisced at family parties, rocking in their chairs on the porches, fanning themselves to keep cool on hot summer afternoons. Each one seemed to recall different versions of the same events, weaving in their biases and opinions. No one denied Father had his foibles as a young man and at times behaved badly. But the explanations were as varied as the changing colors reflected in the facets of a prism.

"When your father volunteered to report to the army in Nashville, your mother was fit to be tied," Aunt Bertha would say. "She was five months along with you, while Mildred was not yet four years old. She demanded that he stay at home. Your father just laughed and said he wasn't going to be a coward and let others do all the fighting."

"Young men were full of spit and fire in those difficult days," Aunt Effie would add. "Like wild stallions, they were raring to fight. It wasn't only your father."

Aunt Bertha would shake her head. "It was a dreadful time. The war changed those fine boys. They went off to battle and didn't know if they were ever coming back. Of course they misbehaved. Men could be excused, given the strain of the war. They took their pleasures where they could find them, unsure if each day was their last. They needed to escape and forget the unspeakable things they saw and did. Most wives understood and found it best to ignore these indiscretions. But not your mother. She couldn't forgive your father for anything."

My aunts, like many sisters, were not blind to Mother's shortcomings, nor were they afraid to talk of them. "Oh, your mother had her faults. Don't we all," Aunt Bertha would say. "She was demanding and downright selfish at times."

Aunt Effie would sigh. "She was too young and spoiled to marry. Barely seventeen years old. Mama and Papa should have made her wait, but they always gave in to whatever she wanted."

Cousin Victoria remembered the balls where Mother danced with the best-looking young men. "She knew how pretty she was and that all the young men desired her. It made her proud."

"Haughty," Cousin Genevieve would add. "She had no thought for anyone but herself."

Cousin Victoria told me once how Mother had stolen Genevieve's beau, Jake Reynolds. "When Jake lost your mother's affections to your father, he ran off to Richmond. He died later in the war. Genevieve never forgave your mother."

"When your father came home on leave, worn down and disheartened by the fighting and killing, your mother never stopped complaining about the trials of her life without him," Cousin Genevieve said. "Soon he didn't come home at all."

"But it was wrong of your father to be so open in his indiscretions," Cousin Victoria allowed. "He went to New Orleans, gambling, drinking, and running around with the worst sort of women. Word spread. People knew. It humiliated your mother, and I felt sorry for her."

Aunt Effie admitted she worried about Mother during the war. "He left her alone much of the time when he could have come home. Deserters or Union soldiers might have raided the farm. She could have been assaulted or killed. That was unforgiveable."

The stories ebbed and flowed. It was the difficult times. It was poor judgment and a lack of fortitude by the young. Father had erred. Mother had made life impossible for him. No one was right. No one was wrong.

I may not have understood the strife between my parents in those early years in Tennessee, but I had other memories of our life there. I could still picture our overseer, Mr. Coulter, with his cruel, dark eyes and his inappropriate attentions toward my mother while Father was away. He terrified me when he threatened our field hands and stable workers with harsh and unforgiving words, his whip on display. Not yet four years old, I had no concept of slavery and didn't understand that my father had bought and sold these people who served us, as if they were horses or livestock. I only knew the inequalities of our lives confused and pained me.

Two of my favorite people were Angela, our cook, and her daughter, Chastity, two years older than me, who helped her mother in the kitchen. Chastity and I often played house together in the warm, smoky spaces near the brick oven, sharing my porcelain doll and her rag doll. We held tea parties with glasses of fresh lemonade and her mother's molasses cookies. I didn't understand why they lived in a crude wooden cabin behind the stables and wore rough cotton dresses. Why did our workers toil long hours in the fields, eating only pork and cornbread cooked on a camp stove? Mother dismissed my questions, saying it was not my place to ask. It was simply the way things were.

After the war when the slaves were freed, Father had no money to replenish his horses or pay for workers. He struggled for a year trying to make ends meet. In April 1866, he announced we would leave the unhappy history of our lives in Tennessee behind and start anew in Lawrence, Kansas.

The three-week ride to Lawrence through Tennessee and Missouri stands out in my mind. We rattled and bumped along rutted dirt roads in an old hay wagon pulled by Father's two last field horses, staying in small inns along the way. We passed camps of former slaves huddled along the roads, living in lean-tos. Many stared at us with open hostility and defiance while others had a wild look of confusion and fear, grateful for their freedom but with no idea where to go or what lay ahead.

Mildred and I rode in the flatbed among a few pieces of our best furniture, crates of clothes, several paintings and mementos, and the good English china and family silver. Mother clutched her jewelry box in her lap, containing a ruby necklace and earrings, a diamond bracelet, an amethyst broach, a gold locket, and silver bracelets. She had buried her jewels and the family silver in the forest during the war in case of looting by deserters or Union soldiers.

Mildred and I viewed the trip as a great adventure, having never traveled more than a few miles to neighboring farms. Father led us in songs and told silly jokes. He promised we would make new friends and go to a real school with other children. Mother cried for most of the journey, sullen and unresponsive.

My parents chose Lawrence, Kansas, to begin anew after Aunt Effie wrote to Mother, urging our family to come north. She had married Uncle Clyde shortly before the war and moved to his hometown. He owned the local newspaper, a bank, and most of the buildings in downtown Lawrence. Kansas had joined the Union as a free state, opposed to slavery, in January of 1861, only months before the war broke out. They fought with the North.

We lived with my aunt and uncle for six months until Father settled into his work and could afford to rent a house. They had no children of their own and relished the chance to fill their roomy home with family. Uncle Clyde loved telling jokes and often acted like a child himself, as Aunt Effie was fond of saying.

Father went to work at Mr. Carney's grain business, which contracted with local farmers to market their wheat, corn, barley, and rye. When Mr. Carney died two years later, he left the business to Father. It made no sense to many. His only son had died in the Battle of Nashville in 1864 fighting with the Union Army. And no one in Lawrence would ever forget the deadly massacre by Quantrill's Raiders, Confederate "bushwhackers," who descended on Lawrence in August 1863, killing a hundred and fifty men and boys. Luckily, Mr. Carney had been out visiting farms and escaped the carnage. People in Lawrence talked about it endlessly, wondering how Mr. Carney could give his life's work to a Southerner. The enemy. Some said it was an act of forgiveness for his son's death. Others called it a betrayal.

Yet with Father's genial nature and honesty, he gradually won over most people in town and the farmers. Growers, large or small, received a fair price and respect for their hard work.

Three years later, Father built a big house and stables on the edge of town, where he could once again keep his beloved thoroughbred horses. Mother never stopped issuing endless recriminations and complaints, a constant, bitter diatribe on Father's neglect and disgraceful behavior during the early years of their marriage and his inability to keep the land in Tennessee. No matter how hard Father tried to please her, she never appeared to forgive him. He bore it in silence.

When I was ten, I discovered *Uncle Tom's Cabin* on a back shelf in the Lawrence library. Only then did I fully comprehend the truth about slavery. I confronted Father over our family's part in such a cruel system. He told me he deeply regretted his role in perpetuating an indefensible practice for his own selfish gain.

"It was flat-out wrong." He shook his head with eyes full of sorrow. "I knew the institution of slavery had to be abolished. I dishonored myself and all that is good by not standing up against it. But I feared the farm would never survive without our slaves, and I lacked the courage to defy my family and everyone around us. Our existence was destined for failure, but we remained too blind and selfish to relent. And so we went to war, bringing unimaginable destruction and the loss of hundreds of thousands of young lives on both sides. I must live with this guilt all my days. I hope God can forgive me." He stared into my eyes. "I hope you can as well."

I always thought of my childhood as relatively happy, despite my parents' obvious antipathy toward each other. Mildred and I were pampered and loved. As sisters, we enjoyed a close relationship until I left home. There were frequent parties and gatherings of relatives and friends to fill

101

our days. Father taught us to ride at an early age and often brought us to the harness races in Kansas City, where his horses competed. As young ladies coming out into society— as much as Lawrence had such a thing—Mildred and I shared our secret crushes and the thrill of being wooed. I was Mildred's maid of honor at her wedding the year before I left for college.

When conflicts arose between our parents, as they inevitably did, we split into camps. Mildred aligned with Mother, while I defended Father. Although he treated both of us with kindness and affection, I was clearly closest to him. I held no grudges for his past. When I was young, father always had time to play with me, explain how things worked, or read a book aloud at bedtime. He taught me how to train horses, and I often accompanied him on his visits to farms in the countryside over the summers when I was out of school. Father imparted in me an admiration for those who worked the land, never knowing when weather, disease, or pests might wipe out their crops and bring them to their knees. He said there was dignity and worth in even the lowliest forms of labor. Every soul must be valued.

Mother never stopped complaining that Father was ruining me, turning me into a tomboy no man would ever marry. She eventually gave up trying to keep me home to conform to her ideals of a "proper young lady."

When I was fifteen Mother gave birth to Evangeline, which came as a great shock to all. The joy of a new baby in the house helped unite the family and eased the discord between our parents, even if it remained under the surface waiting to erupt. Everyone loved our beautiful Eva. I spent my free time holding and rocking my baby sister, in awe of the

102

tiny hands that clutched my fingers and the big blue eyes that followed every movement I made. There was nothing more wonderful than a smile from her sweet lips. As she grew into a toddler, Mildred and I fought over who could read her books each night or hold her hand as she stumbled along on wobbly legs. Eva's sweet disposition defined her from the start, and we proudly displayed her to neighbors and friends to admire. For the first time the notion came to me that I might want to marry and have children of my own one day.

Academics had never been my strength until I reached high school. Mrs. Richards, my history and civics teacher, inspired me with her love of knowledge and excitement for teaching. She revealed the possibilities an education offered for expanding one's world, especially for women. Once I dedicated myself to my studies, I began to excel. She convinced me to further my education, helping me research women's colleges across the country and fill out applications. I could have gone to the University of Kansas in Lawrence, but I wanted more than life in a small, Midwestern town. Once I had read the Smith College brochure, proclaiming its pride in offering intellectual freedom, attention to the relation between a college education and public issues of world order and human dignity, and a concern for the rights and privileges of women, I knew I must attend. I thought it would be thrilling to live near Boston and experience life on the East Coast.

Father supported my ambitions from the start, despite Mother's angry opposition. I think he understood Lawrence was too small in place and spirit to meet my needs. He escorted me on the long train ride to Massachusetts that September to see me safely settled as I commenced my great adventure. We spent a wonderful set of weeks touring Boston and the Massachusetts coast before school began. I remember how he clung to me on parting, making me promise to work hard, but most of all to be happy. It was as if he had a premonition it would be the last time we saw each other. He died two months later of pneumonia. I could not bear to go home that Christmas to face his absence. I grieved alone in my dorm room, staring out at the snowy grounds.

Now, drowning in a lifetime of memories, I stood and gazed around the library. A great longing for William, with his sleepy smile and tender eyes, swept over me. I knew he would have supported me in aiding Eva. Although I had yet to meet Mr. Dearman, my instincts told me he was a good man who would make a wonderful husband. Eva was too smart and capable to misjudge the man with whom she desired to share her life. She had to make her own choices, and I would help her find the courage to not be swayed from her heart's purpose

.

Expected Responses

Wednesday, June 26, 1901

Dear Diary,

I am at sea here with Lida and Eva. They've bonded together, two peas in a pod, and I feel like an unwanted intruder. Even the children flock to Eva, enraptured by her beauty and gentle nature. I am but someone to avoid. I cannot deny my hurt feelings. I can see I was foolish to hope that Lida and I might reconcile and find the closeness we once shared.

The trip seems particularly ill-conceived now that Eva has enlisted Lida in her attempt to convince me Mr. Dearman is a suitable match. I should have anticipated this outcome. Lida spoke with me this afternoon, challenging Mother's and my opposition. I tried to clarify our concerns but found my explanations rang hollow to my own ears. Yet the confrontation raised a contrary demon within me and spurred me to issue defensive, adamant retorts to Lida's counterarguments.

As the night grows late, sleep eludes me. I am mired in a jumble of conflicting emotions. Truly, I want Eva to be happy. At the heart of my opposition to Mr. Dearman is my concern and love for her. I could not stand to see her hurt by someone I fear is feckless in his pursuit of her. But is it fair to compare Mr. Dearman to our father when I understand so little of the man? I am driven by intuition rather than facts. Given Dr. Bartley's diagnosis, I worry about Eva's fragile health. However, Lida claims she is fine, and I admit her medical training is more current. I struggle over who or what to believe.

There are several truths I could not admit to Lida. While Mother's initial physical collapse, which brought Eva home from school three years ago, was not feigned, subsequent episodes appeared highly dubious. Her motives in keeping Eva at her side are quite transparent and not entirely admirable. Mother nears the end of her life and seems consumed by loneliness and, perhaps, regrets. The thought of Eva marrying Mr. Dearman and moving to Boston is too much for her to bear. I confess it is hard for me as well. This possible outcome may have unfairly colored our opinions of the man.

I have remained empathetic to Mother for reasons not conveyed to Lida, as she seems unreceptive to such concerns. Mother has become frail and diminished in her dotage—a gradual decline that began almost twenty years ago with her inexplicable grief over Father's untimely death. Lida's choice to forge a life of her own against Mother's wishes left her defeated and weakened. When Eva decided to go to college in Pennsylvania, this only compounded her sense of helplessness. But Mother is blind to the truth that her obstinacy and attempts to manipulate others only alienates those she loves.

I am quite sure the topic of Mr. Dearman will be raised again. But in the meantime, I can report to Mother Eva is happy in Lida's company and at least physically away from Mr. Dearman's influence.

I received a letter from Mother late today filled with shock and outrage over the news of Lida's conversion to Catholicism. Mother says she could not bear it if anyone in Lawrence found out and assures me I need not worry about her spreading the news. I did smile when she accused Lida of changing religions with the sole purpose of causing her the greatest possible distress. I sincerely doubt that entered Lida's mind. To my opinion, Lida has made a pact with the devil for the purpose of securing a job to support her family. But I cannot condemn her motives, no matter how unacceptable I find her new faith.

Mother is worried about our exposure to Lida's friends who support women's suffrage and other radical causes. I hardly think my beliefs can be so easily influenced. Eva is more impressionable, but I doubt these ladies and their ideas will do her any harm. Better to keep her mind focused on something other than Mr. Dearman.

Aunt Effie is a saint, and I must write to her with my thanks. Mother says she comes by every day to check on her and took her to the Eldridge Hotel for luncheon on Tuesday. Her ability to put up with Mother's tiresome self-indulgence is a testament to sisterly love. This gives me pause as I think of my strained relationship with Lida.

Mother is disappointed Franklin turned down her invitation for dinner this coming Sunday, claiming the demands of his work. I know she tests his patience, but I do wish he could sacrifice a few hours for a lonely old lady. More concerning, he told her he isn't planning to attend church. I agree with Mother that this may strike our congregation as odd given that I am away.

I had hoped to find a letter from Franklin in the post. Perhaps tomorrow. He is as helpless as any man I've ever met, but I am sure he is getting along. His only interest seems to be his work these days, so he may hardly notice I'm gone. I do worry about my sweet Biscuit and how she is faring without me. I sorely miss the comfort of her snuggling in my lap as I pet her silky, golden hair. Pomeranians are known for their intelligence, and my beauty is certainly a compelling example, so aware of her surroundings and attuned to unexpected changes. She is my constant companion and, I fear, the only love I can consistently depend on these days. It is regrettable that she has never really warmed to Franklin. I recognize she is a bit high strung, and her barking grates on his nerves. Perhaps this time together alone will foster a new understanding between them.

I will struggle through the upcoming weeks here in Denver, far from home and my dear little Biscuit.

Chapter 9   **SARA JANE**

The Secret Correspondence

On Thursday I returned home from work at the millinery shop and found a cream-colored envelope addressed to Aunt Eva lying in the silver tray on the entry hall table. The return address read *Mrs. Sylvia Lewis, 14 West Fourth Street, Lawrence, Kansas*. The weight and thickness of the letter told me Aunt Eva's good friend had forwarded a letter from Mr. Dearman as promised. I decided to tuck it in my skirt pocket to deliver to Aunt Eva later in case Aunt Mildred should see it and become suspicious.

The house remained quiet except for the sound of Katherine humming one of her favorite Irish airs as she prepared lunch. I wandered through to the kitchen, knowing I would find a warm smile and ready ear. I could always share a confidence with her and be sure it was safely held between us.

When Mama had started medical school four years earlier, spending long hours attending classes and studying at the library, home had felt empty and lonely. I missed my sweet brother Peter more than ever. Papa was mostly away working at the mines. And then he was gone forever as well and life felt truly desolate. It was Katherine who helped filled the void and comforted me. Many days I cried in her arms, complaining of Mama being gone so much.

"Ah, lass," she would say, "yer ma is a fine woman who loves ye and little Cole beyond all measure, don't ye know. Ye must admire her dedication at this difficult time. Sure we must help her get through school so she can be a great doctor. I know it's hard, but she is doing it for ye and Cole and to help others. How can we let her down?" I took her words to heart and tried to support Mama as best I could, for I knew she was grieving like me.

Katherine glanced up with hands covered in flour as she cut dough into triangles and rolled them into crescent rolls, then lined them up on a baking sheet. The room smelled of yeast and stewed chicken, causing my stomach to gurgle with hunger.

"How was yer mornin', Miss Designer? Have ye dressed the grandest ladies in town this fine day?"

I groaned. "It was *so* boring. Rose stayed home with a headache, and only two customers came in all morning. I spent my time wiping down counters and cutting lengths of ribbon."

I took a plump red cherry from a bowl on the counter and popped it into my mouth, savoring the sweet burst of flavor. "Where are my aunts and Cole? Did they go for a walk?"

"They took a carriage to City Park for an outing. I gave Cole bread to feed the ducks at the lake. I expect them back any minute. I think it's a wee bit warm for yer Aunt Mildred to be out." Katherine lowered her voice to a whisper. "She perspires somethin' fierce. I had to scrub and scrub the blouse to her travelin' suit. But don't be tellin' yer ma I said that."

I giggled. "I won't. That must be why she uses so much lavender scent." I grabbed two more cherries.

"Mind ye, those are for dessert. I've made a lovely chicken salad and the rolls." She put the pan of rolls in the oven and washed her hands in the sink.

"Yer ma sent a message from work. She's been deliverin' a baby for one of the women at the Good Shepherd and can't get away as yet. I'm to serve lunch without her."

After being hired by the nuns, Mama had sat me down and carefully explained the circumstances of many of those she treated at the House of the Good Shepherd. The first Catholic Bishop in Colorado, Joseph Machebeuf, had opened the home almost twenty years before. The sisters who had run it helped many homeless and destitute young girls and women over the years. Recently, they had taken in an increasing number who had fallen into prostitution and wished to escape their unhappy fate.

"I will be completely frank about my new position," she began. "You are old enough for the truth, and I'd rather you hear it from me than from the careless or cruel remarks of others. A great many of the girls and women who end up at the home were forced into a terrible life due to poverty and desperation, selling their bodies to earn money. The economic collapse of the past eight years has only exacerbated the problem. Some are widows with children whose husbands were killed in mining accidents or other disasters. Surely we understand this tragedy after losing your father. Only these poor women have no education or training to fall back on. What jobs are available to them—domestic work or factories—often don't pay enough to keep their families fed and together. Most have no one to turn to for help."

I listened, too shocked to ask questions but admiring Mama's courage for choosing to help these women. And to tell me.

A slight blush had filled her cheeks as my own burned. "You should know there are women—madams who run houses of prostitution, like the infamous Mattie Silks—who choose this immoral work without a thought to society's conventions. They hope to make a lot of money, whatever the human cost. But most of the women have simply fallen into a terrible trap out of despair and hopelessness. They drink or take drugs to escape the shame and horror of their life, which only adds to their woes. Some are mere children as young as you, my darling. These are the ones who truly break my heart. I have come to sympathize, where once I might have harshly judged them. When I hear their tragic backgrounds and how they ended up in this position, I can only feel compassion. They could be ruined forever from living a normal life, but the nuns at Good Shepherd are trying to help. The girls train for work in respectable jobs, and the sisters assist them in resettling in other cities to start fresh. I treat them for diseases and addictions they may have developed through their illicit work. These are human beings who deserve our empathy and prayers." She looked at me with an anxious expression, perhaps wondering how I might react.

"Oh, Mama, I'll pray to Mary Magdalene, the patron saint of repenting prostitutes, and Margaret of Cortona, the patron saint of despairing prostitutes," I said. "They have the most moving stories of how they overcame their past sins by dedicating themselves to God and Jesus Christ."

Mama's eyebrows shot up. "Why...that's good of you, dear. You can see this problem has been a scourge on society throughout the ages." She paused a moment. "And you learned about the saints in catechism class?"

"Yes, from the booklet Sister Mary Claire gave us."

"Goodness. Now you understand why my friends and I find it essential for women to have decent work and wages, and for their children to have a good education. Without these things, they are often forced into unfathomable choices. If all women have the vote, we can pass new laws to help stem the tide of this terrible problem."

"I'm proud of you, Mama, for helping," I had assured her and hugged her close.

Now I turned at the sound of the front door opening and Cole racing through the dining room to the kitchen. He stood before us grinning, his shirt half out of his shorts and his socks falling around his ankles. "We saw three kinds of butterflies, and I caught a shiny black beetle as big as my thumb." He held up a dirt-encrusted hand. "But he got away."

Katherine pulled a kitchen chair in front of the sink. "Stand up here, and I'll wash ye up for lunch. Are ye eatin' with me, then?"

"I want to eat with my aunts." He gave her a pleading look. "Please."

"Aye, but ye'll have to mind yer manners and do as Sara Jane says, because yer ma won't be home 'til later." She ran her fingers through his unruly hair.

"Watch what you say," I added.

We sat down to lunch ten minutes later. Aunt Mildred poured glasses of lemonade. I nodded to Cole as I placed my napkin in my lap, and he followed suit. By now the letter for Aunt Eva was practically burning a hole in my pocket. I couldn't wait to give it to her.

113

Katherine carried a big tray into the dining room and set a basket of hot rolls on the table with a plate of butter and a bowl of her homemade apricot jam. Next she served the chicken salads.

"Did ye see the letters on the hall table, Miss Delacroix and Mrs. Bolton?" Katherine asked.

"Yes, thank you, Katherine," Aunt Mildred answered.

Aunt Eva looked up, alert. "No. I checked the tray but didn't see one."

"I put some letters for Mama on the desk in the library," I said quickly. "I must have accidently picked up yours."

"I can look," Katherine offered.

"No, no. I'll go when we finish lunch," I insisted too loudly. "I mean you have enough to do." Everyone looked at me with puzzled eyes, but Katherine shrugged and returned to the kitchen.

"How was your morning at City Park?" I asked Aunt Eva, hoping to divert attention.

"The gardens are lovely with the roses in full bloom," she replied. "Such beautiful shades of pink and coral."

"I don't know what good they are," Cole said, lifting a forkful of chicken. "You can't pick any of them."

"Of course not. It's a public garden," I said.

He frowned. "How do you know?"

I sighed. "There are signs in the park forbidding people to pick the flowers."

"Oh." He blinked several times. "I can't read them."

"And that's why you must go to school and learn," I said with a touch of impatience. The idea of starting school in September struck terror into Cole's heart. I didn't blame him for not wanting to end his carefree days with Katherine, but

114

we all had to grow up at some point. I certainly had found this out in recent years. I softened my tone. "I'll help you."

"Can't you help me here at home? Why must I go to school?"

"All good children go to school and get an education," Aunt Mildred interjected. "What would become of you if you didn't?"

Cole stared down at his salad, pushing the chicken around. He looked near tears.

"What is it that worries you about school, my dear?" Aunt Eva asked.

Cole raised his eyes to meet hers. "Billy Martin says I'm stupid 'cause I don't know my letters and numbers yet. He learned them when he was four."

"Billy lives in the block behind us," I explained to my aunts. "He's two years older than Cole and a big bully."

"What nonsense," Aunt Mildred said. "I shall help you prepare for school. We'll spend some time each morning."

I expected her offer to alarm Cole even further. She had been nothing but severe and critical with him—and with me, too, for that matter. To my surprise, a broad grin spread across his face.

"Hurray!" he shouted. He proceeded to finish his salad in record time, and I only had to remind him once to chew with his mouth closed.

"May I be excused, please?" he asked.

Aunt Mildred raised an eyebrow. "It's not polite to leave the table before others finish their meal."

"But I have something special I need to do," he insisted.

Eva cocked her head to one side. "He's been very good. I think we could let him go this once."

Cole raced toward the kitchen, nearly knocking over Katherine as she came into the dining room.

"Ach. Where are ye off to?" she asked as he dashed into the kitchen. We heard the back door slam.

"He ate all his lunch and asked to be excused," Aunt Eva offered.

Katherine shook her head. "That wee one has a time keepin' still, but he's a lovely boy altogether." She placed cups, a pot of coffee, cream, and sugar on the table along with the bowl of cherries and a plate of freshly baked icebox cookies.

Aunt Mildred looked up. "Sara Jane told us Lida had an emergency at the women's home, but she'll be back soon."

"Sure enough, she delivered a baby. She'll be home in plenty of time to go to yer tea." Katherine removed the empty salad plates.

"I thought only single women lived at the home," Aunt Mildred said.

"Babies are an unplanned consequence for these poor girls," Katherine said with a sigh.

Aunt Mildred frowned. "I beg your pardon?"

"These unfortunate ones worked in the lowest business known to women out of desperation, don't ye know," Katherine explained. "God bless and save their souls."

A short gasp escaped Mildred's lips as Katherine's meaning came to light. "Good lord. Eva, did you have any idea?"

Aunt Eva winced. "Lida did mention the nature of some of the home's residents."

"Don't worry, Aunt Mildred," I said. "Mama told me that now the women live in the home, they don't have to do those terrible things anymore."

"Your mother explained this to you? A girl of your age?" Aunt Mildred exploded as her face turned scarlet. I thought the buttons might pop off her blouse.

"Mama said it was better I hear it from her than through gossip and the misinformation of others," I said, defending her.

"Yer sister saved my life," Katherine said. "I nearly lost my mind with grief after the loss of my family. I don't know what might have become of me, but Dr. Clayton found me wandering the streets and took me in. She gave me a new family to love and a place to feel useful. And even when money became tight these past few years and I offered to find other employment, she wouldn't consider letting me go. She's a saint, don't ye know."

Aunt Eva cleared her throat. "Thank you, Katherine, for those kind words. That's all we need for now."

Katherine bustled off with her full tray.

Aunt Mildred glared at Aunt Eva and me. "Really, I never in all my life. The very idea."

I thought better of recounting my conversation with Mama about her new employment. Aunt Mildred was unlikely to appreciate the depth of Mama's sympathy and compassion. And it certainly wouldn't do to bring up the saints Mary Magdalene and Margaret of Cortona, since Aunt Mildred was so unhappy about our Catholic faith.

The back door slammed, and Cole reappeared, holding a fistful of sweet peas snatched from the vine out back. He thrust his hand out to Aunt Mildred.

117

"Thank you, Aunt Mildred, for wanting to teach me."

Aunt Mildred's mouth fell open and her shoulders relaxed. "How, how lovely," she sputtered. A gentle smile softened the harsh lines of her face. "Mind you, I shall require hard work on your part."

Aunt Mildred retired upstairs for a rest, and Cole went off to play with his friend Bobby next door.

Aunt Eva and I settled in the parlor. "I took your letter," I whispered, pulling the envelope from my pocket and handing it to her. "I thought it might be best if Aunt Mildred didn't see."

Aunt Eva read the return address. "Aren't you a clever girl?" Her hands trembled as she opened the flap. "Do you mind if I look?"

"Oh, *please*, I can't wait to hear what it says. I mean, if you want to tell me."

She smiled. "Let me see." The color in her cheeks heightened. She pulled out a single sheet of paper wrapped around another white envelope. She glanced at it and dropped it next to me. I read the short note: *Passing along a special letter for you. So exciting. Write me with the latest news. Love from your devoted friend, Sylvia*

Bold letters on the second envelope spelled *Eva*. She put a hand to her mouth and murmured, "As I hoped." She tore it open, pulling out three pages of thick white paper and quickly scanning them.

I turned my face away, wanting to give her privacy. Although it was terribly tempting to peek over her shoulder and read the letter. As she reached the third page, the front door opened. Mama was home at last.

"We're in the parlor," I called.

Mama walked in. "What have we here?"

Aunt Eva raised her head, beaming. "A letter from Mr. Dearman." Her breathing came in short, soft bursts, the way Buttercup's did when she was dreaming. "He arrives in Denver Wednesday—oh, that was yesterday—accompanied by his sister, Mrs. Charlotte Grove from Springfield. He's told me so much about her." She took a deep breath. "I must send him a note as soon as possible to let him know when we can meet. They're staying at the Brown Palace Hotel."

Mama blinked several times. "How wonderful."

"He's looking forward to meeting you." Aunt Eva put the letters in her skirt pocket and placed a hand over her chest. "My heart is pounding like a drum. I can hardly believe I shall see him soon. It's torture knowing he is nearby."

Mama sank down onto the green velvet chair. "Whatever shall we do about Mildred?"

My Admirable Friends

My sisters and I arrived for tea at the Meredith residence a little after four that afternoon. The home had a coziness about it I greatly admired. The family hosted a constant flow of Denver's intellectual and progressive thinkers, leaders for political reform and social equality, providing convivial and stimulating conversations. I always left these gatherings feeling enlightened and inspired.

The maid showed us into the formal parlor where Ellis, my dearest friend, and her mother were gathered with three other friends.

"Lida, dear," Ellis said, rising from her chair and giving me a quick hug. She turned expectantly to my sisters and extended her hand. "Mrs. Bolton and Miss Delacroix, I'm Ellis Meredith. What a great pleasure to meet you. Let me introduce my mother, Mrs. Emily Meredith, and our friends and colleagues," she continued. "May I present Mrs. Louise Forrest, who founded the Women's Industrial Legion, Mrs. Mary Bradford, a teacher and advocate for education reform, and Miss Minnie Reynolds, a fellow journalist at the *Rocky Mountain News*."

I beamed, proud of the accomplishments of these ladies and others who would soon arrive, the women I was lucky enough to call my friends. The individuals in our circle shared a long list of talents, which they put to good use in leading the Colorado suffrage movement and the fight for social justice. We came from different political backgrounds but worked together for the greater good. Some had run for and served in state and local offices, while others marched for causes and toiled tirelessly in women's clubs, raising money and implementing badly needed social programs. The efforts and commitment of these women had inspired me on many occasions when I came close to losing my courage and giving up on medical school. After William's passing, I often felt as if I was trapped at the bottom of a dark well. Some days I could hardly force myself from bed. But my circle of friends had bolstered my resolve to go on, providing not only sympathy but laughter and companionship, which sustained me through the worst.

Mildred managed a tepid handshake, warily examining the assembled women, while Eva shook each hand, murmuring greetings and offering the innocent smile of one still young and discovering life's potential.

"It is an honor to meet such an accomplished group of ladies," Eva said.

"Do sit down," Ellis said. "We all look forward to getting to know you." She was not quite five feet tall with chestnut hair and a vital energy that shone in her amber-brown eyes. Charming and articulate, she could disarm friends and foes alike, arguing anything from women's rights to philosophy with aplomb.

Ellis was staying temporarily with her parents since leaving her husband, Mr. Stansbury. Their divorce had become final only a few days before, and I knew she needed cheering up. While she never aired all their troubles, she had confided in me that Mr. Stansbury had grown weary of supporting her career and activism. He would have preferred she dedicate more time to home and family. Sadly, there had been no children.

"I've been reading your column, 'Woman's World,'" Eva said. "Your report on the disparity of women's wages compared to men's was very enlightening."

"Why thank you," Ellis said. "Miss Reynolds and I do our best to raise important issues in our community. Miss Reynolds cofounded the Denver Woman's Club and the Denver Women's Press Club, both instrumental in achieving many important reforms." She glanced around the room. "We're all members in one or both of these organizations."

Mildred raised an eyebrow. "Surely you're not in the Press Club, Lida."

"I am an associate member for now. But I plan to write a series of articles on the public health needs of Denver's poor," I said. "Since the collapse of the silver market in '93, and the economic depression that followed, mining families and immigrants have flooded into Denver. It's created a terrible disparity in income levels and a great demand for medical care. Thanks to the Woman's Club, we've opened several health clinics to serve the needy. I'm working with them to collect data that will be useful for future planning and treatment."

"Dr. Clayton is a highly valued member, Mrs. Bolton, and we look forward to reading about her research," Minnie Reynolds, another of my closest friends, said. "We adopted rigorous requirements for our associate members in the Press Club. No woman shall be admitted: (1) who is a bore, (2) who holds out on newspaper reporters, (3) who does not have proper respect for the power of the press, and (4) who cannot do something to drive dull cares away." She finished with a flourish, "Otherwise, we welcome all intelligent and congenial women, and your sister excels on both counts."

This seemed to flummox Mildred. "Goodness," she said at last.

Minnie chuckled good naturedly and patted Mildred's arm. She was a vivacious woman in her midthirties, as small in stature as Ellis, with a wonderful sense of humor. She held little store in fussing over her appearance, inciting some to call her frumpy with her wire-rimmed glasses, unbecoming clothes, and unruly gray-streaked hair. But she cared little for others' opinions as she rode her bicycle about town collecting stories from Denver women for her columns in the *Rocky Mountain News*. She was passionate—some said strident—about social injustice, including racial inequality toward the Negroes, Indians, and Chinese. I shared her strong views and tried to be as conscientious and empathetic in my dealings with all people as our dear Minnie. Considered an old maid, she'd sworn never to marry until she could find a man who shared her beliefs and allowed her to continue on her chosen path outside the confines of society's conventions. I feared it would be difficult for any man to meet her expectations. It made me realize how exceptional William had been to support me in my endeavors.

"I love the sentiments of the Press Club," Eva said, smiling at Minnie with an expression of wonder. "My sister told me you ran for the Colorado State Legislature. How thrilling."

Minnie nodded. "Even losing, as I did, there is no headier feeling than being free to vote and run for office. I campaigned hard but faced formidable opponents. No one imagined Colorado would be one of the first to take such a progressive stand. We were only second to the Wyoming Territory."

"How did you ever manage here when one state after another fails?" Eva asked. "Every time a bill shows promise for passing in the Kansas Legislature, the liquor and business lobbies defeat it, leaving the supporters terribly disheartened."

"Oh, we had our failures as well, dear," Minnie assured her. "Our first major effort was in '77, when the Legislature allowed the men of the state to vote on a constitutional amendment. Miss Susan B. Anthony joined us and campaigned across the state, but, sadly, the measure failed.

"In '93 we asked the Legislator to allow another go at the amendment. Thanks to Miss Reynolds's efforts approval for the statewide vote passed the senate, and Mrs. Louisa Tyler ushered it through the house. None of our esteemed lawmakers believed it had the slightest chance of passing."

Minnie smiled. "The campaign began with twenty-eight members in the Non-Partisan Equal Suffrage Association of Colorado and a mere one hundred twenty-five dollars in the treasury."

"Somehow you worked a miracle," Eva said with delight.

"Our secret weapon was Mrs. Carrie Chapman Catt," Ellis said. "I attended the Congress of Women at the Columbian Exposition in Chicago in May that year with the express purpose of meeting with Miss Anthony. I convinced her to loan us Mrs. Catt for the Colorado campaign, even though Miss Anthony remained skeptical of our chances for success."

Mrs. Forrest shook her head. "Mrs. Catt kept us stumping down to the last hour. Many of us traveled to any town that would have us to give speeches and gather donations. We withstood a great deal of heckling from unhappy men, and more than a few women, in the process."

"We encouraged women to convince their husbands to vote in favor of the suffrage referendum," Mrs. Bradford said. "I met some brave souls who threatened to divorce their husbands if the measure failed. A most convincing argument." She laughed. "I must add we did not recommend this."

"It helped to have the support of our governor, Davis Waite. He was a Populist elected the year before," I said.

Mrs. Forrest nodded toward Minnie and Ellis. "Miss Reynolds and Miss Meredith were instrumental. They persuaded seventy-five percent of the newspapers in the state to support the ballot. No easy task."

"Victory was terribly sweet," Ellis said, raising her tea cup to the group. "And we continue to carry the banner forward for national suffrage."

"I am so envious that you've met Miss Anthony," Eva said. "Do tell me what she is like."

Ellis paused a moment before speaking. "At first, I found her a bit stern and intimidating. She peppered me with questions about our plans for the campaign. I argued at length for any help possible. Since the national organization lacked funds to assist us, she finally agreed to loan us Mrs. Catt. I find Miss Anthony a dedicated leader who is extremely courageous."

"You're being generous," I said. "Miss Anthony was most ungracious to Miss Meredith at the '94 National Convention. Miss Meredith was scheduled to present a much-anticipated talk about Colorado's historic victory at the start of the program. At the last-minute Miss Anthony moved her to the

126

end of the agenda on the last day. And when Miss Meredith finally spoke, Miss Anthony tried to cut her presentation short. The delegates protested and insisted on letting Miss Meredith finish."

Ellis smiled. "No harm done. Clearly she was frustrated that we managed to pass the ballot without her. And there is the ongoing debate of whether to pursue the vote state-by-state or hold out for a constitutional amendment on the national level. Miss Anthony prefers the later."

"She is getting on in years so a bit of prickliness is understandable," Mrs. Bradford offered.

Ellis nodded. "Ever since the first suffrage convention at Seneca Falls in '48, Miss Anthony has spent her entire life, day in and day out, staunchly working for the cause. She has educated and inspired a generation of American women to stand up for their rights. I can't begin to express how much I admire her."

"Did you know that when she attended the International Council for Women in London two years ago, she was invited to tea with Queen Victoria?" Mrs. Forrest asked.

"She went to Windsor Castle, along with Mr. Booker T. Washington," I added. "How appropriate that the queen would host two of America's leading activists for human rights together."

"Imagine." Mildred appeared quite impressed. "Miss Anthony must have been saddened to hear of the queen's death this year."

"Undoubtedly," Minnie agreed.

Ellis held her hand out toward Minnie. "Our Miss Reynolds recently returned from back east, where the *New York Times* and *New York Post* published a number of her articles. She wrote brilliant accounts on the passage of Colorado's suffrage amendment and our successes in passing reforms since Colorado women began voting. The articles were so well received that I fear we are losing her to the national effort."

Minnie gave a rueful smile. "The National Association has asked for my assistance, so I've resigned my post at the *Rocky Mountain News*. I leave next week for New York to dedicate myself to the cause."

"How thrilling," Eva exclaimed.

"We shall sorely miss you," I said.

"And I all of you," Minnie replied. "But the time is ripe for success. I must be part of it."

"What of Lawrence, Miss Delacroix? Do you have an active suffrage organization?" Mrs. Bradford asked.

"I am part of a small but dedicated group who does their best to educate men *and women* on the importance of granting the vote," Eva answered, glancing briefly at Mildred. "Women have the right to vote for Kansas school board and local elections, but universal suffrage has proved elusive."

Mrs. Forrest turned to Mildred. "And you, Mrs. Bolton?"

Mildred's mouth twitched as she held her head high. "I'm quite active with the Christian Women's Temperance Union and a number of charities, but not the suffrage group."

"Most of us are ardent supporters of temperance as well," Ellis said, hesitating a moment. "Are you associated with Carry Nation and her Home Defenders Army?" Mrs. Nation had made national headlines over the last two years with her radical antiliquor organization. The members were infamous for marching into Kansas saloons and smashing bottles of liquor with bricks or hatchets. They had left a trail of terrified owners. The women had been arrested and fined numerous times, but continued their campaign.

Mildred gasped. "Mercy, I should say not. That crazed woman does far more harm than good. We must remain civilized and lobby for new laws."

Mrs. Bradford nodded. "Which makes a strong case for women voting. Colorado is much in the spotlight these days as others evaluate how the women's vote has led to new laws and social changes. We have achieved a number of significant improvements. I was able to shepherd the passage of a law requiring compulsory education for children through the age of fourteen."

Mrs. Forrest leaned forward. "And we managed to get laws passed raising the age of consent for marriage to eighteen and for mothers to have equal guardianship over their children."

"The creation of the State Home for Neglected and Dependent Children was a major accomplishment," Mrs. Bradford continued. "None of this would have happened without women's enfranchisement. The legislators can't afford to ignore us if they hope to be reelected."

"But you've failed to outlaw alcohol after eight years," Mildred countered as her voice grew testy. I cringed, wondering what she might say next.

Mrs. Bradford seemed unperturbed. "How true, Mrs. Bolton. There are so many reforms that remain to be passed. It takes a great deal of time and patience to convince the men in power to support our proposals. In this case, we are up against a very powerful liquor lobby."

Mildred shifted in her chair, looking as if she were under attack. I knew none of the ladies intended this; they were simply actively engaged in the issues and enthusiastic about discussing them.

Eva touched Mildred's arm. "My sister does much to help orphaned children in Lawrence." Eva described Mildred's work in raising money for the orphanage. "She insists the children receive not only an education and life's basic necessities but the joy of small pleasures, too. She collects new toys for them at Christmas and organizes picnics at the river in summer."

Before any more was said, the maid escorted four new arrivals into the room.

Ellis introduced the new guests, giving each their due. "This is Mrs. Helen Robinson, a teacher and well-known writer, Mrs. Martha Conine, who served in the '97/98 State Legislature, and Mrs. Katharine Patterson, who organized the YWCA in Denver and cofounded the Denver Woman's Club with Miss Reynolds. Last but certainly not least, this is Mrs. Susan Hall of the Republican Women's Club, who founded the nonpartisan Civic Federation of Denver to unite those of us from different political parties to fight for common causes."

"Mrs. Bradford and Miss Meredith must take credit as cofounders," Mrs. Hall protested. "We joined forces—a Republican, a Democrat, and a Populist—determined to work for social changes without letting politics interfere. Our individual parties often oppose the legislation we support, so we formed a coalition to get bills passed."

"It's been very effective," Minnie added.

I thought once again how these attractive, elegant women, so talented and confident, made a statement by the grace and strength of their accomplishments. They had provided a deeper meaning to my life.

Ellis poured tea as the newcomers settled into their seats. Soon the din of multiple conversations filled the room.

"Did you hear Mrs. Brown returned to Denver this week?" Mrs. Conine asked Ellis and me.

"I heard from my housekeeper, Katherine," I said. "She's a close friend of Mrs. Brown's housekeeper, Mary Mulligan."

Mrs. Margaret Brown was one of the wealthiest and most active members of Denver society, who had worked with me in setting up medical clinics for the poor. At her invitation, I had joined the planning committee for the Catholic Fair, a charity fundraiser she was organizing for September. I admired her a great deal and hoped my sisters would have an opportunity to meet her.

"Mrs. Brown left at the start of the year to study at the new Carnegie Institute in New York," Ellis told Eva and Mildred. "She had to leave school at a young age, so she is pursuing a formal education now. She says you're never too old to learn new things."

"I heartily agree," Eva said.

"Mrs. Brown is particularly fascinated with languages and travels a great deal abroad," I said. "I do envy her."

"But tell us, Miss Meredith, when shall we see your book?" Mrs. Robinson asked. She turned to Eva and Mildred. "We are very proud, as her first novel has just been published."

Ellis beamed. "According to my publisher, it will be in bookstores in two weeks. If the trains are to be trusted."

Eva sighed, looking awestruck. "I can't imagine having the fortitude to write a novel. Tell us about it."

"It's titled *The Master-Knot of Human Fate,*" Ellis said.

"From the poem by Omar Khayyam?" Mildred asked.

"Exactly. I describe it as a parable that draws on the tales of Adam and Eve and Robinson Crusoe, only it's set in a postapocalyptic Rocky Mountains. It examines the meanings of life and love."

Mildred's eyes opened wide. "That's certainly original."

"I'll be giving a talk about it at next month's Press Club meeting," Ellis said.

"I'm sorry it didn't come in time for my talk at this Sunday's meeting," Mrs. Robinson said, turning to Eva and Mildred. "I'll be speaking on recent literature. I hope you can attend."

"We wouldn't miss either event," I assured her.

"Speaking of new novels," Ellis said, "I read a delightful book, *My Brilliant Career,* by a young Australian woman, Miles Franklin. Remarkably, she's only nineteen. The story centers on the heroine's struggle to determine her future, whether to choose a career or marriage. It seems particularly timely, since the Australian territories formed the country this year and adopted universal suffrage. We need literature with independent-minded women who don't automatically forsake everything for a romance. I loved this young character's pluck and courage."

"I read a nice review of it recently," Eva said. She paused a moment, glancing at me. "Courage is certainly what we need in life."

"I shall loan you the book." Ellis popped up from her seat and went to a small bookshelf in the far corner of the room. She returned and handed the novel to Eva. "I know you'll enjoy it."

The conversation turned to upcoming events. Mrs. Bradford reminded us of the meeting of the Nonpartisan Colorado Equal Suffrage Association on the following Wednesday, where we would finalize our plans for the Denver Fourth of July parade. "Any and all who care to join us, are most welcome."

"I plan to participate," Eva said. Mildred kept quiet.

Ellis's mother, Mrs. Meredith, moved over to sit next to Mildred, perhaps sensing her discomfort among such an outspoken group. She had been instrumental in the early suffrage movement in Montana. After Ellis was born, she and Mr. Meredith had moved to Colorado. Her continued dedication to the cause provided inspiration to the women of Denver who also devoted themselves to women's rights. She was a lovely woman, an older version of Ellis, whom I viewed as a surrogate mother. I had cried on her shoulder more than once after Peter and William passed.

"I feel certain you are a reader, Mrs. Bolton," Mrs. Meredith said.

"Why, yes. I belong to a literary group and read a great deal. Of course, I take *The Bookman* for reviews and articles on new publications." They continued to discuss their mutual interest in literature, unconcerned by the chatter around them.

Ellis turned to Eva and me. "I received a note this morning from a dear friend. She came to Denver unexpectedly yesterday, which is a lovely surprise. I first made her acquaintance at the Woman's Congress in Chicago back in '93, and we've corresponded ever since. I've been with her at several of the National Suffrage conventions, including last month in Minneapolis."

"Have I heard of her?" I asked.

"I may have mentioned her to you. Mrs. Charlotte Grove of Springfield, Illinois. She's quite well known in the state's suffrage movement."

Eva gasped and stared at me. It seemed an incredible coincidence, but how many Charlotte Groves from Springfield could there be?

"She's traveling with her brother, Mr...." Ellis began.

I grabbed her arm and interrupted. "Ellis, I must speak to you privately at once." She gave me a queer look as I stood up. Eva had turned quite pale.

Mildred glanced over. "Are we leaving so soon?"

"No, no. I need to discuss some club business with Miss Meredith." I dragged Ellis behind me out of the room and down the hallway.

"Whatever is the matter, Lida?" she asked.

"I hardly know where to begin." I explained Eva's predicament with Mr. Dearman. "He's coming here to see Eva and asked Mrs. Grove to accompany him. We can't let Mildred know yet. Please don't mention his name."

"Oh my, what a small world. I think highly of Mrs. Grove. She's spoken to me of her brother as one of the dearest men alive. What are you planning to do?"

"Eva wants me to meet him first, so I can argue his case to Mildred. It's essential we keep this confidential."

"If I can do anything to help." She paused. "Perhaps Mother could keep Mrs. Bolton busy while you meet with Mr. Dearman."

And we set about fashioning a plan.

Trials at Home

Wednesday, June 26, 1901

Dear Mildred,

I received your letter today. I know it was a long and tiring journey, but I hope you will enjoy your time in Colorado. I have always been very fond of Lida and found her husband, William, most agreeable and interesting. The falling out with your mother was regrettable.

Your strange little dog, Biscuit, is acting out. She yaps incessantly at the slightest noise and, according to Jessie, has relieved herself in the house twice now. The dog stays at Jessie's heels all day, which is hampering her ability to clean and cook. Biscuit refuses to come near me when I return from work and sleeps in your room on the bed at night, looking quite forlorn and whimpering for hours on end.

I am very busy at the bank with an unusual number of loan applications to consider and an upcoming audit by the accountants for which I must prepare. I am working my way through stacks of paperwork. Mr. Anderson, the new teller I hired, is not working out as well as I hoped. I fear he is too young to understand the importance of hard work and wastes a great deal of time chatting with customers and other employees about frivolous matters. I may have to let him go and start the search anew.

Your mother has called twice and invited me to dinner. I told you when you left I can't be running over there to suit her whims. Of course if there is a real emergency, I will take care of it. But you know how she invents problems out of nothing and craves attention. Aunt Effie is better suited to the task of keeping her occupied.

Lida's children sound like they are good at heart and need understanding and compassion after the losses they have experienced in their young lives. I am sure you will enjoy their company and find each has admirable qualities.

My best to Eva, Lida, and the children.

Your husband, Franklin

A Private Appointment

I pulled items from the display case and gently placed them on the glass top: a wide purple grosgrain ribbon suitable for a hat band, a double satin bow in bachelor-button blue, three goose feathers dyed deep rose, and a spray of silk lilacs. Mrs. Mattie Silks, the famous madam whom Mama had told me about, stood across the counter, surveying the wares.

When I had arrived at work Friday morning, Mrs. O'Malley made the shocking announcement. "Mattie Silks asked for a private appointment," she said in a hushed voice, although there was no one in the shop except Rose and me. "She'll be here late morning."

"Why a private appointment?" I asked.

"You girls understand the nature of her business. She knows no respectable lady wants to be seen in my store while she is here."

Rose's deep green eyes grew rounder. She loved nothing more than a bit of gossip and, better yet, something scandalous. "But, Mama, what if someone sees? What will they say?"

"Her money is as good as anyone else's, and she's a loyal customer. I would have scheduled her when you were both away, but this was the only convenient time we could find." She gave us a stern glance. "You girls must keep this to yourselves, please."

All morning Rose and I awaited Mrs. Silks's arrival, falling into fits of giggles every time our eyes met. I had never seen her or any other "soiled dove," as far as I knew. Mrs. O'Malley's shop on Lawrence Street in downtown Denver was only half a dozen blocks from the stretch of Market Street where Mrs. Silks had three houses of ill repute alongside other establishments of a similar nature. That area of the city remained a world apart. Mama forbade me to go anywhere near it. Never had I imagined meeting such a person at my place of work. I wondered what Mama might think.

Mrs. O'Malley closed the shop at eleven twenty to accommodate our special customer, drawing the blinds and locking the door. A small sign in the window of the door read *Gone for Lunch, Open at 12:30*. At exactly eleven thirty, Mrs. Silks rapped three times and, a moment later, three more times.

When Mrs. O'Malley greeted Mrs. Silks, Rose and I had yet another shock. Here was the woman we had seen talking to the two gentlemen outside the ice cream parlor Wednesday afternoon. I recognized the round face and the false golden curls on top of her head.

A number of things about Mrs. Silks surprised me. She appeared at least ten years older than Mama, with wrinkles crowding the edges of her eyes and mouth. She was several inches shorter than me: portly, with a ruffle of multiple chins. I had expected someone scandalous, perhaps wearing a red satin gown with a deep-cut neckline, a boa scarf, or heavy eye color and rouge. But everything from her leather shoes to her

138

dress and hat were the latest fashions from Paris, modest and sewn with expensive materials. Only her dyed blonde hair and ruby-red lips stood out as inappropriate to her attire.

Rose and I remained unsure exactly what the women prostitutes in these establishments did to entertain the men. We had spent long hours in Rose's room whispering back and forth about the possibilities. Our only source of information came from Laura Jean Libbey's novels, like *A Dangerous Flirtation or Did Ida May Sin?,* stories of unscrupulous men seducing young women with lies and ruining their lives. It seemed to involve a great deal of unchaste kissing and touching, but beyond that, it remained a mystery. Part of me was afraid to learn more.

Mrs. Silks picked up the spray of silk lilacs, holding it against the front of her dress. The color complimented her lavender organdy and lace dress.

I wondered how she had fallen into such a desperate life.

"I must have these," she said in her high-pitched voice. She ran her fingers along the rose-colored goose feathers and then leaned in to peer at other items in the case. The scent of lemon verbena filled the air. "What are these dark feathers with the spots?"

"I believe they're guinea hens, ma'am," I said. Mrs. O'Malley nodded her approval from the small table and mirror where she was arranging a variety of hats for Mrs. Silks to try on.

"So many lovely things to choose from," Mrs. Silks crooned as she fingered a two-inch long diamond cross hanging on a delicate silver chain around her neck. She studied my face. "You are so lovely, dear." She glanced at

Rose. "Both you girls, in the bloom of your youth." A small sigh escaped her lips.

I felt the heat rise from my neck to my face until I must have matched the red geraniums in our window boxes at home. Her smile made me uneasy, as if she were considering me for employment at one of her bawdy houses. Rose's stifled giggles drifted across the room, and I dared not look at her.

Mrs. Silks turned away and took a seat at the table in front of the mirror. "Let's see what you have, Mrs. O'Malley." She let out a deep, throaty laugh. "Can you make me look ten years younger, please?"

For the next half hour Mrs. Silks tried on hats in all sizes, colors, and shapes. Mrs. O'Malley showed her the latest styles in the June issues of *Harper's Bazar* and the *Delineator*, suggesting hats that would complement different types of outfits. She selected three hats—one for afternoon and two for evening—to be adorned with a variety of feathers and ribbons. Satisfied with her selections, she thanked us and slipped out the front door, stepping down the sidewalk toward her forbidden world.

I thought of my prayers to the saints for the women at the House of the Good Shepherd. I would add Mrs. Silks to my appeals to Mary Magdalene and Margaret of Cortona. Only, unlike the saints or the girls in the home, Mrs. Silks didn't seem the least bit repentant or despairing about her profession. She seemed quite content. Her businesses provided her with ample funds to buy nice clothes and jewelry, despite the immorality of the trade. What a terribly confusing world.

My aunts arrived at the shop by carriage at twenty to one, missing Mrs. Silks by only fifteen minutes. After receiving Mr. Dearman's letter the day before, Aunt Eva had insisted she needed a new hat. Aunt Mildred had agreed to go shopping with her and offered to take us out for luncheon. She had no idea Aunt Eva's desire for a new hat was prompted by Mr. Dearman's arrival in Denver.

I introduced my aunts to Mrs. O'Malley and Rose.

Aunt Eva shook Mrs. O'Malley's hand and smiled. "I'm so pleased to meet you. Did Sara Jane mention that I need a new hat? She assures me you have the best in town."

"How very nice. Please take a seat and tell me what you have in mind." Mrs. O'Malley settled Eva at the same table where Mattie Silks had sat a short time before. She spread pictures of different fashions before her. "Is it for afternoon or evening?"

"Afternoon," Eva answered.

As they talked of hats, Aunt Mildred slowly circled the shop, inspecting the accessory cases and emitting an occasional *humph*. She stopped in front of Rose, looking her up and down until poor Rose bent her head, looking as if she wanted to curl into a ball like one of Cole's pill bugs.

"May I show you anything, ma'am?" Rose asked.

"Perhaps you'd like a new hat, too, Aunt Mildred," I said, trying to rescue poor Rose from Aunt Mildred's scrutiny.

"I have no need for another hat. As Franklin always says, it's nonsense trying to keep up with the latest fashion trends. These frivolous magazines prey on insecure and needy women."

"We have many basic styles, ma'am," Rose offered in a timid voice. "My mother calls them classics."

Aunt Mildred patted her black straw hat, the same one she had been wearing when they stepped off the train. "This is a classic hat, young lady. Five years old and still perfectly fine."

Another customer entered the shop and greeted Mrs. O'Malley. Rose stepped forward. "I'll get Mrs. Wilson's order, Mama." She scurried off to the back of the store.

"Sara Jane, come help me choose," Aunt Eva called, turning to me wearing a large pale pink hat trimmed with cream satin ribbons and two goose feathers like the ones Miss Silks had admired. "What do you think? It's perfect for my rose afternoon suit."

I stood next to her. "I love it. Everything looks pretty on you."

Aunt Eva chuckled. "Just the answer I wanted to hear."

"You train your workers well, Mrs. O'Malley," Aunt Mildred called out from across the shop.

"But it's true," I protested.

Aunt Eva took my hand in hers. "I hope I have a daughter exactly like you someday."

She tried on three other hats, but, in the end, none caught her fancy like the pink one. She paid Mrs. O'Malley and arranged to come back for the hat after lunch.

I guided my aunts down Lawrence Street past the dressmaker and shoe shop next to Paris Millinery. We turned onto bustling Sixteenth Street, crowded with businessmen returning from lunch and shoppers loaded with packages. The hot summer sun shimmered off the sidewalks and streets. Shade from the window awnings of the multistoried brick buildings provided only a modicum of relief. Carriages and a horse-pulled tourist bus rolled past, the sound of the horses' hooves clip-clopping a steady beat. The conductor rang the electric tram bell as he stopped at each corner to let passengers on and off. We reached Daniels and Fisher Dry

Goods, one of my favorite stores. A window filled with women's afternoon suits caught Aunt Eva's eye.

"That green one with the gray piping is lovely," Aunt Eva said. "I may have to try it on later."

"Really, Eva. What has gotten into you?" Aunt Mildred sputtered. "You brought a trunk full of new ensembles with you. How will you even find time to wear them all?"

Eva winked at me. "I'm sure I'll find many occasions."

As Aunt Mildred walked on, Aunt Eva whispered in my ear. "I can't help searching the streets, wondering if we might run into Mr. Dearman. It's so difficult knowing he's somewhere close by, and I won't see him until tomorrow. But Mildred must not find out."

Aunt Mildred stopped and turned, narrowing her eyes. "What are you two conspiring about?"

"Some ideas for a new dress," Aunt Eva answered.

I hurried ahead until Aunt Mildred pulled on my arm, breathing hard. "Do slow down, Sara Jane. This is not the way a young lady comports herself, sprinting down the street like a racehorse."

"Can you walk five more blocks?" I asked. "Or should we take the tram?"

"For heaven's sake, I'm not feeble," Aunt Mildred sniffed.

"But I..."

"Sara Jane only wants you to be comfortable, Mildred," Aunt Eva interjected.

I forced myself to match Aunt Mildred's snail pace until at last we reached Pell's Oyster House. I loved the leaded glass windows and doors and the gold lettering across the awning out front. Inside, the welcoming aroma of steamed clams and fried fish filets enveloped the air. Mama waved to us from a table in the ladies' section, having already arrived from work.

Aunt Mildred had instructed Mama, "Pick a fine eating establishment and not some common soda fountain or café frequented by riffraff." Mama chose the Oyster House, a popular spot for businessmen and Denver society. It had been Papa's favorite restaurant.

Memories of my only dinner at Pell's with Mama and Papa on my fourteenth birthday brought a lump to my throat. I had loved the bright lamps, wooden bar, and cozy tables. Most of all I loved an evening alone with my parents. Papa had called me his special princess. A few months later he was gone forever, and the ache never went away.

The host escorted us to our table and handed out menus. The cover touted *We Bring the Sea Shore to Denver Every Day.*

"I hope you like it," Mama said. "The fish is very fresh. It comes by train encased in ice. It takes three days from the Atlantic coast and two days from the Pacific."

Aunt Eva smiled. "It all looks delicious."

"William and I loved coming here. It reminded us of our early years on the East Coast, when we were courting," Mama said. "I had never really eaten seafood before. Mother certainly never served it. William took me to funny little places along the Atlantic seashore and convinced me to try cod and lobster. We ate big piles of clams until I couldn't take another bite." She drifted off momentarily. "It seems so long ago."

"This is a lovely treat," Aunt Mildred said, her voice tender with a sympathy I had not heard before.

We scanned the menu. I copied Aunt Eva and ordered the filet of sole. Mama asked for fried oysters, and Aunt Mildred chose the lobster with drawn butter.

Mama smoothed her napkin in her lap. "We're lucky, as they close next week until September. Mr. Pell finds it too hard to keep the fish fresh in the heat of summer."

Aunt Mildred started to comment as a voice called out, "Lida." We turned to find Mama's friends Miss Meredith and her mother, Mrs. Meredith, coming from the far side of the restaurant. They stopped at our table.

"I'm so glad to run into you. We'll see you tonight for dinner at your house, of course, but I wanted to extend an invitation," Miss Meredith said. "My friend Mrs. Grove, who is visiting from Illinois, invited us for tea at the Brown Palace Hotel tomorrow afternoon. She is most anxious to share the news from the Suffrage Association's membership committee meeting she attended last week. As I mentioned before, Mother and I saw her at the national convention in Minneapolis in May. Lida, I thought you and your sisters might enjoy joining us."

"Of course," Aunt Eva said. "It will be most enlightening to hear their progress in enlisting new members."

Aunt Mildred's mouth formed a tight line. "That's kind of you, but I might feel out of my element in such a gathering."

Mrs. Meredith smiled at Aunt Mildred. "I rather thought you would prefer to come to tea at my home instead, Mrs. Bolton. We can continue our discussion of literature."

Aunt Mildred's face flushed with obvious pleasure. "I would enjoy that immensely."

I caught an exchange of subtle smiles between Aunt Eva and Mama.

On the Streets of Denver

Luncheon at Pell's Oyster House had proved a great success. Not only was Mildred impressed by the restaurant and thoroughly pleased with her meal, but our scheme had worked to perfection. Ellis and her mother performed their parts with the craft of seasoned actors. Best of all, no one actually told a lie. Mrs. Grove had in fact attended the membership meeting of the National Association and undoubtedly wanted to share the latest news. The only omission was Mr. Dearman's presence at the tea, a detail of which Mildred need not be the wiser. I felt a twinge of guilt for the ruse, but it wouldn't have been necessary to go to such lengths if Mildred hadn't been so uncompromising.

We didn't leave the restaurant until almost three o'clock, lingering over dessert and coffee. Lapis blue brushed the sky free of clouds, and I found myself perspiring in the heat. We had barely gone a block down Sixteenth Street on our way to pick up Eva's new hat when a tall, powerfully built man halted directly in front of me. He wore a charcoal-gray suit, a white shirt with a well-starched collar, and a blue striped tie, looking as crisp as an autumn morning. With the sunlight behind him, I could make out only his chin and mouth beneath the shadow of an enormous gray cowboy hat.

"Why, Dr. Clayton, I hoped I might run into you." He removed his hat, revealing his identity, although I immediately recognized the deep, rich voice of Mr. Wallace Abbott. He was a cattle baron who had traveled north from Texas as a young man over twenty-five years before to make his fortune. Now he owned a vast stretch of rangeland between Denver and Colorado Springs. A life spent outdoors had turned the sharp features of his face a deep brown. Startlingly light gray eyes sparkled warm and inviting amid the crinkled lines etched in his skin. Ribbons of silver threaded his abundant dark brown hair and moustache.

"This *is* a surprise," I managed at last, stepping back to gain my equanimity. Sara Jane and my sisters stared at me with perplexed expressions. After a moment's hesitation, I introduced them.

"A pleasure to meet you lovely ladies on this fine day," he said. "Your daughter looks just like you, Dr. Clayton. Lucky girl."

My face burned as if scorched by the sun. "I met Mr. Abbott, w-when I did my internship…at the Homeopathy Hospital," I stumbled on.

"This here is the best doctor this side of the Mississippi. I got tossed from a wild stallion I was trying to break, and my leg ended up in a dozen pieces." He chuckled. "Dr. Clayton put me back together and made me stay in the hospital until it mended properly. Not even a limp to show for it. I am eternally grateful."

"Luckily, our hospital had just purchased one of the new X-ray machines," I explained to my sisters, a bit too eagerly. "Or we wouldn't have known the extent of the damage and how to set the bones." I took a deep breath, my heart

148

pounding as I stared into his eyes. "We...we must be going, but it's so nice to see you."

"Yes, ma'am, that it is. I'm staying at the Brown Palace for the next week." He turned to my sisters and Sara Jane. "It would be an honor if you all joined me for dinner one night."

"What a kind offer," Eva said in a noncommittal tone.

"Thank you, but now I'm working, and with my sisters visiting, well, we have engagements every evening," I said hurriedly. "Perhaps another time, Mr. Abbott."

His face clouded briefly. "I understand, Dr. Clayton. Have a good day, ladies." He doffed his hat and went on.

I watched as he continued down the sidewalk, the shadow of my regrets trailing after him. My mind slipped back over the past months. Wallace Abbott had been my patient for almost three weeks with the complicated fracture in his left leg. Our brief moments together each day became the highlight of my busy rounds at the hospital. I stayed at his bedside longer than I should have, laughing as he regaled me with tales of his colorful youth. He was a widower of five years with one daughter who now attended Pembroke College in Rhode Island. He understood the yawning void in my heart after losing William.

When the day arrived for him to go home, he had taken my hand. "Dr. Clayton, it would make me the happiest man in the world if you would allow me to call on you soon. Perhaps I could take you out for dinner." His pleading eyes reflected a depth of loneliness I knew too well.

My heart fluttered with pleasure like a young girl being courted by her first beau. The reality of my situation soon overshadowed this fleeting moment, though. Beyond the fact that it would be a breach of the patient-doctor relationship, I was a middle-aged widow with two children to raise. "I am flattered, Mr. Abbott," I said, "but I'm not ready to entertain the thought of another man in my life." I knew I might never be ready and gently pulled my hand from his.

"I appreciate your position. I've never considered the possibility of taking another wife until I met you. You are the loveliest woman I've ever met next to my dear late wife." His eyes searched mine as if looking for any sign that my resolve might weaken. "I won't give up hope just yet. Somewhere down the road you may at least need a friend."

He wrote to me in mid-March, a letter filled with news of his ranch and a trip to visit his daughter in Rhode Island. He assured me his feelings remained the same. He signed it: *Your ardent admirer and friend, Wallace Abbott.* Another letter and a huge bouquet of red roses arrived at the end of April, congratulating me on my graduation from medical school a few days prior. All I need do was contact him at any time, and he would come to town. I sent a brief note thanking him for his thoughtfulness, but insisted nothing in my situation had altered.

These events wore at my heart and good humor, like the swirling clouds that swept across the Rocky Mountain peaks, turning shadows to light and back again. In truth I found myself drawn to Mr. Abbott in a way I never anticipated feeling about another man. His offer sorely tempted me. But every time I gave it consideration, guilt riddled me, reigniting my grief for William. I could not betray our happy years of marriage. Moreover, I refused to take the coward's way out by marrying another man to solve my financial woes. Would he expect the children and me to move to his ranch in the countryside? If so, four years of medical training might be for naught. My first responsibilities remained with the children and my long-fought-for career. In truth, I hardly knew the man and had no idea if he shared my sentiments regarding women's rights and other issues dear to my heart.

I often marveled at my good fortune in finding a man like William. Only on rare occasions did he express frustration over the strain my ideals and activities put on our domestic life as we struggled to balance the needs of family and our respective work. Many of my friends' husbands espoused agreement with the fight to improve the lot of women, but when it came to running the house and raising children, they still expected their wives to carry the load. Their true colors came through as they condescendingly referred to their wives' efforts for women's suffrage and social change as mere hobbies, distractions from their real duties at home. It had proved the ruin of more than one marriage, including my dear friend Ellis.

Fate led me to William through his sister Beatrice Clayton. She spilled into my life our freshman year when we shared a dormitory room at Smith College. She was a gentle-tempered soul: bright, inquisitive, and quick to laugh, filled with unrestrained enthusiasm for fairness and justice. I had finally found a compatriot to share my strongly held beliefs of equality for all men and women, regardless of color or background. With the exception of Father and sometimes Mildred, life among family and friends in Lawrence had grown uncomfortable as my outspoken opinions chaffed at their prejudices and conventional sense of propriety. While I was mildly homesick for my family, I knew my decision to go east to college had been the right one. Beatrice and I joined the campus suffrage club and distributed pamphlets demanding the vote for women. One Saturday each month, we volunteered at the Home for Little Wanderers in Boston, which helped orphaned or abandoned children. Young and naive, we fancied ourselves intellectuals and provocateurs, who also loved to have a lark now and again.

Beatrice "hailed" from New London, Connecticut, as she liked to tell new acquaintances. Her grandfather had founded a gun and rifle manufacturing company in the 1820s, which her father took over thirty years later. It was the Civil War and the Union Army that had made the Claytons their considerable fortune, the fact my mother found most objectionable about William.

I returned home the summer after my first year at Smith. While I was happy to be with Eva and Mildred, it soon became clear that I could no longer tolerate the narrow-minded attitudes of Lawrence. Mother and I were barely speaking when I left in mid-August. Thankfully, Father had provided me with four years of college tuition and expenses, perhaps anticipating potential conflicts if he should not be there. I never knew, if it had been left to Mother, whether she would have denied me the money or given it gladly, relieved for my departure.

Beatrice had invited me to her family's home in New London for the two weeks before school began again. Her only sibling, William, was home for the summer. All through the school year I had gazed at William's picture on Beatrice's desk and listened to hilarious stories of their childhood capers. She often said, "You two would get on famously. You must come home and meet him." And so I did.

William was three years older than me and studying engineering at Cambridge University in England. I first spied him leaning against the edge of a chair in the family parlor, holding a tennis racket, his head tossed back, chortling over a joke his cousin Robert had told. As Beatrice and I entered the room, he turned his broad, toothy smile on me. A mass of sandy-blond hair curled down his forehead, giving him an air of mischief and irreverence. He took my hand, holding onto it longer than proper. "You're Miss Delacroix. I'd know you anywhere from Beatrice's letters."

Perhaps we had met in a previous life and were destined to find each other again. I fell under the spell of his lively blue eyes and unrelenting good humor. The two weeks flew by with clam bakes on the beach, tennis games, and late-afternoon sailing trips. We attended parties at the homes of Clayton family friends and danced until the early hours. I returned to school pining for William, wondering how I would ever survive until I could see him again. Over the next nine months we wrote back and forth across the sea, exploring each other's hearts in a slow and measured way.

The following summer, I found a job in the library at Smith for June and July, then spent August at the Clayton's home. William had graduated from Cambridge and was searching for a job. His father wanted him to go into the family arms business, but he took an engineering job with a small firm in Boston for the time being to be closer to me. That decision prompted a growing rift between father and son. During our Christmas break at the Clayton home, William knelt beneath the mistletoe, asking for my hand in marriage and presenting me with an engagement ring. His parents embraced me as one of their own, particularly his mother. Beatrice was thrilled beyond words, rightly claiming credit for the match.

I knew if my father had been alive, he would have loved and approved of William. But Mother, as expected, vehemently opposed the match. She wrote a curt note: *How could you entertain the idea of marrying a Northerner whose family made the arms that killed my brothers, cousins, and many of our dearest friends? Do not expect him to be welcome in my home.*

We married a year and a half later, shortly after I graduated from Smith. It was a small ceremony in the garden of the Clayton home. To my great sadness, no one in my family attended. Mildred wrote she could not travel after the loss of her recent pregnancy, and Eva was still a small child. Even my aunts and cousins cowered to Mother's wishes and sent their apologies. Whatever the consequences of my choices, I had never regretted a single day with William.

William was gone, but to marry again now would only bring difficult adjustments for the children. I was only beginning to find my footing as a doctor. Yet I often thought of Mr. Abbott, especially at the end of a long and challenging day, when duties weighed me down. How lovely it would be to have someone to share my troubles and joys with once more, a warm set of arms to encircle and comfort me.

"Mama, are you all right?" Sara Jane asked, pulling me back from my reverie. Eva and Mildred had drifted over to peer into the window of a shoe store, as if giving me time to compose myself.

I put an arm around Sara Jane's waist. "Yes, darling, I'm fine."

A great commotion could be heard. We looked up to see at least twenty young women strutting down the walkway on the opposite side of the street. When they drew closer, I realized the girls were part of an unsavory profession. They wore evening dresses of bright silks and satins, which exposed a good deal more skin than any lady would deem proper. They displayed a crude boldness that was shocking to encounter on one of Denver's main commercial streets. An older woman with blonde curls, in a black satin gown, led the others as she smiled and called out to half a dozen men crowded in the doorway of a popular saloon. Ladies and gentlemen along the sidewalk quickly stepped aside with scandalized expressions. Whistles and catcalls could be heard as the tram passed and the conductor clanged the bell.

"What is going on?" Eva asked, eying the parade. "Oh my goodness."

Sara Jane gasped. "It's Mattie Silks."

"And her girls," I added. I'd heard stories that once or twice a year Mrs. Silks marched her best girls through town to attract new customers, although I had never before witnessed the despicable display. They handed out little red books to the saloons and hotels. It was a directory of the major brothels in town, which described the attributes of each house and the "bawdy women" who worked there. The police and city officials overlooked this brazen behavior, thanks to the regular and generous "contributions" Mrs. Silks and other madams were rumored to provide.

In the past few months I'd learned more about Mattie Silks and her "palaces of pleasure" than I had ever dreamed of knowing. Maryellen, a sweet nineteen-year-old girl with a lovely face and ginger-colored hair, had worked for Mattie Silks before taking refuge in the House of the Good Shepherd. Maryellen came from a good family in Philadelphia, but she'd foolishly run off with a handsome young man who promised

155

to marry her when they reached Colorado. He soon disappeared, leaving her destitute and stranded in Denver. Scandalized, her parents disowned her and refused to send help. She turned to Mattie Silks in desperation. Her three months in the "sporting life" brought only misery and shame. She told me Mrs. Silks had been a fair employer and paid her well, but soon agreed that Maryellen was not cut out for the life. She steered Maryellen to the Catholic home.

Mildred stood with her mouth agape, watching the tawdry show across the street. "Mercy. I never in all my years."

"Let's go," I said. "No point in giving them the attention they desire."

Eva and Mildred hurried down the sidewalk. I took Sara Jane's arm as we followed behind them. "How is it that you recognize Mattie Silks, my dear?" I whispered, startled that she had identified one of the most infamous women in Denver.

She blanched, then explained about the private appointment at Paris Millinery that morning. I bristled, distraught at Mrs. O'Malley's poor judgment in scheduling the visit while the girls were present.

"Mama, Mrs. Silks didn't seem like a bad person really. How could she run such an immoral business?"

"As I explained before, women fall victim to desperate circumstances, poverty, and abandonment. They are forced to make terrible choices in this cold and unjust world. But some, like Mrs. Silks, appear to choose this life without any qualms. We must pity them all and try to help when possible."

The glow of our pleasant afternoon had dimmed with this unfortunate display, casting an unsavory shadow over Denver. I could only imagine what Mildred would have to say.

156

Chapter 14   **MILDRED**

Life in the Wild West

Saturday, June 29, 1901

Dearest Mother,

More adventures from the reaches of the Wild West, for surely that moniker fits this unruly place. I find myself longing for the simple, yet civilized, life of our dear Lawrence. The day of our return home looms too far in the future for my comfort.

I will not relay to you the most shocking and sordid event we encountered yesterday afternoon, but suffice it to say that I never dreamed I'd witness such base behavior in the middle of the day on a main street of Denver. I am certainly not naive about the world and the vile nature of many men and women. Yet, the worst you can envision is openly flaunted here in front of decent citizens.

That being said, we have enjoyed a number of pleasant days since I first wrote. I am happy to find a congenial group of people in Denver who have an appreciation for the arts. Tuesday night we attended a piano and violin concert with about fifty others put on by the Tuesday Music Club. The musicians, both Denver residents, exhibited impressive talents, playing two Mozart études and a lovely piece by Chopin. Most enjoyable.

Wednesday evening Lida took us by carriage on a tour around town to see some lovely new homes and impressive office building. The city seems to be expanding rapidly. We also drove past the medical school and hospital where she trained, and the home for needy women and orphanage where she works. The last two were rather dreary looking establishments. She is understandably proud of her accomplishments, which required many years of hard work and determination. It can't have been easy with William's passing. I admire her, even if her chosen field is ill-suited for a woman.

Thursday we attended the tea at the Meredith home, which I mentioned in my last letter. As expected it was a group of progressive women intent on pushing women's suffrage throughout the country. (You'd think it would be enough for them to have the vote in Colorado.) However, I found many of the ladies most companionable. I particularly enjoyed Mrs. Meredith, Miss Meredith's mother, who cohosted the party. We had a most stimulating conversation about literature and music.

Before our encounter with the seedier side of Denver yesterday afternoon, Eva and I visited Sara Jane at her job at Paris Millinery. It's a grand name for the likes of Denver, but the shop proved a bit smarter than I expected. The owner, Mrs. O'Malley, seems proper enough, so I feel better about Sara Jane's apprenticeship. Eva insisted on buying a new hat, which she needs like another bout of scarlet fever, but she had a great time selecting one. Sometimes she behaves like she's Sara Jane's age.

After shopping we met Lida for luncheon at an excellent seafood restaurant and had the pleasure of running into Miss Meredith and her mother again. Mrs. Meredith invited me to her home for tea tomorrow afternoon, a tête-à-tête between the two of us. My sisters and Sara Jane will accompany Miss Meredith to have tea with a suffragist friend visiting from Illinois, a meeting I am happy to miss.

As we walked downtown after eating, Lida ran into Mr. Abbott, a man she treated for a broken leg while in training at the hospital last winter. She told us later that he owns a large cattle ranch and is extremely wealthy. He is nice looking in a rough, outdoor sort of way. He wore an expensive tailored suit, although his cowboy hat and boots distracted from the overall impression. He seemed exceedingly pleased to see Lida and invited us to join him for dinner at his hotel. Lida quickly refused. It was difficult to discern her reaction to his obvious admiration, but the meeting left her quite flustered and blushing. One would think she'd be amenable to marrying a nice man—a Southerner from Texas, no less—who could care for her and the children. I shall never comprehend my sister.

Yesterday evening, Miss Meredith, Mrs. Meredith, and Miss Minnie Reynolds (another journalist friend of Lida's) came for dinner. It was a farewell party for Miss Reynolds. She gained notoriety these past months for her articles on the suffrage movement in Colorado published in the New York Times and other Eastern papers. She leaves this week to live in New York and work for the National American Woman Suffrage Association, hoping to publish more articles pushing

159

their agenda. I find it amazing that these women devote their lives to the cause without a thought to their personal needs. I suppose such conviction should be admired. Fortunately, political discussions were kept to a minimum last night. After a delicious meal, Miss Reynolds played the piano while we sang, followed by several games of charades. This resulted in a great deal of laughter, which I must say did me good.

Lida has planned any number of interesting excursions to gardens and nearby towns for us. And her friends continue to invite us for teas and other events. I hope we are not tiring poor Lida out with so much activity on top of her demanding work schedule.

Yesterday morning, I began spending half an hour teaching Cole the alphabet and his numbers to prepare him for school in September, something he has resisted up until now. Lida takes the attitude that he will learn when he is ready, but that approach has come home to roost. He is afraid of going to school, fearing he is behind the other boys his age. He has a good memory and is bright as a button, which may account for the inventive ways he finds to be naughty. I engage him by using toys and animals to help him remember his letters and reading his favorite books. We count the bugs in his collection, stones out in the yard, and anything else that interests him. I may be out of my depth, but he has taken to it, and I dare say to me!

The best news is that Eva is in better spirits than I have seen her since before her illness. She appears stronger and healthier and has lost the pallor of recent months. She is eating well at last and takes regular walks each morning.

I'm sorry Franklin has been too occupied with work to visit you, but we can't fault him for his dedication. You know he will be there for you in an emergency.

Keep busy and take advantage of Aunt Effie's offers to dine with her. I hope the summer heat and humidity are not too much for you. Please give my regards to Aunt Effie and the rest of the family.

With deepest regards,
Your devoted daughter Mildred

The Handsome Mr. Dearman

T wo doormen in red waistcoats and gray striped jackets opened the glass doors to the Brown Palace Hotel as we stepped out of Ellis's carriage. Eva swept through the entrance in her rose-colored afternoon suit and dramatic new hat, looking as beautiful and exotic as a wild flamingo.

Well-dressed patrons bustled about the high-ceilinged reception hall near the front desk, speaking in discrete voices. A plush, red-flowered carpet blanketed the floors below marble walls and sparkling chandeliers. It always thrilled me to enter the hotel no matter how many times I had been there. I saw the same expression of delight on my daughter's face.

Sara Jane wore her white dress that Eva had helped alter to accommodate her ever increasing height. They had placed an inset at the waist and covered it with a wide blue satin ribbon. An inch of new lace lengthened the hem and sleeves. Eva had arranged Sara Jane's hair in a loose pompadour adorned with two peacock feathers. My dear girl suddenly appeared terribly grown-up and lovely, a butterfly emerging from her chrysalis.

We stepped into the atrium where tea was served each afternoon. Broad, marble columns soared eight floors up to a glass dome. Cast-iron panels with intricate designs and elegant arches framed the balconies on each floor, overlooking the tea room. Light flowed from the frosted glass roof, diffusing into a gentle glow over the patrons seated below. A piano played softly at the far left side of the room as waiters glided past, delivering pots of tea with china cups and multitiered stands filled with plates of hot canapés, finger sandwiches, and delicately iced cakes and bonbons. Delicious aromas filled the air amid the hum of muted conversations. The tea salon was crowded for a Saturday afternoon, but each summer Denver attracted a growing number of tourists from around the county.

Ellis and Eva stood side by side, scanning the tables. I had worried Eva might collapse of nervous exhaustion after two long days anticipating this momentous meeting. Mildred mentioned Eva had not been able to sit still all morning while I was at work and had barely touched her lunch. At the last minute, Mildred suggested that she and Mrs. Meredith might join us at the hotel after all. Eva turned as pale as Sara Jane's white dress. I convinced Mildred it would be impolite to suggest changing plans at the last minute and sent her off in a carriage to Mrs. Meredith's home. By the time Eva finished her toilette and fussed endlessly over the placement of her new hat, Ellis had arrived to fetch us.

All the intrigue had left me unsettled and anxious as well.

The maître d' greeted Ellis. "Miss Meredith, welcome. Your friends are this way." We followed him across the right side of the room, weaving through tables. I nodded to three ladies from the Women's Club, who called a hello. Several men stared openly with admiration as Eva and Sara Jane passed.

A tall, slender man rose from his seat. He locked his eyes on Eva, wearing a smile of tenderness and the wonder of a child on Christmas morning. Mr. Dearman—surely it was him—stepped forward to meet us, clasping Eva's hand as if he would never again let go. His pale skin stood out in stark contrast to glossy black hair and a neatly trimmed moustache that curled ever so slightly at the ends. I thought him almost too beautiful for a man. A narrow, straight nose and long dark lashes framed smoky gray eyes. His smooth forehead, high cheekbones, and prominent chin defined his striking appearance.

Ellis took the hand of the woman seated next to Mr. Dearman. "Mrs. Grove, how delightful to see you again." A more delicate, feminine version of Mr. Dearman smiled at us, although she had hazel eyes and light auburn hair, which was pinned up under a pale yellow hat. The swell around her middle surprised me, for she had to be close to six months with child.

A round of introductions and handshakes followed. Mr. Dearman wrapped his slender fingers around my hand with a surprisingly hearty grip. His palms felt cool and damp. He swallowed hard before speaking, his Adam's apple bobbing up and down above the stiffly starched collar of his white shirt. "Dr. Clayton, I can't begin to tell you how much it means to me to meet you. Thank you for bringing your dear sister and joining us for tea."

I nodded my head, feeling embarrassed by the intensity of his gaze. His words carried the cadence of a proper Boston gentleman. "The pleasure is mine. I've heard so much about you."

"Please sit next to me," he said as his sister moved down a chair to be near Ellis. He held my chair then raced around to seat Eva on his other side.

Once we had settled and made the introductions around the table, two waiters delivered the tea. Ellis and Mrs. Grove carried the conversation with small talk about the train trip, the warm weather, and the beautiful mountain views from Mrs. Grove's room. Eva and Mr. Dearman stole glances at each other every few minutes, their eyes burning with deep fervor. Eva's lovely cheeks flushed pink and a slight smile never left her lips. Memories flooded back of those early years with William when we could not stand to be apart and our hearts beat wildly whenever our eyes met. We needed to constantly hold hands or lean against each other to convince ourselves the dream was real. Perhaps there was little else I needed to know about Mr. Dearman beyond the adoring gaze he fastened on Eva.

I glanced at Sara Jane, who wore a stunned expression, as if she had just heard news of a terrible accident. I could not imagine what prompted her to stare unblinking at Mr. Dearman, her mouth slightly agape. Her behavior bordered on rude. He was extremely handsome, of course, but this fact hardly warranted such a reaction. Fortunately, Ellis drew Sara Jane into their conversation as she talked with Mrs. Grove about her family in Illinois: a husband and two children.

Mr. Dearman leaned toward me, speaking in a low voice. "Eva tells me you came to Colorado many years ago, Dr. Clayton."

"My husband and I moved to Leadville in '84 shortly after we married. Since Mr. Clayton trained as a mining engineer, he was drawn to the West. We lived four years in Leadville then moved to Denver after our second child, Peter, was born. The winters in the mountains were too severe." I didn't add how I hated the harsh, uncivilized conditions of the mining camp, always in fear for the children's health. Peter especially was susceptible to the diseases constantly spreading like wildfire through the crowded town. After the rough and tumble population of miners, saloon owners, and worse, Denver had seemed the embodiment of civilization.

"I traveled to Denver briefly on business four years ago. It has certainly expanded since then." He played with the edges of his napkin.

"Does your legal work in Boston often take you to other locales?"

"Not normally, but this last year has been unique. I acquired a new client who spent many years in the West and has holdings in California, Colorado, and Kansas. In fact, I must attend to a piece of business for him while I'm here in Denver."

"Then the trip has a dual purpose." I took a sip of tea.

"Only by chance. Your sister is my greatest concern, both her health and her happiness." He gazed into my eyes with a worried frown. "I'm anxious to hear your professional opinion about her recovery from the scarlet fever. Do you find her well? Do you think she'll have any long-term problems?" He paused a moment, pressing his lips together. "I couldn't bear losing her."

"Rest assured, Mr. Dearman, Eva is doing well. I examined her on Monday, and her prognosis is very positive. She simply needs to gain her strength and a bit of weight."

"I can't tell you what a relief it is to hear those words. I've had my doubts about the family doctor in Lawrence. He seems a bit out of touch with modern medicine, but I feel confident in your diagnosis."

"Thank you." I felt myself flush with pleasure, warmed by his trust in my abilities.

"Eva explained about your current employment caring for children and young women at the Catholic homes. It is admirable that you devote yourself to the less fortunate who have nowhere else to turn."

"I find it rewarding," I said. "And your family is from Boston originally?" I asked, navigating the conversation to a lighter note.

"My ancestors settled in Boston before the revolution as merchants. My grandfather studied law and founded the firm that my father and I now run."

Eva had already filled me in on his background—born into a comfortable life. By all accounts he came from a loving and supportive family and enjoyed his profession.

I often wondered how different things might have turned out if William had honored his father's wishes and taken over the family arms business. Instead, with my support, he followed his own path, seeking adventure and challenges in the West. His father had never really forgiven him, seldom writing and refusing to visit us. My heart broke for William's mother, who ended up losing both her children. Shortly after our wedding, Beatrice married a friend of William's from Cambridge and moved to England. She died in childbirth two years later, leaving us bereft. I could only think that when William died, his father regretted his harsh stance. The unbending righteousness of both our families when we did not bow to their desires left me puzzled and angry. They seemed to care nothing for our happiness, wanting only to impose their will. Mr. Clayton had sent the children and me a moderate sum of money upon William's passing, which I accepted gratefully because we desperately needed it, even though I knew William would have probably preferred I return it.

Eva glanced at me, eyebrows slightly raised with a hopeful expression. She could not fathom that I would do anything but admire Mr. Dearman. I did find him agreeable. Undoubtedly, he would be a loving husband and make her happy. The danger lay in the risk of losing her relationship with her family. Even though I had no regrets about my decision to marry William, could I in good conscience recommend Eva forfeit everything for Mr. Dearman?

I considered my next words carefully. "I would be remiss if I did not ask of your intentions regarding my sister. Forgive me for being so indelicate, but it is obvious you care deeply for her."

"I assure you they are entirely honorable," he said. "I want nothing more than to make Miss Delacroix my wife, but I would not ask her to forsake her family for me. I know the situation is awkward for you, Dr. Clayton, and I hope you will not think me too forward, but I ask for your assistance in reaching out to your family. I do not understand your mother and sister's objections to me or how to overcome them."

A long sigh escaped my lips. "I'm afraid my mother and sister oppose the match for reasons that confound me as well.

I'm sure Eva told you they did not support my marriage either. They left me no option but to abandon my family for my husband. Our only visit to Lawrence after our marriage was a most unhappy event. I don't regret my choice, for my husband and I had a wonderful life together, but losing my family's love and support was difficult. I hope I'm not embarrassing you by revealing something so personal."

Mr. Dearman cleared his throat. "Not at all. I am very sorry for the loss of your husband and young son. I can't imagine what you have endured." He looked up at me. "I want your sister to enter into marriage without sacrifice."

I smiled. "We shall find a way through the forest of dissension, Mr. Dearman. Do not despair."

"Thank you. Your sister promised we could depend on you. She is most devoted to you."

"And I to her."

We left it at that and joined the others in conversation. Ellis and Mrs. Grove were discussing the recent national suffrage convention in May. Eva and Sara Jane sat forward, hanging on their words.

"Mrs. Catt did an excellent job running this year's convention," Mrs. Grove said. "She kept the committees on track, raised a substantial amount of money, and attracted many new members." The national organization had voted Mrs. Carrie Chapman Catt as their new president at the convention the previous year, after Miss Anthony stepped down following her eightieth birthday.

Ellis nodded. "Miss Anthony has many strengths and is still vitally engaged, but Mrs. Catt excels at organization and taking action. We couldn't have won the vote in Colorado without her." She turned to Eva. "Mrs. Bradford, whom you met at my house, presented Mrs. Catt with a gavel this year on behalf of the women of Colorado. It's a stunning piece made of Colorado wood decorated with gold, silver, and amethyst."

"What has become of Mrs. Elizabeth Stanton?" I asked. "Her name is hardly mentioned of late."

"I heard she is in ill health and rarely leaves her New York apartment," Mrs. Grove said. "She's eighty-five years old, so it's not surprising."

Ellis started to speak again but stopped as she glanced toward the lobby. "Oh my."

I followed her gaze to the large, imposing woman with a somewhat hawkish face who stood chatting with several ladies at one of the far tables. Her expansive gestures and slightly elevated voice drew attention. Mrs. Leonel "Nell" Anthony, a journalist with the *Denver Post* until earlier that year, wrote under the pen name Polly Pry. She had created a storm of controversy after working to free Alfred Packer from prison. Packer had been accused of cannibalism after being caught in a blizzard in the Rocky Mountains with four other men in 1874. He survived while all the others died. Thanks to Polly Pry's campaign to reverse his conviction, he was cleared of the charges and set free in January 1901. A few months later Mrs. Anthony parted ways with the *Denver Post* and began her own weekly magazine, *Polly Pry*. She gathered gossip from Denver society members to print in her publication.

"Let's hope she doesn't see us," I murmured, ducking my head.

In her usual intrusive manner, Mrs. Anthony worked her way across the room until she spotted our group and appeared at our table. "Why, Miss Meredith, how nice to see you," she said. She nodded at me, most likely having forgotten my name. I had never done anything of note to merit mention in her gossip columns.

There was nothing Ellis could do but introduce our guests, gracious as always. "Let me present my friend Mrs. Charlotte Grove, a noted suffragist in Illinois and her brother, Mr. Bertram Dearman, of Boston. You know Dr. Clayton, of course, and this is her daughter, Sara Jane, and her sister Miss Evangeline Delacroix, who is visiting from Lawrence, Kansas."

Mrs. Anthony smiled. Her keen eyes bored into our small group, as if she sensed an underlying secret. Did we somehow look guilty? "How long will you be staying, Mrs. Grove?" she asked at last.

"Only a week, I'm afraid," Mrs. Grove responded with a generous smile.

"And you, Mr. Dearman?"

"A bit longer," Mr. Dearman answered coolly. "My sister accompanied me to see Miss Meredith, as I'm here on business."

"And what type of business is that?"

"I'm an attorney, madam."

"Are you working with one of our illustrious business owners?"

"I'm not at liberty to say."

"And you, Miss Delacroix?" the interrogator continued. "How long will you be visiting?"

"Until the end of July," Eva answered. "The wonderful weather and beautiful mountains are a welcome respite from our summers in Lawrence. I'm having a delightful time."

"That's a pretty hat you're wearing," Mrs. Anthony said.

Eva beamed. "Thank you. I bought it at Paris Millinery. They have an excellent selection."

Mrs. Anthony stood for a moment, as if grasping for a way to extract useful information from the assembled group. "Do enjoy your time in Denver, ladies and Mr. Dearman. I hope we meet again." She moved on to her next victims.

Perhaps I worried too much. Surely there was nothing for her to report, and even if she did write something, Mildred would never see a copy of *Polly Pry*. Certainly not in my home.

Chapter 16   **SARA JANE**

Another Chance Meeting

I cannot begin to describe my disbelief on meeting Mr. Dearman. The exceptionally good-looking gentleman gazing into Aunt Eva's eyes with an expression of unwavering love was none other than the man I'd seen talking with Mattie Silks in front of the Barr City Creamery. I couldn't tell if he recognized me as well, although I detected a slightly puzzled frown when Miss Meredith introduced me. The air became heavy and my breathing shallow as I stared at his face, wishing it to be untrue. Whatever had he been doing with the notorious Denver madam? A second wave of dismay rolled through me. What if he had seen Rose and me getting out of Jimmy's car and mentioned our encounter? The thought turned my stomach upside down.

My mind raced as I pretended to listen to Miss Meredith chat with Eva and Mrs. Grove. Surely he couldn't be a customer of Mrs. Silks. The thought was too horrifying to imagine. There had to be a simple reason for his association with this deplorable woman. After all, he had only been conversing with her and the other man. I remembered how stiff and uncomfortable he had appeared, backing up when Mrs. Silks advanced toward him.

I had no idea what to do. Once again I longed to confide in Rose, but that was impossible. Should I tell Aunt Eva or Mama? If I did, it might create a terrible misunderstanding, when there must be an innocent explanation. The two lovers already faced enough barriers with the disapproval of my grandmother and Aunt Mildred. For the next hour, I watched Aunt Eva and Mr. Dearman exchange longing glances. The apparent pureness of their love for each other deeply touched me. I decided to keep what I'd seen to myself for the time being and have faith in Mr. Dearman's good character. With a little luck, he wouldn't mention my ill-advised ride with Jimmy and Fred.

When Mrs. Anthony approached our table and questioned each person with interest, Mama's expression turned from annoyance to concern. I had never met the famous author of *Polly Pry*. Mrs. O'Malley often purchased the magazine, feeling she needed to stay current on social events and other gossip in order to chat with her customers. Rose loved reading the latest tidbits to me. I found the stories mostly boring, except for the detailed accounts of what society women had worn to the theater and charity ball. I tried to sketch the dresses, hats, and cloaks from her descriptions and use them to develop ideas of my own.

Shortly after Mrs. Anthony moved on, Mrs. Grove stood, placing a hand on her lower back. "I apologize, but I'm still worn out from the long train ride and must have a rest."

Mr. Dearman jumped to his feet. "Are you all right, Charlotte? Shall I escort you to your room?"

"I'm fine. Please continue without me." Mrs. Grove walked around to Eva and took her hand. "Would you join me for luncheon Monday, just the two of us? I so want to get to know you better."

Aunt Eva smiled. "That would be lovely."

"I'll meet you here in the lobby at twelve thirty."

Miss Meredith looked at her silver watch pendent. "It's getting late, and Mother will be looking for me. I'll accompany Mrs. Grove to the elevator, but you ladies stay."

Aunt Eva turned to Mama. "Would that be all right?" Anyone could see my aunt was not ready to leave Mr. Dearman.

I didn't blame her. And I convinced myself once more that nothing could be amiss with this dignified man.

"Thank you, Ellis, we'll get a carriage home," Mama said. "Perhaps we might take a stroll with Mr. Dearman before we go."

"An excellent idea." Mr. Dearman waved to the waiter to settle the bill as Mrs. Grove and Miss Meredith said their goodbyes.

The four of us stepped out to the street in front of the hotel and headed in the direction of Sixteenth Street. I spotted Mama's acquaintance, Mr. Abbott, coming toward us. After meeting him the day before, I'd asked Mama why she'd become so flustered and distracted. She brushed it off, saying he was simply a former patient and no one to concern myself about. But the way her eyes avoided mine and the tone of her voice produced an uneasy feeling in the pit of my stomach. The idea that Mama might be interested in this man, any man, was inconceivable. No one could replace Papa.

Mr. Abbott bowed his head. "Dr. Clayton, what a treat to see you again." He gazed at Mama with a hopeful smile.

177

"Mr. Abbott. Of course…you're staying at the hotel," Mama faltered.

Aunt Eva greeted Mr. Abbott, introducing Mr. Dearman. "We're taking a short stroll after taking tea at the hotel. Would you care to join us?"

Mama's eyes widened. "Why yes, please do."

"Thank you. I could use some fresh air and good company. I've been in meetings with bankers and lawyers all day. A stuffy lot," he said in his sonorous voice that carried well beyond our group.

Mr. Dearman chuckled. "I understand completely. I'm an attorney and find most business meetings stifling as well."

Eva took Mr. Dearman's arm while Mr. Abbott, Mama, and I trailed behind. Occasionally Mr. Abbott placed his hand under Mama's elbow to protect her from people hurrying past. We strolled down Tremont then turned up Sixteenth Street, where the wider sidewalks provided more room amid the bustling crowds.

Mr. Abbott stepped around to be on the street side of the walkway and directed his attention to me. "As I recall, Sara Jane, you're fifteen."

"I'll be sixteen in August." I wondered how he knew this about me.

"I have a daughter who is eighteen, Bernadette, my only child. She's been back east at Pembroke College this year. I've missed her something fierce. She comes home Thursday for the summer, and I can hardly wait to see her." The skin around his eyes crinkled as he broke into a broad grin.

"How nice," I murmured, unsure what else to say. I turned for help from Mama, but she was busy pointing out a restaurant to Mr. Dearman and Aunt Eva.

"Do you like to ride horses?" Mr. Abbott continued.

"I rode when I was younger. With my papa," I added.

His expression turned to one of sympathy, an uncomfortable, sad look that adults wore when they talked to me about the passing of my father or Peter. Silence followed. "I'm very sorry for your losses," he said at last. "I would like to invite your family to visit my ranch soon. I have a stable full of horses and miles of trails for riding. You and your little brother would enjoy yourselves. And Bernadette would love the company. She'll be lonely back home after her busy year."

I glanced at Mama, willing her to rescue me. How could this stranger be so bold as to suggest we visit his ranch? He didn't even know us, and surely it wouldn't be proper to go. I didn't care about his daughter or their silly horses. I wanted him to leave us alone.

To my great relief, Aunt Eva called me over to look at a pair of earrings in a jewelry store window. I remained with her and Mr. Dearman as we continued on, glancing over my shoulder periodically at Mama and Mr. Abbott. As they chatted, Mama laughed a great deal—not just polite titters but unrestrained giggles. The tense lines in her face eased, and her thin shoulders relaxed.

As shadows grew longer and the warm afternoon began to wither, we circled back to the hotel. A doorman hailed a carriage for us. Mr. Dearman offered to escort us home, but Aunt Eva grew alarmed at the suggestion. "Mildred might see you," she whispered. "We'll meet Monday after I lunch with your sister." He reluctantly agreed as he helped her into the carriage and kissed her hand. It was terribly romantic.

Mr. Abbott smiled at Mama. "Think on what I said, Dr. Clayton. Send me a note." Then he turned to me. "Take care, young lady." He winked before I climbed into the carriage.

The two men waved as we started off. They turned to go in the hotel, and Mr. Abbott slapped Mr. Dearman on the back, his booming voice drifting in the air. "Let me buy you a drink, sir."

Not only was he trying to woo Mama, but now he wanted to befriend Aunt Eva's Mr. Dearman. The nerve!

I thought about Mr. Abbott as we rode home. Clearly his interest in Mama was a serious matter. Did he want to marry her? I needed to find a saint to pray to who would help prevent the invasion of this man into our lives.

The cuckoo clock in the entry hall struck six as we came through the door. Aunt Mildred and Katherine were most likely worried about what had become of us, yet total silence greeted us.

"Mildred must be upstairs resting," Mama suggested. "But where are Katherine and Cole?"

Aunt Eva unpinned her hat and hung it on the hallway tree. "Is it possible Mildred hasn't come back yet from Mrs. Meredith's?"

I peeked into the parlor and waved to Mama and Aunt Eva to come. Cole lay curled up on the settee under Aunt Mildred's arm with his head resting on her ample bosom, while Buttercup snuggled next to him. All were sound asleep. Aunt Mildred's head had fallen back, and her mouth was open as she softly snored. Cole's favorite book, *Robinson Crusoe*, remained open in her lap.

"How dear," Mama whispered. "Let them sleep until dinner is ready."

We heard the back door close. Katherine's unmistakable solid footsteps came from the kitchen into the dining room. She stopped short when she saw us gathered in the parlor doorway. Mama put a finger to her lips as Katherine took a peek at the scene in the parlor.

Aunt Eva headed upstairs while Mama and I followed Katherine to the kitchen. I smelled something delicious baking. I was starving. I'd been too unnerved by meeting Mr. Dearman to enjoy the beautiful sandwiches and cakes on the tea platters.

"I went next door to borrow some butter," Katherine explained. "Mrs. Bolton said she'd keep an eye on Cole. Ye said to keep dinner light tonight, so I prepared a platter of meats and cheese with some fresh rolls." She dipped her head to me. "And yer favorite chocolate cake, lass."

"You're wonderful," I said and gave her a hug. I vowed to say a special prayer to Saint Laurence, the patron saint of cooks, to ensure we always had the comfort of Katherine and her delicious meals.

The Leading Ladies of Denver

Wednesday, July 3, 1901

Dear Diary,

Once again you await me after many days of neglect. I must recount my thoughts, as my head is swimming with new ideas and experiences.

I have taken great joy in tutoring young Cole, who is progressing splendidly. Once we finish reviewing numbers and letters each morning, we take our daily constitutional about the neighborhood with Eva (Cole on his tricycle). If time allows before lunch, Cole and I toss his rubber ball about in the backyard. He can be the sweetest boy, and I am growing extremely fond of him. I never felt as close to any of my cousins' children, but then I never spent time with them in such a meaningful endeavor. While Lida is a loving mother, I believe Cole sorely feels the loss of his father. He has a never-ending need for attention and affection. Perhaps I am becoming too soft hearted in my old age, but I cannot deny his requests for my time.

Sara Jane has been attentive toward me as well. She is an earnest child, even if she sometimes oversteps her place. I am fascinated with her drawings and feel she has a future in art, whether it be designing clothes or something else. My mind turns to finding a way to support her in this pursuit.

Our days here remain a whirlwind. I had a delightful time at tea with Mrs. Meredith at her home on Saturday afternoon. We talked for almost two hours about literature and a variety of issues, including women's suffrage. I find her personal story fascinating. She became a supporter of women's rights during her years growing up in Montana where the rigors of frontier life required women to be particularly hearty to survive. She is soft-spoken and presents her views in a logical, straightforward manner that does not make me feel put upon or defensive. I found myself listening with new interest and a sense of appreciation for the struggle.

A person of deep compassion, Mrs. Meredith works to help women in difficult situations at the Mothers' and Children's Home here in Denver. The group watches over young children of mothers who must work long hours in factories. She related a story of one young girl named Colleen that is all too common. At the age of nineteen the girl and her new husband struck out from Ohio for the mining town of Golden, Colorado. But her husband died in an accident three years later, leaving the young woman destitute with one-year-old twin daughters. She had no family back home to aid her. The Methodist church stepped in to relocate the family to Denver. She finally found work in a flour mill, where she makes barely half what the men earn performing the same tasks. The wages are so meager, she turned to the home for someone to care for her babies and provide regular meals. Mrs. Meredith says the

*story is repeated many times over in Denver and across our
country.*

*I mentioned this sad tale to Lida that evening, and she told
me there are dozens of young girls in the House of the Good
Shepherd and other charitable homes in Denver with similar
stories. Her housekeeper, Katherine, endured a terrible
tragedy some years back. She and her husband immigrated
from Ireland to New York City in 1878, then ventured out to
Leadville, Colorado, two years later. Lida first met Katherine
when she and William lived there. Lida was teaching
elementary school and pregnant with Sara Jane. She needed a
part-time housekeeper. Katherine answered her advertisement
in the local paper and worked for Lida until the family moved
to Denver when Peter was a baby. The next winter a smallpox
epidemic took all three of Katherine's children. Not six
months later her husband was killed in an accident at the
silver mine. The poor dear was crazed by grief. Through the
charity of the Catholic church, Katherine was sent to the nuns
at Saint Elizabeth's Orphanage in Denver as their cook.
Despondent and hopeless, she often wandered aimlessly
through the streets during her free hours, pondering the sin of
taking her own life. Fortunately, Lida found her downtown
one day and brought poor Katherine into her home. As you
can imagine, Katherine is devoted to Lida and the children.
Any misgivings I had about her have long faded. Life can be
so cruel to all of us, but particularly to those who have the
least.*

*There but for the grace of God...it could have been Lida,
had she not come from a more privileged background. This
great and wealthy country must provide adequate aid for
women in dire situations. I do my small part in Lawrence, but*

it feels insignificant in light of the tremendous need. I've always found questionable the argument that once women had the vote they would force legislators to pass necessary reforms. But the sterling successes of the women in Colorado offer a worthy example. Colorado women have led the charge to pass many commendable reforms. It forces me to rethink my former opinions.

On Sunday. after attending our respective churches, we took a tram to the famous Elitch's Zoological Gardens. I must say I found it a remarkable place where one can wander at will through sixteen acres of beautifully groomed flowerbeds, fountains, and orchards. To her credit, the owner, Mrs. Elitch, maintains a wholesome family entertainment park and wisely bans dancing and alcohol.

Lida promised we will return another day to attend one of the summer stock plays performed by renowned thespians from across the country at the impressive theater. There are also musical concerts by visiting artists or the Elitch's Garden Orchestra. Several times during the summer, the theater shows moving pictures on one of Thomas Edison's Vitascopes. Sara Jane said she watched the film Burglar on The Roof *last summer. I was touched when she asked if I'd like to go with her to see* A Wringing Good Joke, *which is playing in a few weeks. Oh, this modern age! We certainly never had such diversions when I was young.*

I believe Franklin might be enticed to come here for The Naval Spectacle, a reenactment of the famous Civil War battle of the Merrimac and the Monitor. The most astonishing attraction is the hot air balloon, which carries brave souls fifteen hundred feet into the sky while tethered to the ground with rope. You certainly won't find me doing that!

Katherine packed us a hamper, and we picnicked on the lawn beneath the willow trees while the orchestra played in the bandstand. I enjoyed watching Cole frolic in the playground, beside himself with excitement. Eva accompanied him on the new miniature railroad, chugging around the grounds. Then we toured the zoo, which houses all manner of exotic animals from bears, lions, and camels to monkeys, elephants, and ostriches. Apparently Mrs. Elitch received a number of the zoo's denizens from her friend P. T. Barnum.

After returning home for a brief rest, my sisters and I spent the evening at a meeting of the Denver Women's Press Club. Mrs. Helen Robinson, whose articles appear in many papers and magazines, spoke on "recent literature." I had read all but one of the books discussed and found Mrs. Robinson's reviews and insights thought provoking, even if I did not always agree. She compared and contrasted the novels Anna Karenina *and* The Awakening, *both sad tales of women who abandon their husbands and children to commit adultery. Mrs. Robinson argued that Anna Karenina killed herself because of a broken heart after her lover abandoned her, while Edna Pontellier of* The Awakening *took her life as a final act of independence against society's unfair constraints on women. I offered that both tales, whatever the motives of the characters, led to the same unhappy conclusion.*

The discussion soon turned to the unflattering portrayals of women in novels as shrews, hopeless gossips, or empty-headed souls wanting nothing more than to find a husband. She referred to stories by Mark Twain and Frank Norris. Miss Meredith agreed that on the whole this was true but brought up the exception of Henry James's book, The Bostonians, *which provides a more nuanced look at women's divergent roles. Lida added that some women writers are as bad as the men, such as Mrs. Humphry Ward, author of* Eleanor. *Mrs. Ward argues adamantly against women's suffrage, claiming women are best served by influencing politics indirectly through their husbands and male friends. I did not volunteer that I previously aligned my views with those of Mrs. Ward. My beliefs are now in a state of flux, and I have much to ponder.*

Yesterday, late in the afternoon, Lida, Eva, and I attended a meeting of the Colorado Non-Partisan Equal Suffrage Association to finalize plans for participation in tomorrow's Fourth of July parade. I might not have gone to the gathering, but the hostess, Mrs. Bradford, who we have met several times, insisted Eva and I come as her guests of honor. Lida's friends have been most gracious by turning every event into an occasion to welcome us into their circle.

I find our new acquaintances interesting and often inspiring, prompting me to reexamine long-held opinions. Franklin has always looked askance at women in the suffrage movement, dividing them into several categories: (1) a collection of ill-informed, misguided young women such as Eva and her friends, (2) discontented wives and widows who married poorly, and (3) bitter, old maids with strong masculine tendencies. I daresay I used to agree, for the most part, but these biases are falling away. The leading ladies of Denver are well educated and politically astute. They are accomplished in many fields dominated by men, yet they remain gentle and good humored, and most are devoted wives and mothers. I feel a bit inadequate when they speak so eloquently about their convictions without being overbearing, and to the contrary, maintaining an admirable equanimity.

Even if I don't always agree on specific issues, I approve of their dedication to the plight of women.

I find this organization particularly commendable, as it attracts Colorado women from different backgrounds and political parties who have put aside their differences and banded together to further their cause with an air of bonhomie and a view to the larger canvas of life. It was a surprise when Mrs. Bradford introduced me to Mrs. Elizabeth Ensley, a mulatto woman born in the Caribbean. She is a college graduate, teacher, journalist, and activist for women's suffrage and social justice. Miss Meredith told me Mrs. Ensley was instrumental in getting the colored vote in '93 for the Colorado suffrage amendment, helping tip the scales for its passage. I am ashamed to admit she is the first colored woman with whom I have enjoyed a substantive conversation, a circumstance which left me ill at ease at first. I found her refined and a most worthy participant, thoughtful and unassuming in her comments and opinions. While I can't imagine such an encounter at a gathering in Lawrence at present, it gives me hope for the future of relations between the races in our country.

The cooperative and congenial nature of the women here brings to mind my frustrations with my associates in the Lady's Benevolent Society of Lawrence. While the ladies may be well meaning, they exhibit a parochial view of the issues, bickering about petty details and arcane rules, to the detriment of those we strive to help. I had to fight to get their approval to take the orphanage children on a picnic to the river last summer. Those parsimonious, narrow-minded ninnies on the committee didn't want to spend the money, complaining that they and other mothers they knew were

189

worried about something so irregular. What if the orphans ran away and mixed with the town's other children? As if losing one's parents were a contagious disease that could contaminate their precious sons and daughters.

Mrs. Bradford announced forty-two of the group's sixty-three members have signed up to march in the Fourth of July parade tomorrow, including Lida, Eva, and Sara Jane. It has been the topic of discussion between Sara Jane and Lida for some days. While I question if it is appropriate for someone so young to participate, Sara Janes impressed me with her thoughtful reasoning. "Mama, this is about my future and the future of my friends, the next generation. If we are to enjoy independent and successful lives as women, we must make our voices heard now." Imagine this from a girl not yet sixteen. Of course, Eva supported her, and I admit I did as well in the end.

All of this put me in an awkward position being among such ardent supporters. So as not to embarrass my sisters and niece, and with the greater good of temperance and helping the poor in mind, I added my name to the list of marchers.

The group's first banner will urge Congress once again to introduce and pass an amendment to the US Constitution for national women's suffrage, despite the fact that the only time Congress paid any heed to the demand was back in 1887. The amendment was roundly defeated after being held in committee for nine years! It seems unlikely the position of the congressmen might change anytime soon. One can only give credit to these women for their fortitude in continuing to lobby year after year.

The second banner is aimed at members of the Colorado Legislature, voicing support for the implementation of stricter

190

child labor laws. Here in Colorado boys as young as thirteen are working in the mines, and ten-year-olds labor in factories in dangerous conditions. It's shameful. I cannot help but support the Denver ladies' efforts.

I will not mention this to Mother or Franklin for now. Neither would hold any sympathy for such activism. There is no rush to write Franklin anyway, as I have not heard from him since his first letter. I expect he is busy with work, but it is disappointing.

Chapter 18   **LIDA**

The Fourth of July Parade

The morning of the fourth dawned crisp and clear. Thundershowers had rumbled through the city the evening before and into the night, washing down the dusty pavement and leaving the scent of rain in the air. Dew glistened on garden flowers, and droplets of rain pooled in windowsills.

We rose early to enjoy Katherine's special, fortifying breakfast of eggs, ham, fried potatoes, and fresh biscuits dripping in butter and honey. She fussed about the table, insisting we eat second helpings to keep up our strength on the mile-and-a-half march through downtown.

"Sure Cole and I shall cheer ye on from the sidelines," she crooned, glancing out the window. "What a fine day for a parade."

"Thank you, Katherine," I said. "We'll watch for you near Tremont Street."

"And ye stand tall and proud," Katherine admonished Sara Jane. "Such a vision in white ye are, lass."

After breakfast, we waited for the carriage due to arrive at nine fifteen. I still marveled that Mildred had volunteered so enthusiastically to join us on the march. At times the thought of it made me chuckle to myself. I could only imagine Mother and Franklin's shock if they discovered Mildred's growing support for the cause. Was it possible she had written to them about it? I didn't dare ask.

In recent days I'd caught glimpses of the Mildred I'd known when we were young: a lighter, more animated soul. Slowly she shrugged off the weight of convention and the confinement of small-town life, fettered by gossips and the judgment of others. Less scowling marred her face, replaced by smiles that softened the wrinkles and warmed her eyes. I pondered what Eva had said about Mildred and Franklin's relationship, sad to think they had grown apart, leaving a stale and loveless marriage without the joy of children to fill the empty spaces.

Mildred glanced in the mirror over the entry hall table and smoothed her new skirt over her protruding stomach. "You did a lovely job, Eva, but I look like a stuffed pig," she grumbled. "White never flatters anyone except the young and slender like you and Sara Jane." She glanced at me and hurriedly added, "You're the exception, of course, Lida. Thin as a rail still."

Our suffragette attire required white skirts and blouses to symbolize purity and emphasize our femininity, while our green sashes represented hope. But the costume proved a problem for Mildred. While she had a presentable white blouse, she owned nothing but black or drab gray skirts, and her beige traveling skirt. Eva quickly set about making her a white skirt with an attractive flounce along the bottom out of some white poplin I'd bought two years before for kitchen curtains but had never had time to make.

"I believe you've lost weight," I said.

"Mama's right, Aunt Mildred," Sara Jane agreed. "You look thinner."

Mildred feigned disbelief, but a hint of a smile pulled at her lips. "Then I must double my daily walks."

The carriage dropped us at the corner of Market and Sixteenth, where the parade would begin. A few blocks down Market the illicit houses of the red-light district remained shuttered tight at this early hour. I knew Denver society would be in an uproar if they saw the list of stellar male citizens who frequented these establishments—at least according to the stories of the girls at the House of the Good Shepherd. The complicity of these prominent men, the police, and city officials in keeping the businesses thriving enraged me, but it was not my place to spread unsubstantiated rumors.

Red, white, and blue bunting and American flags hung from storefronts along the length of Sixteenth Street as far as the eye could see. Elderly, stooped-shouldered veterans of the Civil War stepped into formation, dressed in their tattered and faded Union uniforms. The morning sun glinted off their well-shined bronze medals. About twenty younger men lined up next to them, smartly dressed in army uniforms from their brief adventures in the Spanish-American War of 1898.

Two steam-powered fire trucks waited as their horses impatiently stamped the ground to get underway. Three men rode unicycles up and down the block while two couples pedaled about on tandem bikes, the latest rage. Paper flowers in bright colors adorned bicycle-powered floats made of tin and plywood. The wagon beds of larger floats, which were sponsored by local businesses, carried the owners and their children, dressed in their Sunday best, ready to wave to the crowds lining the route. Cowboys in full regalia, with

195

enormous cowboy hats, leather vests, deerskin chaps, and silver belt buckles, rode sleek horses sporting their finest fittings, evoking the untamed quintessence of Colorado.

We joined other members of the Colorado Non-Partisan Equal Suffrage Association. The ladies were indignant after discovering our group had been relegated to the second-to-last position in the parade.

"Mrs. Bradford has gone in search of Mayor Johnson," Ellis said. "She'll take care of it."

Mrs. Bradford, always a formidable presence, returned shortly. "We'll be moving up, ladies." A satisfied smile crept across her face. "I had only to remind our esteemed mayor of what the Women's Democratic Club meant to his election." The club, which Mrs. Bradford had founded, had been instrumental in making Henry Johnson mayor of Denver the past three years. We quickly found ourselves positioned near the start of the parade behind the carriage carrying the mayor and his wife.

After numerous false starts, the parade finally got underway at ten twenty. The Denver High School marching band led the way, playing John Philip Sousa's *Stars and Stripes Forever*, which had grown immensely popular over the past few years. The good citizens of Denver stood three-deep along the sidewalks, spilling into the streets. Children waved small American flags and cried out with delight.

Our group represented the largest contingent in the event. We walked six across, proudly holding our banners. Many women and men cheered as we passed, but as always, there were detractors. Angry men and a few women scowled and turned away or, worse yet, called out disparaging remarks. As we passed the front of a saloon, several men, already inebriated at this early hour, booed and hissed.

"Harpies, go back home where you belong," one man yelled. "Leave us men alone, you old biddies."

Mildred straightened her shoulders and responded in a decidedly loud and unladylike voice, "Not until the likes of you drunken brutes are removed from decent society." She continued on with new resolve, her face flushed, her arm tightening over mine. Eva and I couldn't help giggling.

"An excellent response, dear," I said. "But we do find it best to ignore those kinds of remarks."

"Some people must be put in their place," Mildred huffed. "Imagine using that language with ladies. We have every right to proclaim our views."

As we passed Curtis Street, Rose, her five siblings, and Mr. and Mrs. O'Malley called out gaily to us. I waved to several friends from the literary club and the Populist Party. Near Tremont Street, Katherine and Cole pressed forward out of the crowd, whooping and yelling to get our attention. Thankfully Katherine had a tight grasp on Cole's hand, or he would have run right out to join us.

The procession continued amid the press of cheering bodies. Bright sunshine heated the streets and sent a trickle of sweat down my back. I looked over at Mildred and Eva, worried the excitement and long walk might be too much for them both. But they seemed immensely happy. Sara Jane flashed a wide grin. A surge of pride rushed over me, yet I still worried if it had been wise to expose her to the public like this at such a young age. Hopefully the good sisters at St. Mary's Academy would not find out and scold her for unseemly behavior.

As we neared Broadway, the parade turned to march past the front of the State Capitol. I spied Mr. Dearman, Mrs. Grove, and Mr. Abbott standing on the corner. I glanced over at Eva and gave the slightest nod of my head in that direction. She scanned the crowd and blushed as her heart's desire raised a hand of greeting. Then Mr. Dearman stepped back into the shadows, out of view, knowing it would not do for Mildred to discover his presence.

Eva and Sara Jane had met Mrs. Grove for lunch on Monday under the guise of a shopping trip, and Mr. Dearman had joined them afterward. The more duplicitous we were with Mildred, the worse I felt, but Eva had wanted to wait until after the Fourth of July celebrations to confess our secret activities. We had agreed to talk with Mildred the following evening and announce Mr. Dearman's arrival in Denver in the company of his sister. We would try to persuade Mildred to meet with him and allow him a chance to make his case.

Mr. Abbott doffed his cowboy hat, breaking into a bemused smile that wrinkled his friendly face. I nodded and grinned back. The brief time I had spent walking with him the previous Friday afternoon had buoyed my spirits. In a light-hearted tenor, he suggested we take time to get to know each other better. It would not be a courtship but a friendship developed over as much time as I saw fit to grant him. He insisted I need not feel uncomfortable or pressured. As we strolled down the street laughing and chatting, his words made perfect sense. I might not be ready to change my life or that of my children; however, I could entertain the idea of a friendship. Let people think what they might.

Mortal Sins and Errors of Omission

Sister Mary Claire, a young nun recently arrived from Ireland, transformed catechism class from a dreaded duty to a palatable means of learning about the Catholic faith. Unlike grouchy Sister Agnes, she was young and pretty with a joy for her faith that sparkled in her eyes. Her contagious smile and indisputable belief in God inspired me to try to embrace the church. If only I didn't have so many nagging questions.

Due to the large number of catechism students and our varying ages, the sisters had broken us into two sections. After Sister Agnes gave a general introduction to the day's topic—which always sounded more like a threat—we separated into our groups. Thankfully, Sister Mary Claire taught those of us ten years and older, while Sister Agnes terrorized the younger ones, roaming between desks with her ruler, rapping the knuckles of anyone who misbehaved or didn't know the answers to her questions.

The day after the Fourth of July, I sat in class puzzling over the lesson, "Sin and Its Kinds," as explained in the Baltimore Catechism booklet. I understood we were all born with original sin, the result of Adam's sins in the Garden of Eden. It seemed unfair to me that everyone had to inherit his sins, but luckily baptism washed them away. However, I found the distinction between the mortal and venial sins much harder to decipher. In her introduction to the lesson, Sister Agnes warned even the most minor misdeeds could be interpreted as mortal sins, which had dire consequences if we ever hoped to get to heaven.

Once we broke into groups, Sister Mary Claire stood before us with wisps of dark auburn hair peeking from the sides of her habit, softening her angular face. She smiled brightly. "Children, please open yer catechism books to lesson six. Jeannette, can ye please read the description of actual sins?"

Jeanette, a plain-looking girl with long blonde braids, read the text in a voice not much louder than a whisper, "Actual sin is any willful thought, desire, word, action, or omission forbidden by the law of God."

"Very good," the Sister said. "In the next part, we learn that actual sin includes both mortal sins and venial sins, with the first being more serious than the second. Sara Jane, please read to us about mortal sin."

I cleared my throat. "Mortal sin is a grievous offense against the law of God. To make a sin mortal, these three things are needed: (1) the thought, desire, word, action, or omission must be seriously wrong or considered seriously wrong; (2) the sinner must be mindful of the serious wrong; and (3) the sinner must fully consent to it." The next part caused my stomach to tighten. "Besides depriving the sinner of sanctifying grace, mortal sin makes the soul the enemy of God, takes away the merit of all good actions, deprives it of the right to everlasting happiness in heaven, and makes it deserving of everlasting punishment in hell." Could I possibly commit such a grave crime?

"So as ye see, we must do everything in our power to avoid committing a mortal sin." Sister Mary Claire scanned our faces with a benevolent gaze. "I know ye all have pure hearts and would never purposely commit such a sin."

I didn't feel as confident as Sister in that assumption, having observed the actions of several of my fellow students outside of catechism class. I could think of a number of my past actions that might be considered mortal sins. I hoped they could be excused, as I had been a Baptist at the time and unaware they were potentially serious sins.

Twelve-year-old Frank Corte's hand flew up. "Sister, can you tell us what things would be considered a mortal sin?"

Sister nodded. "A very good question, Frank. For example, if ye knowingly told a lie to yer parents or teachers, that would be a mortal sin. Or if ye hurt someone on purpose or stole someone else's property. Even thinking bad thoughts about others is wrong."

Tense lines formed on Frank's brow. "What if you tripped your sister almost by accident and she broke her arm?"

Sister Mary Claire tipped her head to one side and bit her lower lip for a moment before responding. "Well, Frank, I know ye must be most sorry for such a thing. As we'll learn in lessons seventeen through nineteen starting next week, there is a way to atone for our sins. We can make a confession to God to ask for his forgiveness and do penance to be absolved of our sins."

This aligned with Rose's assurances that sins needn't be a problem. I prayed it was really that simple.

Frank let out a whoosh of air as his shoulders relaxed. "Thank you, Sister."

"Thank God in all his mercy," Sister replied. "Now, ye may read us the description of venial sin."

Frank wiped his sweaty brow on his shirtsleeve and began. "Venial sin is a less serious offense against the law of God, which does not deprive the soul of sanctifying grace, and which can be pardoned even without sacramental confession." He looked up from his book. "Shall I read the next part, Sister?" She nodded.

"A sin can be venial in two ways: (1) when the evil done is not seriously wrong, (2) when the evil done is seriously wrong, but the sinner sincerely believes it is only slightly wrong." Frank sat back in his chair.

Hannah Webber raised her hand above her head. "Sister, what if you had something important to tell your parents, which they might not like, and you forgot to say anything?"

"If ye simply forgot, this is a venial sin. Ye can rectify it easily by telling yer parents and asking God to help ye to be more mindful." Sister paused. "But if ye purposely didn't tell them, ye have committed a sin of omission, which is a mortal sin."

Hannah blanched. "Can I tell them now and ask for forgiveness?"

Sister Mary Claire smiled. "Aye, of course, lass. Talk to your parents, then pray to God and do a good deed as a way to repent."

This exchange raised my deepest fears. I found myself in a quandary over keeping several important secrets I knew might cause others pain. Should I have told Aunt Eva about the encounter I had witnessed between Mr. Dearman and Mrs.

Silks? Was keeping this to myself a sin? And clearly Aunt Eva's secret meetings with Mr. Dearman would cause Aunt Mildred a great deal of distress, yet we all continued to deceive her. I doubted it mattered that we thought Aunt Mildred's stance against Mr. Dearman unreasonable. In addition, I had omitted telling Mama about riding in the horseless carriage with Jimmy and Fred when I knew she would disapprove. These errors of omission must be considered venial sins, at best, but more likely mortal sins. I could think of no way to justify them as anything less. Perhaps if everything turned out well in the end, my sins would be erased or forgotten?

Sister talked of circumstances where we might be tempted to sin, encouraging us to stop and think before we acted. "Be watchful of situations where others might lead ye astray." I admit, her warning brought Rose to mind. All this prompted more questions from guilty-looking students who obviously feared they were headed straight to hell.

I thought the hour would never end. Mama had let me invite Rose for dinner, and I was anxious to get home.

"A most productive discussion today," Sister Mary Claire said at last. "Next week we'll cover the lessons on confession, and in three weeks ye'll be ready to make yer first confession."

The day of reckoning was coming sooner than I expected. Whatever would I do?

Ten minutes after I arrived home from class, I answered Rose's knock at the front door. My aunts and Mama were out back enjoying glasses of lemonade in the gazebo. Dinner would be served shortly.

203

Rose burst into the entry hall, and Buttercup slipped in on her heels, bolting up the stairs. Rose hopped about and waved a magazine in the air. "Wait until you see. Polly Pry wrote an article about your Aunt Eva's visit, and she mentioned you! Why didn't you tell me you went to the Brown Palace Hotel for tea?"

My heart lurched. "Don't say anything," I whispered, pulling on her arm. "Come to my room quickly."

Rose looked puzzled, but followed me upstairs. We reached my room, and I closed the door. "Let me see."

Rose opened the magazine to the second page and folded it over, pointing to a column titled *About Town*. "Why are you being so quiet?"

"It's complicated. I'll tell you in a minute." I scanned the column and found the dangerous description in the third paragraph. I read it aloud, glancing up nervously at my door to make sure no one was coming.

NEW IN TOWN: Summer brings distinguished visitors from across the country to our metropolitan hub. On Saturday, I encountered a cozy group having tea in the Brown Palace atrium. Dr. Lida Clayton and her pretty daughter, Sara Jane, are hosting Dr. Clayton's sister, Miss Evangeline Delacroix from Lawrence, Kansas, on an extended stay. The beautiful Miss Delacroix, with silver hair and brilliant blue eyes, wore a stunning afternoon suit of rose peau de soie topped by a lovely crepe de chine hat from none other than Denver's own Paris Millinery.

"Mama is thrilled she mentioned the shop," Rose interrupted. "She thinks we'll be busy tomorrow after ladies read this."

I nodded and continued reading.

Also in attendance were Miss Ellis Meredith and her guests, the charming Mrs. Charlotte Grove of Springfield, Illinois, accompanied by her handsome brother, Mr. Bertram Dearman, of Boston, Massachusetts. Mrs. Grove and Miss Meredith met through their activities in the national suffrage movement. Mr. Dearman is an attorney in Denver on business, but to these prying eyes his business appears to include Miss Delacroix. The two could not turn their gazes away from each other. Do I detect romance floating on Colorado's summer breeze?

I let out a long sigh. "Oh dear, Rose. This is terrible."

"She called you pretty! What's wrong with that?" She stared at me, perplexed. "But who is Mr. Dearman?"

"Where to begin. I'll tell you about Aunt Eva and Mr. Dearman, but you can't repeat this to anyone. And I mean anyone, not even your mother." After she put her hand over her heart and swore herself to secrecy, I explained about their romance, the struggle with Aunt Mildred and my grandmother, and the secret rendezvous at the Brown Palace Hotel. "Aunt Eva and Mr. Dearman are so in love. They absolutely must find a way to be together," I concluded, omitting my discovery that Mr. Dearman was the man we had seen talking with Mattie Silks. It hardly seemed relevant in this moment of crisis.

"It's like a fairytale," Rose said, clasping her hands together in delight. "I've never known anyone in a secret romance. When it's all decided, I shall write a story and send it to *Harper's Bazar*."

I looked at Rose, feeling glum. "Let's hope it doesn't end in tragedy."

The door flew open, and Cole burst in. "Mama says to come to dinner." He gazed at the magazine. "What's that?"

"Just a fashion magazine." I pulled a pillow over the top of it. "We'll be right there." Cole scooted back downstairs.

"Maybe your aunt will decide to elope," Rose said. "That would be thrilling."

"Isn't it terrible that a grown woman can't decide her own life without making such difficult choices?" I paused, thinking about the gravity of what I had revealed. "You absolutely must not tell anyone about this, Rose. I'm sorry. Now you'll be committing the mortal sin of omission."

Rose let out a hearty laugh. "You worry too much." And we went down to dinner.

Lightning Strikes

The dinner went well, although Sara Jane seemed unusually tense and quiet. I had been a bit nervous about Rose joining us. Once when dining at our house she became so animated she tossed a forkful of food into the air and across the room. Another time she let loose with an inappropriate word, which Cole repeated numerous times over the following weeks. But this evening she remained subdued, smiling with obvious admiration at Eva and politely answering questions about her family.

"And what are your interests, young lady?" Mildred asked. "Do you have plans beyond finishing school at St. Mary's Academy?"

"Yes, ma'am. I plan to go to college and be an author," Rose said, ducking her head with an uncharacteristic shyness.

Aunt Mildred hesitated, looking as if she might laugh. "How ambitious."

"She writes wonderful short stories," Sara Jane said.

Rose looked up and took a deep breath. "My father read that a company is developing an electric typewriter to sell soon, and he's going to buy one for his business, and the best part is he's going to give me the old one, a Remington that's only four years old, and I'll be able to write ever so fast then, and won't it be thrilling." Here was the Rose we knew so well.

"Do you know how to type?" Aunt Mildred asked.

"Well, not yet. But Papa said he'd send me to business school to learn. He says I can be a secretary while I'm waiting to become a famous author."

"Very practical, indeed," Mildred said. "And are you a great reader as well?"

Rose nodded. "Oh yes. I love Jane Austen, Louisa May Alcott, and Martha Finley's Elsie Dinsmore series. At least I did when I was younger, but this summer I discovered two wonderful books, Charlotte Bronte's *Jane Eyre* and Leo Tolstoy's *Anna Karenina.*"

"Mercy," Aunt Mildred said, raising an eyebrow. "Those are rather…adult stories for someone your age."

Katherine entered with her tray and began to clear dishes.

"You've outdone yourself once more," Mildred said to her. "I don't know how you keep the pork so moist, and the lemon chiffon cake melted in my mouth."

"Thank ye, Mrs. Bolton. I'm glad ye enjoyed the dinner."

"Why don't you bring us coffee in the parlor, Katherine?" I suggested. "And I think we should light a few lamps. Those dark clouds mean rain is coming soon." As if on cue, a streak of lightning illuminated the room, followed by a deafening clap of thunder. By the time we walked to the parlor, a cascade of rain battered the roof and streamed down the windows.

We settled in the parlor. Rose sat down at the piano, pounding out Cole's favorite, "Yankee Doodle," as we sang along. Cole loved to march around the room acting out the lyrics, pretending to ride a pony and stick a feather in his cap.

Sporadic bolts of lightning and ear-splitting thunder made his antics all the more dramatic, giving us a good laugh.

Upon request Rose played everyone's favorites, "My Sweet Irish Rose," "A Bird in a Gilded Cage," and "When You Were Sweet Sixteen." Eva sat at her side singing in her fine soprano voice.

Cole sidled up to Mildred and leaned against her knees as a big yawn engulfed him. Mildred whispered in his ear. He nodded enthusiastically and disappeared upstairs.

Eva and Rose moved on to a new piece I hadn't heard before, "Eyes of Blue, Eyes of Brown." Another crack of lightning brought Buttercup streaking across the parlor and jumping into Sara Jane's lap as the music ended.

Cole reappeared with a book in one hand and a magazine of some sort in the other, which he dumped into Mildred's lap.

"What have we here?" Mildred asked, picking up the magazine and glancing down the page.

"Will you read it to me, Aunt Mildred?" Cole asked, peering over the edge of the page and pointing. "Don't these letters spell Clayton, the way you showed me?"

Sara Jane leaped up, unceremoniously tossing Buttercup onto the floor. Her face took on a deathly pallor. She strode across the room, reaching for the magazine. "You won't be interested in this, Aunt Mildred."

But Mildred pulled it away, holding the pages up in the air. Her eyes narrowed to slits, and her breathing grew short. "You think I'm blind? That I can't see what this is?"

Sara Jane turned to me, stricken with horror. A knot gripped my middle. I was unsure what Mildred held, but it threatened something disastrous.

Mildred's voice acquired an unnaturally hollow tone, like someone in a tunnel, as her words echoed off the walls. "You've made the press, Eva. Let me read it to you. 'On Saturday I encountered a cozy group...'" and she read through to the end.

Polly Pry! Rose had most likely brought the magazine to the house with her usual enthusiasm, thinking we would find it exciting. Eva's hand flew to her mouth as she glanced at me with panicked eyes. While most unfortunate, possibly it was for the best that the truth was finally out in the open.

"How could you deceive me this way?" Mildred sputtered, her chest heaving. "It's unthinkable. My own sisters."

Cole turned to me with doleful eyes, unsure what he had wrought by delivering the magazine.

I rose from the settee and escorted him from the room. "Find Katherine and go up to bed." Two big tears rolled down his cheeks. "It's not your fault, darling. This is a grown-up problem. We will resolve it. Now give me a hug, and you're off." I leaned down and kissed his cheek, as he clung to my neck and sobbed. He scurried off to the kitchen.

The thunder and lightning had moved on as quickly as it had arrived, leaving only the steady patter of raindrops. I returned to the parlor and put a hand on Sara Jane's shoulder. "Take an umbrella and walk Rose home."

Rose stood up, staring at the carpet with a guilty expression. "Thank you for the dinner, Dr. Clayton. Goodnight Mrs. Bolton, Miss Delacroix." She and Sara Jane hurried out the front door.

Eva sat frozen on the piano bench, mute and shaking. I perched on the settee again and drew a deep breath. "First, Mildred, I'm dreadfully sorry that you found out this way. We

210

had planned to tell you tonight." I waved an arm through the air. "We only…"

"It's my fault," Eva blurted out. "I wanted Lida to meet Mr. Dearman and form an opinion before we talked with you about him again. I was wrong, terribly wrong."

Mildred stared at us. "I cannot begin to express my anger and disappointment. My own sisters conspiring behind my back. The egregious duplicity of it." Her pinched expression spoke of pain rather than anger. Then a new emotion flitted across her face, a wave of alarm and distress. "Now I understand Mrs. Meredith was part of your elaborate scheme, inviting me to her house on the pretense of enjoying my company." Her voice trembled and tears welled in her eyes. "You've humiliated me."

Her words and tears felt like knives plunging into my heart. How could we have been so callous and insensitive to wound our sister this way? I should have known our ruse would be discovered and end with overwhelming remorse.

Eva rushed over and put her arms about Mildred's shoulder. "Dear sister, please forgive me. I was wrong. But you don't understand how much I love Mr. Dearman."

Mildred pushed her away, rising to her feet. "I am going upstairs to pack, and you shall do the same. We are leaving for home on the train tomorrow morning."

Eva stumbled back, her eyes wide. After a moment she spoke in a soft but firm voice. "No. I'm remaining here. I am a grown woman and shall make my own decisions." With that she tore from the room, her footsteps disappearing up the stairs.

Mildred closed her eyes and swayed slightly, as if she might collapse. I rushed over and took her arm, but she shook me off.

"It's all your fault, encouraging her to pursue this…this ruinous match," she stammered.

The situation felt hopeless. Perhaps it would be better for Mildred to leave, for Eva to move forward with her own life. And yet, was there not some way to mend the divide and salvage our family? Each day of my sisters' visit, Mildred had visibly relaxed, becoming more comfortable with the children and me. Her unexpected kindness with Cole touched my heart. The ability to repair our long estrangement seemed within grasp.

"I beg of you to think this through. If you leave now, Eva could be alienated from her family the rest of her life. I know you don't want that. She tells me you only met Mr. Dearman once and didn't have a conversation of any consequence with him. You condemn him unfairly for his good looks and charming manners with the absurd assumption that he'll be like our father. Please, consider staying and taking the opportunity to get to know him. You'll soon find you have misjudged the man."

Her face twitched with emotions I could not read. "It's out of the question." She marched from the room.

Everyone but Cole remained sleepless most of the night. It took me an hour to calm Sara Jane when she returned from walking Rose home. We spoke in hushed tones as I explained what had transpired. In her young, excitable way, she apologized profusely amid a flood of tears, as if the entire misunderstanding had somehow been of her making. I assured her Eva and I were to blame for keeping Mildred in the dark.

"Sometimes life simply unfolds as fate would have it, mistakes and all," I said. "We have to take responsibility and do our best to make it right." Yet I couldn't envisage how to alleviate the pain and distress we had inflicted on Mildred. Or how to convince her to stay.

I tossed and turned in my bed, haunted by the sounds of Mildred packing in the room next door, the squeak of her armoire door, and the scrape of dresser drawers opening and closing. Across the hall Eva paced in her room, periodically collapsing into tears. Footsteps pattered down the hall to the water closet and bathroom, followed by the rush of running water. At one point I heard Sarah Jane rap on Eva's door and the two of them whisper back and forth. Poor Buttercup was locked out of the comfort of her home, huddled on the back porch emitting plaintive cries that drifted through the open windows, mirroring the pain of those within.

Dread and guilt churned in my middle, resurrecting memories of William's and my disastrous trip to Lawrence eleven years before. It had been an ill-fated undertaking long before we boarded the train and settled with Peter and Sara Jane for the long journey. I had been a fool to believe in any other outcome.

Up until that fateful encounter, I corresponded with Mildred, sending updates on the children and careful accounts of our lives in Colorado, omitting the hardships and worries. Mildred responded in her matter-of-fact, formal manner, as if writing to a casual acquaintance. Yet I had still felt connected to her.

When Eva turned fourteen, she began sending me letters every month, recounting events at school and adventures with her friends. With the innocence of a young girl, she set in motion the doomed encounter. She convinced me that Mother would welcome my family in her home. She claimed Mother longed to meet her grandchildren and let past misgivings be forgotten. I should have paid attention to the missing words in her and Mildred's letters. Neither one ever confirmed they had actually spoken to Mother about the trip before writing to encourage me to come.

William and I debated over many days whether to risk going. At first he opposed the idea. "I worry it will cause you more unhappiness," he said, putting his arms around me and holding me tight. "Or maybe you and the children should visit without me? That might ease the tension. But I'll do whatever you want."

The thought of traveling alone with two small children to face Mother overwhelmed me. I wanted my family to know the wonderful man I had married and accept him into their fold. This was the whole point of the trip for me. While I remained skeptical, it was worth a fair chance to recover my family.

We arrived in Lawrence early Friday afternoon on July 3, 1890. William would return to Denver the following Friday, as he couldn't be away from work any longer, but the children and I would stay an additional week. Mildred and Eva came to fetch us from the train station. The town remained sleepy and quiet in the smothering heat of midday, exactly as I remembered it. Mildred acted genuinely happy to see me and meet the children. She offered a courteous hello and handshake to William, asking after our journey.

The site of my childhood home evoked a flood of emotions, a deep longing for happier times. The spacious Greek revival house had been fashioned after our home in Tennessee. The ionic columns, wraparound porch, steeple roofline, and dormer windows remained unmarked by time. I thought of all the contented hours I had spent reading in the window seat of my room on lazy summer days. The two elm trees shading the sloping front lawn had grown taller and wider, lending an air of grace. I ached for my father, to hear his soft southern drawl calling me to go with him to the stables or the cackle of his laughter as he teased me. If only I could feel his reassuring embrace once more, all my doubts would disappear.

Mother met us in the hallway with a stoic expression, approaching us like an unpleasant burden to be endured. Her slightly worn dress and the untidy bun at the nape of her neck startled me. Her middle had grown thick and her face puffy, nothing like the pretty woman with flashing dark eyes I remembered. She always had been vain and meticulous about her appearance, retaining her slender figure and dressing in the latest fashions. Now gray strands dominated her auburn hair, and deep crevices marked the skin around her eyes and mouth. She gave the impression of someone defeated by life, resigned to her decline. It tugged at my heart, and I wanted to forgive her for my exile.

I tried to give her a hug, but she managed to elude me by looking down and patting Peter's head. William, his brow and upper lip damp with sweat, awkwardly offered a hand to shake as I introduced him and the children. She pretended not to see it. Gazing at Sara Jane and Peter without a modicum of warmth, she called for her maid, Serena.

215

Serena, wearing a plain black cotton dress and white apron tied around her abundant middle, emerged from the kitchen with a fearful, apologetic expression. Her eyes darted warily between Mother and me, but she shined a warm smile on the children.

Mother leaned down to Sara Jane and Peter. "I'll thank you not to run or make loud noises in the house. Serena will be watching you. Under no circumstances are you to enter the parlors or touch anything without an adult present."

"Come, I'll take you upstairs," Eva said, grabbing my hand. "You and William will be in your old room. There are lots of changes since you left. We had a bathroom installed upstairs last year." And so the stay began.

Mildred and Eva had planned a full slate of activities around the Fourth of July holiday. That first evening, Mildred and Franklin hosted the entire clan of cousins, aunts, and uncles for dinner at their home. A pack of six children of varying ages belonging to my cousins, Lois and Charlotte, soon had Sara Jane and Peter running from house to yard and back, shouting and giggling with wild abandon. William fell into convivial conversation with Franklin and the other men, discussing business and politics. I felt disoriented suddenly back in Lawrence, chatting and laughing with family members I had not seen since leaving for my second year of college, as if I had never left. Everyone was welcoming and kind, never mentioning the intervening years. They remarked on the sweetness of my children and how well and happy I looked. Throughout the evening Mother sat on a straight-backed chair in the parlor scowling, eschewing the company of everyone but Auntie Effie.

Saturday began with the Fourth of July parade in downtown Lawrence, followed by an ice cream social and picnic on the banks of the Kansas River. Right after dusk, the annual display of fireworks showered the sky with an effusion of brilliant colors. Dear William could not have been more solicitous toward Mother, but she ignored him, impervious to his attempts to win her over. It sorely disappointed me, but I decided the best way to keep peace was simply to avoid her.

On Sunday afternoon, the folly of our visit reached a boil. Mildred and Franklin came for supper, arriving at half past one. The adults gathered in the family parlor, with its faded furniture and spinet piano. We did not warrant being entertained in the formal parlor.

Mildred and Franklin sat at either end of the settee as if not wanting to intrude on each other's territory. Even then the distance between them caught my attention. In his midthirties, Franklin had grown portly. His strawberry-blond hair had thinned considerably on top, and he attempted to conceal it by combing a few strands of hair from one side to the other. Always taciturn, he struck me as having resigned himself to a life of predictability and boredom, doing Mildred's bidding.

We struggled through halting exchanges about the heat and humidity shrouding the day. Mildred repeated some news she'd heard in church that morning about a neighbor's son leaving for Harvard University in the fall. My mind drew a blank when I tried to think of something to say to engage Mother.

William turned to business matters in desperation, commenting on Congress's passage the week before of the Sherman Anti-Trust Act. "We shall see if it's successful in breaking up the big monopolies."

Franklin nodded. "One can only hope. It's remarkable that Congress had the fortitude to pass the bill almost unanimously when they're all on the dole from these same entities."

Eva rolled her eyes at me as if she would rather be with Sara Jane and Peter, who were in the backyard playing under the watchful eyes of Serena. The room grew quiet again. We sipped tall tumblers of cold lemonade, drops of moisture dripping down their sides. The smell of roasting beef drifted from the kitchen.

"Do you hunt in the Rocky Mountains?" Franklin asked, tugging at his shirt collar and tie, which seemed at least a size too small.

"The occasional deer," William answered. "I'm not much of a hunter, but my employer enjoys the sport and invites me along." He gave a soft chuckle. "I find it hard to say no."

"Do you enjoy killing?" Mother asked in an icy voice. These were her first words since we had sat down. "After all, you come from a family that manufactures arms for that purpose."

William's face remained passive. "I prefer to be home with my family, as I'm away a great deal for work."

I glared at Mother, contemplating a retort to her snide insinuation. But Sara Jane and Peter burst into the room, breathless and pink-faced. Peter's white shirt had mud down the front, and his blond curls hung over his forehead damp with sweat. He was still wobbly on his thin little legs. He approached Mother's chair and stumbled, knocking her arm. Lemonade sloshed over the lip of her glass and down her skirt.

"Look what you've done, you thoughtless boy," Mother cried, blotting the liquid with her handkerchief.

218

Mother turned to me. "Can't you control these children, Lida?"

"He didn't mean to," Sara Jane spoke up. "He's only two."

Mother glared at her. "Such impertinence."

"Why are you so mean?" Sara Jane asked with consternation.

"Sara Jane, that's enough," William said. "Take Peter back to the kitchen and ask Serena to bring a towel for your grandmother."

"What kind of parents are you?" Mother sputtered, her face flushed. "That girl is the most spoiled and naughty child I've ever met."

"Calm down, Mother," Mildred said.

Sara Jane took Peter's hand and led him off, turning at the doorway for a parting shot. "I don't like you either. I wish we'd never come here." She stuck her tongue out before pulling Peter down the hall.

Mother flew out of her chair. "I'll teach her a lesson she'll never forget." I recalled the many times she had swatted me across the backside for minor infractions.

William sprang up and stepped in front of her. "Stop right there. That's *my* child. Who do you think you are, saying such terrible things to my wife and daughter?"

Mother tried to skirt around him, but he grabbed her arm and held her back. All the while I sat mute, unable to move as the thin veneer of civility unraveled.

"Let go of my mother," Mildred said. "Franklin, do something."

Mother took a step back, pulling her arm from William's grip. She turned her wrath on me, pointing a finger in my face. "I want you and your family out of my house. I never wanted you here in the first place."

"Oh no," Eva gasped. "Mother, don't do this."

I stood up to meet Mother eye-to-eye. "Gladly. You're still the same intolerant, vindictive person you've always been. How could I have believed you'd be any different?"

"Really, Lida, to speak to your own mother like that," Mildred said. "You should be ashamed. But you were always willful and selfish. Just like Father."

I swallowed hard, feeling even more betrayed that Mildred would defend Mother and not stand up for me. "Of course you'd take her side, Mildred." I wondered what sway Mother had over my older sister to turn her against me.

William and I retrieved the children and packed our bags. Eva walked us out to the street, sobbing and apologizing for Mother as she hugged us goodbye. Franklin drove us in his carriage to the train station, silent the entire way. He shook William's hand and kissed me gently on the cheek. "I'm sorry, Lida," he whispered.

We boarded a train west late that evening.

After some hours of reflection, I understood Mother had directed her anger with me toward my husband and children. Under different circumstances, she undoubtedly would have loved them—at least as much as she was capable of loving anyone. But I had scorned her by aligning myself with Father during my years at home, becoming his closest companion and ally, his pet. I had dared to form my own opinions, denouncing our terrible past in Tennessee and condemning her for supporting slavery, bigotry, and hate. With Father's blessing, I had escaped her clutches and gone off to college to create a life of my own. Marrying a Northerner had only been the final betrayal. She would never forgive my transgressions.

I woke very early after only a few hours of fitful sleep, occupied by dreams where Mildred refused to wait for me as I ran after her, begging her forgiveness. I ventured downstairs in the early light and made coffee as Katherine was not yet about. I sat at the empty dining room table with my cup, overwhelmed by sadness and anxiety. My neck and back muscles felt as tense as a stretched rubber band about to snap.

Mildred descended the stairs a few minutes later, wearing her traveling suit. She placed her small carrying case on the floor in the hallway, then stood in the dining room doorway. The dark circles beneath her eyes and slump of her shoulders cut at my core. How callous I had been to deceive her and dismiss her feelings as unimportant. Her stance on Mr. Dearman might appear unreasonable, but at the heart of it I knew she wanted to protect Eva out of love and perhaps a misguided sense of duty to our mother. Mother had never taught us lessons of compromise or compassion from which Mildred could draw.

I jumped up. "Can I get you some coffee?"

"No thank you. There is a train at one o'clock. Please instruct Katherine to bring my bags down and call a carriage to pick me up. I'll wait at the station."

"Mildred, please reconsider. I'm so sorry. How can I convince you to stay? For Eva's sake and mine." She put up a hand as if to stop me. "Please listen," I continued with the words I had composed during my sleepless night. "It's not only about Mr. Dearman." I took a gulp of air to control the waiver in my voice. "There was a time when we were close...I long to recover what we've lost. You are my sister, and I love you." I could no longer speak as tears flooded my eyes.

I thought I detected a glimmer of uncertainty in my sister's eyes. The kitchen back door banged shut as Katherine arrived and began running water and placing pans on the stove.

"I don't see..." Mildred started, but she stopped as Cole clambered down the stairs and landed next to her.

Cole glanced at the carrying case and then up at her. "Aunt Mildred, where are you going?"

Mildred pressed her lips together for a moment. "I'm afraid I must go back to Lawrence today."

"I don't want you to leave." Cole's face crumpled. "Who will teach me my letters? I'll be better and not cause any trouble. I promise." He threw his arms about her knees, nearly knocking her over. "Don't go," he wailed.

"Now, now, dear boy," Mildred said, patting his head. Her face slackened as tears teetered on the rims of her eyes.

I put a hand on her arm. "If you'd only give us another chance. You can go home any time."

She pulled a handkerchief from her sleeve and dabbed at her cheeks as several teardrops spilled over. "I suppose...I could wait," she said, her voice sounding like a thin reed.

"Yes," Cole shouted, releasing Mildred and skipping around the table. "Will you teach me to write my name today? And later we can go to the park."

Mildred chuckled. "Only if you calm down. Why don't you return my bag to my room for me?" Cole grabbed the carrying case and carted it upstairs, his little legs and arms straining with the effort.

"Thank you." I put my arms around her shoulders, and she leaned into my embrace. "We'll start fresh."

222

"I would like that." She pulled away. "But don't ask for too much regarding Mr. Dearman."

She sniffed and dabbed her nose with her handkerchief. "How will I hold my head up among your friends? They'll all think me a great fool."

"Oh, Mildred, no one knows. And they would only think Eva and I were the fools if they did."

Chapter 21   **MILDRED**

Forgiveness

Saturday July 6, 1901

Dear Diary,

I write with a troubled heart, given the betrayal of my sisters. They deceived me in a way I could not have fathomed, a cruel and heartless act. However, I have forgiven them, as I believe their apologies and regrets are sincere. My first reaction was to flee back to Lawrence, but Lida's teary request for me to stay touched me deeply. So I remain as planned, for in the end, I dearly love Eva and Lida, and of course Sara Jane and little Cole (even Katherine). Lida and I are slowly rebuilding our once-close relationship, like a loving memory reawakened by a gentle word or touch. I cannot allow this trying situation with Mr. Dearman to cause me to lose her again. And I certainly don't want to lose Eva. Their dishonesty deeply wounded me, yet I acknowledge that my uncompromising position on this romance might have prompted them to go to such lengths. Why couldn't they have told me the truth? Am I so fearsome that it felt impossible to do so?

Elaine Russell

My sisters and I are as different in temperament and nature as the changing seasons. Eva is a gentle soul with a tender heart and quiet inner strength. I agree with Lida that her sense of duty to Mother has stolen too many years of her young life. I have selfishly enjoyed her presence back in Lawrence, but I know it is unfair. She must have a life of her own, and I will support her plan to return to college.

Lida was rebellious from a young age, outspoken and stubborn (traits I must confess to as well), but underneath she is as kind and dear as Eva. Her wonderful children reflect this goodness. Observing Lida with her friends and colleagues, I've come to appreciate her ability to listen to others and open her heart to new ideas and opinions. It is a strength from which I can learn.

In removing myself from life in Lawrence these past several weeks, it has become clear I've spent far too many years under the influence of our unhappy, bitter mother. It is a tragic truth that Mother never moved beyond the disappointments of her early life and marriage with Father, and the untenable existence she left behind in Tennessee. I am at fault for tolerating her disgraceful prejudices rather than raising objections. She meted out love to her daughters conditioned upon compliance with her wishes and not on our best interests. At times I have pitied her while, more often than naught, I have harbored great resentment over her bullying. Everyone in the family, except Lida, coddled her rather than incur her wrath. We would have done her a service long ago by standing up for what was right. She remains angry with the world and her lot in life, as petulant and self-absorbed as a spoiled toddler.

Conflicting emotions buffet me about, like a ship at sea tossed on the waves by a fierce storm. For better or worse, I've agreed to give Mr. Dearman a chance to prove himself worthy. I recognize how important this is to Eva. Perhaps I misjudged him. We are to go out to dinner tonight.

What to do about Mother? Should I write her and explain the situation, knowing how it will upset her? Keeping it from her may be worse. I shall no longer hold back in telling the truth and expressing my feelings.

As if the turmoil with my sisters is not enough, I received a letter today from Mother, which has given me quite a turn. She relayed a rumor regarding Franklin, which originated with Aunt Effie's friend, Miss Henrietta Hamilton. It seems Miss Hamilton has a cousin who lives in Eudora. While visiting her last Monday, she saw a man who looked exactly like Franklin go into the house next door. The cousin's neighbor, Mrs. Becker, is an attractive, middle-aged widow who moved there two years ago and makes a living teaching piano. The cousin claims to have seen Franklin (or his double) visit Mrs. Becker on several occasions, and assumed he was a piano student.

Whatever am I to make of this? My first reaction is to laugh. Franklin surely isn't taking piano lessons and would have no reason to be in Eudora on a Monday afternoon. Another possibility, too dreadful to imagine, sends a chill through my heart. Could Franklin be having an illicit assignation? He is not the kind of man to do something so despicable. It is true that our romantic life has faded over the years, for which I blame myself. After the two miscarriages early in our marriage, Dr. Bartley's pronouncement that I would never have children, stole the happiness from our relationship. My longing for a child was so painful that Franklin could not bear to talk to me about it. A wedge formed between us as we both turned to other interests. It is possible that Franklin might seek comfort somewhere else. He is a man, after all, and has needs.

I hardly know what to think or believe. Mother advises me not to jump to conclusions, then negates her words by reminding me of Father's indiscretions—as if I need reminding. But Franklin is nothing like Father. He's never been a ladies' man or anything close to charming. He is a solid, loyal person who works diligently without complaint. There was a time when he made me laugh and feel loved. I have almost lost the memory of those days. Can I forgive him if this proves to be true?

Lida is calling me. Miss Meredith and her mother are here to speak with me. I know they want to apologize for their part in this misguided ruse over Mr. Dearman. Despite the humiliation I feel at being duped, I do not hold a grudge toward them. We shall move on and not mention it again. I find them both very agreeable people and do not wish to cause any further discomfort.

Making Amends

On Sunday, my sisters, Sara Jane, and I rose early to meet Ellis and her mother at the train station for an outing to the Chautauqua camp in Boulder. We boarded the Colorado and Southern Railroad eight twenty train for the hour ride. The small town, some thirty miles west of Denver, was near the base of the Flatiron Mountains.

"What unusual cliffs," Mildred remarked, gazing up at the distinctive range as we stepped onto the station platform. The reddish brown, triangular-shaped rocks had sheer, flat sides.

"They've been dubbed the Chautauqua Slabs since the arrival of the camp," Ellis said.

Eva took in a deep breath. "The air feels cooler already."

"And healthier, since we're free of the haze from Denver's manufacturing plants," Mrs. Meredith added. "You can see why people come for a weekend excursion in the summer."

"Boulder is one of the early mining settlements," Ellis explained, "but it grew steadily after the University of Colorado opened in 1877. Now the Chautauqua development is bringing even more growth."

A group of Texans had partnered with the Boulder city government three years before to build the Texas-Colorado Chautauqua, or Texado, as some called it. The summer retreat for teachers and families stemmed from the popular Chautauqua movement, which had spread across the country. The centers were dedicated to cultural and educational opportunities, as well as recreational experiences in nature. Boulder offered a perfect location.

We walked three blocks from the train station to the town center and strolled along Pearl Street, a broad avenue lined with shops and hotels. I pointed out the new Armory building and the impressive brick Boulder County Court house with its tower and cupola.

"The town seems a bit rough and tumble," Mildred said, lifting her skirt as we crossed the dusty dirt street to the wooden walkway on the other side.

"That's part of the charm," Ellis said, chuckling. "An authentic Western settlement."

Eva gazed in the window of Frank Hiskey's Boot and Shoe Store. "Look at these darling shoes. Too bad it's Sunday and they're closed."

"Thank heavens," Mildred said, urging Eva along.

The window displays of the Golden Rule Store on Pearl and Broadway showcased goods that catered to visitors at the Chautauqua, including hiking and camping equipment, stools, folding tables, musical instruments, books, journals, outdoor clothing, and cooking utensils.

I checked William's watch, pinned at my waist. "We have a little time before lunch. I want to show you the more elegant side of Boulder." Our small contingent wandered several blocks over to Mapleton Hill known for its impressive Victorian and Queen Anne homes. I was surprised by the number of new houses under construction since my last visit a few years back. A gentle breeze kept us refreshed as we climbed up the street's gentle slope. White, cotton-puff clouds skittered across a blue sky like errant children escaping from school.

"I feel invigorated," Eva enthused, slipping an arm through Mildred's. "I'd like to hike to the top of one of those mountains."

Mildred laughed. "Hopefully not today."

"My church youth group—that is my former church group—hiked in the hills here one Saturday last fall," Sara Jane said. "We saw some beautiful birds, a wild turkey, and a giant green snake." She spread her arms out to show the length of the reptile.

Mildred shuddered. "Mercy. I'll view the mountains from a safe distance, thank you."

"Shall we head back to catch the streetcar?" Mrs. Meredith asked.

Emotions had calmed over the past few days, following the events that had nearly sent Mildred back to Lawrence. Eva, Sara Jane, and I fussed over her with extra kindness, trying to assuage her wounded feelings. But it was Cole who had a miraculous influence, bringing smiles to Mildred's lips with his loving embraces. We were moving forward on a new path, the success of which surprised me. We had gone to dinner the night before with Mr. Dearman, Mrs. Grove, Mr. Abbott, and his daughter, Bernadette. It went better than either Eva or I had dared to hope. Although I thought poor Mr. Dearman looked on the verge of collapse by the end of the evening. Surely he loved Eva to go through such an agonizing ordeal. I was grateful for Mr. Abbott's presence, lightening the mood and rescuing Mr. Dearman during awkward gaps in the conversation.

I had sent Ellis a brief note Saturday morning to tell her of the terrible upset the previous evening. She and her mother insisted on coming over to talk with Mildred immediately. I couldn't help but eavesdrop from the kitchen window as they sat with Mildred in the gazebo out back. Overflowing with regret and embarrassment for their part in our scheme, they apologized profusely. Mrs. Meredith took Mildred's hand, a few tears rolling down her cheeks, reassuring Mildred how much she enjoyed her company and the conversations they had shared. Mildred graciously accepted their regrets and suggested they never speak of it again.

Ellis and her mother invited us to join them for the lecture at the Chautauqua on Sunday, and we accepted enthusiastically. The 1901 summer season had just opened on the Fourth of July.

We joined eight other people at the electric streetcar stop in front of the train station, waiting for the tram to the Chautauqua grounds and facilities at the edge of Boulder.

"What a perfect day to visit the Boulder area," Mrs. Meredith said brightly. "I think you'll enjoy the campgrounds, even though they are still rather basic. The facilities are designed to blend into the natural surroundings."

"William and I heard the Kansas City Philharmonic play three years ago during the Chautauqua's opening season," I said, remembering that happy day. "That first summer the only buildings completed were the auditorium and dining hall."

"All the visitors camped outdoors or in tents to start, but each summer more cottages, and other amenities are added," Ellis said. "This year they opened an academic hall for classes and lectures."

Streetcar No. 202 arrived, clanging its bell. I searched my coin purse and handed my sisters and Sara Jane each a nickel for the fare. "Good day, ladies, and a fine one it is," the conductor greeted us with a smile and tip of his cap. We handed him our money and found seats on the wooden benches.

The streetcar rattled down the tracks, rocking gently back and forth. A lovely breeze came through the open windows. The car turned south on Broadway and headed out of the downtown. There were stops at the electric power plant and University Hill, where the brick and stone halls of the University of Boulder sprawled up the hill on our left. Soon we passed through open fields.

It took only fifteen minutes to reach the Chautauqua entrance. A stone gateway fanned out on each side into low, curved walls to welcome visitors. We stood in line at the ticket booth to pay the entry fee of fifty cents. The ticket allowed us to visit all the facilities and activities on the property, including exhibitions and the afternoon lecture.

A path led up a slight incline through a large expanse of grass, known as the Green. Families and groups of young people sat on the lawn enjoying picnic lunches and relaxing in the sun. Children ran back and forth playing tag, throwing rubber balls, and flying kites.

The expansive two-story dining hall stood at the top of the rise. The maître d' seated us on the outdoor porch, which wrapped around the front and left sides of the building overlooking the Green. The Louis Rischar Band, a fifteen-piece ensemble, serenaded patrons with "The Band Played On."

"This is lovely," Mildred said and turned to me. "Lida, you remember my friend Molly Harris. She and Mr. Harris went to the original Chautauqua camp in New York for two weeks last summer. She thoroughly enjoyed the experience." She unfolded her napkin and placed it in her lap, a small sigh slipping out. "I suggested to Mr. Bolton that we might visit, but he didn't think he could take that much time away from the bank. His work is terribly demanding."

Mrs. Meredith took off one of her lace gloves. "Mr. Meredith is greatly occupied with his work at the paper as well. We are lucky to have our women friends to enjoy such times as today. We can always count on one another." She paused. "That reminds me. August first will be the start of a grand three-day jubilee celebrating the twenty-fifth anniversary of Colorado's statehood. I believe you will still be here. There are events planned both in Boulder and Colorado Springs. Boulder is hosting a parade downtown and a distinguished list of dignitaries who will speak at the Chautauqua Auditorium, including Governor Orman, Senators Teller and Patterson, and other officials."

"All fine orators I'm sure," Ellis said with a short laugh, "but you must come to the festivities in Colorado Springs instead. They are holding a Women's Conference to report on women's accomplishments and progress in different professions in Colorado. I'm to speak on women in journalism."

"We must attend," Eva said. "I would love to hear you speak."

Ellis put a hand on Eva's arm. "I've been meaning to ask you. How did you like *My Brilliant Career*? Or have you been too busy to read it?"

234

"I'm almost finished. It's amusing at times but also rather poignant."

"What is the story about?" Sara Jane asked.

Eva pulled her mouth to one side, as if thinking how to best describe the book. "A young Australian woman named Sybylla is sent to live with her grandmother and aunt on their ranch. Her family has fallen on hard times because the father turned to drink. Sybylla meets the handsome, wealthy neighbor, Harold, who falls in love and wants to marry her. But she's unsure of her feelings. She really wants to be a writer and strike out on her own in the world."

"Oh, I'd like to read it," Sara Jane said.

Ellis nodded. "You're more than welcome to pass it along."

"The story gives one a great deal to think about, Sara Jane," Eva said. "I find myself empathetic to Harold, who is rather awkward and guileless. He can't understand why Sybylla would possibly reject him. I'm not sure how it's going to end. I'm rooting for both sides—for her independence but at the same time his ability to convince her to love him."

"The story beautifully captures the dilemma women face in succumbing to the safety and comfort of marriage, a life devoted to a husband, in lieu of following their heart's desire," Ellis said as her voice turned a bit melancholy. "Sybylla's words spoke to me: 'Ah, thou cruel fiend— Ambition! Desire!' Sybylla longs to feel the rolling billows of the ocean beneath her and hear the grandeur of music in a great hall. 'To be swept on by the human stream,'" Ellis quoted.

"A lovely sentiment," Eva agreed. "But isn't it possible to follow your ambition and also have a happy marriage?"

Ellis shrugged. "I'm not the best person to answer. Lida was fortunate with William. He supported her interest in women's rights and tackling medical school."

"I was lucky. But, lest you think William a saint, he did issue complaints on occasion when life became too overwhelming. He was human, after all."

"If you find the right man, I feel sure it can work," Ellis said. "But you must make it clear what you expect *before* you marry. I still hold out hope I'll meet my perfect match one day."

"I have no doubt someone as worthy as you will encounter the proper mate," Mildred offered Ellis with a great deal of tenderness. "A woman must be very sure of a man's character and beliefs before ever considering marriage," she added. "People aren't always what they appear."

"Indeed," Mrs. Meredith said. Then, as if to change the subject, she glanced at her menu. "What shall we order? The roast lamb sounds nice."

After considering the luncheon choices, everyone ordered the meal of the day. We savored fried trout from nearby streams, roasted quail with fresh carrots as a second course, and a rich devil's food cake for dessert.

Sara Jane ate heartily. As she speared her last bite of cake, she murmured, "This is so delicious."

"Imagine, the whole meal for thirty-five cents," Mildred marveled. "How can they manage such a fine luncheon for these large crowds?"

"Katherine would be hard-pressed to match it," I said.

"Oh, Lida, our Katherine outshines everyone," Mildred said indignantly. "This cake is nice, but Katherine's is twice as light."

Once we had paid the bill, Ellis stood. "We have time to see the grounds and some of the exhibitions before the lecture starts."

Beyond the enormous auditorium and dining hall, row upon row of small wooden cottages and canvas tents stretched across the dirt fields. We passed a family lounging in rocking chairs and stools on their cottage porch, while another group sat in a circle playing guitars and a fiddle. A striped canvas tent, looking like it belonged to a circus, was labeled Gymnasium.

"Ah, here is the art exhibition," Ellis said, leading us into a large tent filled with paintings and sculptures by Chautauqua artists.

"It's nice to see how many of the artists are women," Eva said, examining several charcoal drawings of the surrounding mountains. "Some of them are quite good."

"Sara Jane is much better than any of these," Mildred scoffed.

Ellis smiled at Sara Jane. "You're very talented, my dear. I've been wanting to ask if you might be interested in doing some sketches for the paper. It doesn't pay a lot but offers good experience. I can speak to my father. They're always looking for artists to cover local stories."

Sara Jane gasped. "Oh yes. That would be so exciting." She turned to me. "Mama?"

"As long as it doesn't interfere with your schoolwork," I said, "I fully approve."

"You can use the paper as a reference when you apply to art school," Mildred added, puffed up with pride like a prairie chicken doing a mating dance.

A little before two o'clock, we entered the auditorium, which seated several hundred people. It was quickly filling up, so we scooted into a row midway back from the front and settled on the hard pine benches. The hall was basically a giant wooden tent with dirt floors covered in sawdust and open-air sides, which allowed a pleasant breeze to filter through. A five-piece band was tuning up in the front. Heavy curtains darkened the stage, where a white screen had been erected. The afternoon's entertainment featured the silent film *Joan of Arc*, by a French filmmaker. While full-time movie theaters were opening in other cities, Denver's only venue was at Elitch's Gardens, which offered only a few films each summer.

"We saw *Cinderella* by the same filmmaker last summer," Mrs. Meredith said. "It was delightful."

"The way the fairy godmother transformed the rats into footmen and the pumpkin into a golden coach amazed us," Ellis said. She went on to describe the dancing clocks, scolding Cinderella in front of all the royal court for not getting home from the ball before she turned back into a maid and the scene with the evil stepsisters trying on the glass slipper.

Mrs. Meredith became quite animated. "There was a wonderful celebration with dancers and a ballerina at the end as Cinderella and the prince married."

"It was only six minutes long," Ellis said, "but the costumes and colors were remarkable."

The auditorium had filled to standing room only as the lecturer—Mrs. Sherwood, an art teacher at the Chautauqua—stepped up to the podium. "We have a great treasure to share with you today. French filmmaker Monsieur George Méliès has taken the art of filmmaking to a new level with his creativity and innovation. And what better choice of subjects to represent art breaking free of convention than the classic tale of Joan of Arc, a tragic story of courage and faith. At eighteen years of age, young Joan overcomes the constraints of her role as a woman to lead the French army into battle. For her bravery and dedication, she paid the ultimate price, unjustly accused of heresy and burned at the stake. After the film, I will detail how this remarkable film was made. Please enjoy."

The projector hummed to life, and the band played dramatic music to match the action and emotions of the story. Young Joan, in all her religious fervor, hears God's angels order her to guide France in its war against the English. Disobeying her father, she dresses in men's armor and swears her allegiance to the Crown Prince Charles of Valois. She convinces the prince to allow her to lead the French army to the besieged city of Orléans. Her army achieves a momentous victory over the English and their French allies, the Burgundians. After seeing the prince crowned King Charles VII, Joan is captured by Anglo-Burgundian forces. She is tried for witchcraft and heresy and burned at the stake. She becomes a great martyr for God and France. The film only lasted ten minutes, but it was captivating. I found myself filled with admiration for young Joan, then moved to pity and sadness at her unhappy fate.

Mrs. Sherwood stepped before the audience again and spent the next half hour explaining Méliès' editing technics for creating special effects and his method of colorizing the movie by hand-painting each frame of the film. "This artistic form of filmmaking is the promise of the future. I believe we shall see it reach great heights," she finished, receiving an appreciative round of applause.

"I thoroughly enjoyed it," Mildred said as we worked our way outside with the rest of the crowd, "but I am happy to leave that hard bench and stuffy auditorium."

"It did get rather close," Mrs. Meredith agreed.

"Poor Joan of Arc," Sara Jane said. "She was so brave and daring. I understand now why the church made her a saint."

"Did you learn about Joan in school?" Eva asked. "She's always been one of my heroes."

"I read about her in my Catechism booklet on the saints," Sara Jane said. "Was she a real person, Mama?"

I linked my arm through my daughter's. "Definitely. Watching the film made me think of all the struggles women have faced through history, including my own challenges in medical school." I laughed softly. "I think a few of the doctors and male students wanted to try me for heresy and burn me at the stake as well—at least metaphorically."

Mildred smiled at me. "You were extremely brave, Lida. I'm afraid I'd never find the mettle to persevere in the way Joan of Arc, or you, did. But I admire you both."

"The basic message of the story is as true today as ever," Mrs. Meredith said. "Women have fought for their rights from the beginning of time and almost always met with great resistance from men. The male species cannot stand to have their authority challenged."

"We must have faith in our cause," Ellis joined in. "Great changes are coming in your lifetime, Sara Jane. I believe women will achieve equality, the vote, and success beyond anything we can imagine right now."

"Here, here," said Eva. "There is strength in solidarity."

"Mercy. I can see you won't stop at merely getting the vote," Mildred said, chuckling. "Next you'll want to run the country."

"Why yes," I said. "I believe we should."

Chapter 23   **MILDRED**

An Unexpected Change in Circumstances

Sunday, July 7, 1901

Dear Mother,

Eva and I are having a marvelous time. We could not feel any more welcome and continue to be busy with a variety of activities. It may surprise you to hear that I marched in the Fourth of July parade with the Colorado Non-Partisan Equal Suffrage Association. As you might surmise, I have reconsidered my position regarding the vote for women. I now find myself a supporter, despite past doubts on the issue. What a heady feeling it was to step down the street, arm in arm with my sisters, Sara Jane, and the other ladies, adorned in our white dresses and carrying our banners. It filled me with a sense of freedom I've never before experienced. Exhilarating! The people of Denver cheered us on—except for a few drunkards stumbling out of saloons and yelling rude words, which I could never repeat.

Today brought a lovely outing with Miss Meredith and her mother to the Chautauqua camp in Boulder, not far from

Denver. After an excellent lunch at the dining hall, we attended a showing of Joan of Arc, *by filmmaker George Méliès, and heard a fascinating lecture. I never expected the Denver area to offer so many excellent cultural opportunities. More so than Kansas City, I dare say.*

This coming Thursday we have tickets to see a New York production of The Mikado *at the Tabor Opera House. Gilbert and Sullivan shows are always a delight, and the opera house is said to be very elegant. They attract the best theater companies from around the country.*

There has been an unexpected change in circumstances here in Denver. I know of no other way to broach the subject than to tell you straight out. Please try not to get upset, as I have the situation well in hand. Unbeknownst to me or you, Eva has been secretly corresponding with Mr. Dearman ever since you forbade her to see him. He turned up in Denver a week ago with his sister, Mrs. Charlotte Grove. Eva introduced Mr. Dearman to Lida, who is favorably inclined to his cause. When Lida raised the subject with me, I informed her of our objections; however, I found it difficult to clearly explain our reasoning. In regard to concerns for Eva's health, Lida has given her a thorough examination and vows that she is quite fit. She suffers no ill effects from the scarlet fever, which would keep her from marrying. If Lida is correct, this certainly changes my thinking on the subject.

Lida and Eva pleaded with me to become better acquainted with Mr. Dearman before forming a final judgment. After much agonizing, I have decided to comply with their request. Though it may lead me to the same opinion as before, I owe it to Eva to give him a fair hearing. Foolhardy or not, she is desperately in love with him. If I do not honor Eva's wishes, she will never forgive me (or you). And I cannot allow another split in our family. So we shall see.

Saturday night, Lida, Eva, Sara Jane, and I (Cole remained at home) joined Mrs. Grove and Mr. Dearman for dinner at the Royal Restaurant, an elegant establishment. An unanticipated addition to the gathering was Lida's friend, Mr. Abbott, whom I mentioned meeting in my last letter. He came with his daughter, Bernadette, who has just returned from her first year at Pembroke College in Rhode Island. The entire assemblage started the evening as skittish as racehorses waiting in the starting gate, but we soon relaxed and enjoyed some pleasant banter.

Mr. Dearman sat to my right, stiff and formal, making comments on the weather and other nonsense, while Eva nodded encouragement from across the table. I could have been more accommodating, but I let him squirm a bit. As the dinner commenced, he talked on and on about Eva's fine qualities—her wit, intelligence, kindness, and beauty—as if I were not acquainted with her.

Mr. Abbott, obviously more at ease and perhaps not encumbered by the same level of scrutiny, brought a much-needed dose of humor to the table. He and Mr. Dearman struck up a friendship, as they are both staying at the Brown Palace Hotel. While a bit rough around the edges, I find Mr. Abbott's directness and honesty refreshing. The only behavior of concern was his consumption of a large whiskey and a glass of wine with dinner. Despite my feelings on the evils of alcohol, he did not drink to excess, so perhaps can be excused. (I must add that Mr. Dearman did not partake, most likely as he knows my aversion to liquor.) Mr. Abbott appears completely smitten with Lida. I hope she will put aside her grief for William and give him a chance. She would do herself and the children a favor to marry again.

Mr. Abbott's daughter, Bernadette, is a poised and pretty young woman. She and Sara Jane became friendly by the end of the evening.

I had an opportunity to talk privately with Mrs. Grove, Mr. Dearman's older sister. She favorably impressed me as a person of good breeding and manners. She lives in Springfield, Illinois, where Mr. Grove is a bank president like my Franklin. Without overstepping propriety, I flushed out the details of the Dearman family background. They have been part of Boston society ever since settling there before the War of Independence. If we made inquiries through appropriate channels, we could verify this. As might be expected, Mrs. Grove remarked often on her brother's fine qualities, declaring him honorable, steadfast, and loyal. She appears to be very close to him and quite anxious to argue on his behalf. Of course, we know how family members often overlook the faults of their loved ones.

Mrs. Grove, who is expecting a child in three months, departed for Illinois this morning accompanied by her maid. The train ride could not be easy in her condition. She told me Mr. Dearman had fussed about her health and insisted she return home without further delay to avoid any problems. Meanwhile, Mr. Dearman also leaves today for Leadville on business for a mysterious client he cannot reveal. Most irregular. He is to return on Thursday and will accompany us to the opera.

Mr. Abbott and Bernadette are returning to their ranch tomorrow morning but have invited our family and Mr.

Dearman to visit them in the coming week. To my surprise, Lida agreed. She will arrange for a friend, a fellow woman doctor, to fill in for her at work. We leave this Friday and will combine the trip to the ranch with an additional two nights in Manitou Springs to see Pikes Peak. I've been told by Lida's friends this is a highlight of any visit to Colorado. We will return to Denver next Tuesday.

It is my belief this excursion will show Mr. Dearman's true colors one way or the other. When Eva spends an extended period of time with him in different surroundings, she may find he is an unsuitable match. As for Lida, I hope the time with Mr. Abbott in his environs will foster a different outcome.

Eva and I are feeling a bit of trepidation for our trip home next month, given the brazen robbery this past week of the Great Northern train by Butch Cassidy and his wild bunch near Wagner, Montana. Lida says, two years ago, they robbed a Colorado and Southern train in New Mexico. It is shocking that this type of crime continues in this modern age. Why can't the authorities catch these despicable men? We must hope our train does not carry large sums of cash or gold.

I shall write soon to keep you updated on our situation. Feel confident that I am proceeding in the right direction.

As to the gossip regarding Franklin, I refuse to believe it. He is not that sort of man.

> *Your daughter,*
> *Mildred*

Acts of Grace

My aunts surprised me on Tuesday afternoon, arriving at Paris Millinery as I finished at work. Mrs. O'Malley greeted them warmly and then continued with a customer who was trying on hats.

Aunt Eva gave me a big hug. "We are taking you shopping for a new dress for the opera," she announced. "Your much-altered white dress, while still serviceable, simply won't do."

My hand flew to my mouth. "And Mama agreed?"

"Yes. It's our treat; an early birthday gift," Aunt Mildred said, smiling. "We'll find something sensible that you can wear for other occasions as well."

Rose emerged from the back of the shop with a box of ribbons and halted on seeing my aunts. Her eyes went wide, and she turned several shades of red, looking like she wanted to sink into the floor boards. She was mortified about bringing *Polly Pry* to our house the previous Friday, unwittingly creating a near-disastrous situation. The worst part had been witnessing the untimely revelation unfold. I could not convince her none of it was her fault or assuage her guilt any more than I could my own.

"Hello." Rose managed, ducking her head as she placed the box of ribbons on the top of the counter.

"How nice to see you, Rose." Mildred glanced at me and cleared her throat. "We're taking Sara Jane shopping for an evening dress. Perhaps you'd like to come?"

A broad grin broke out across Rose's face. "Oh yes."

Aunt Mildred turned to Mrs. O'Malley. "Can you manage without her for a short while?"

"Of course." Mrs. O'Malley said. "But come right back after, Rose, to unpack the ribbons."

I had been starving and looking forward to lunch at home, but my hunger disappeared as we glided into Daniels and Fisher's Dry Goods and headed to the ladies' formal wear department. Aunt Eva explained what was needed to a young saleswoman who had dark hair arranged in a fashionable pompadour. She looked askance at my basic white cotton blouse and faded blue linen skirt but led us to an array of gowns displayed along the back wall.

Aunt Eva held out a lilac peau de soie with a multitiered skirt and smocked bodice dotted with tiny pearls. "It's a beautiful color, but perhaps the front is too low at your age."

"I should think so," Aunt Mildred said in her most severe tone. "What of this one?" She lifted a hideous thing in taupe with strands of gold running through it from the rack. The collar fell in folds down the front that was sure to obscure any hint of a figure—not that I had much of one to show.

"Perhaps," I murmured. Over Mildred's shoulder I caught Rose making a terrible face and had to look away. "But I think I'd like something with more color."

"That is more appropriate at your age," Aunt Mildred agreed.

Rose and I selected four dresses for me to try on. My aunts took seats in the viewing area, with its ring of mirrors. Rose followed me into the dressing room and helped me strip to my camisole and bloomers.

"I wish I'd known we were coming here," I whispered to Rose. "I would have worn my good bloomers. I've mended these in a half dozen places."

The saleswoman appeared with the first dress, a pale pink confection of taffeta, which Rose had insisted I try. It was sleeveless with thin straps at the shoulders and several rows of ruffles that ran from the left side on a diagonal across the front. She undid the buttons and lifted it over my head and arms. The ruffles felt scratchy and seemed to stick out at least a foot.

I stepped out to show my aunts. "It makes me look like a puff of cotton candy," I said.

"Or as if you were wearing someone's bedroom curtains," Aunt Eva said, laughing. Aunt Mildred simply shook her head and sighed.

Next came a green organza with layers and layers of cream-colored lace covering the elbow-length sleeves and running down the bodice and skirt.

Aunt Mildred grimaced. "That looks like one of my tablecloths." We all giggled.

The next two—a deep pink gown scattered with sprays of rosebuds and a lavender gauze, embroidered with bows and dripping in ribbons—quickly garnered negative votes from the entire group.

"How I wish we had thought of this earlier and had a dress made for you," Aunt Eva said. "You could have designed it yourself."

251

The saleswoman paused a moment. "We got in a new shipment from New York this morning that's being unpacked right now. Let me see if I can find something."

She returned five minutes later with a pale blue dress of chiffon. I loved the modest off-the-shoulder neckline and high draped belt of satin in sapphire blue. The flowing skirt swirled around me in soft folds, rustling like a happy sigh. It fit me perfectly and was too wonderful to even imagine.

"Lovely, just lovely," Aunt Eva said. "We shall have to keep a close eye on the young men at the opera Thursday night."

Aunt Mildred smiled. "I should think this is the one. Very becoming and nothing too fussy."

Rose glanced at me with a touch of envy. "You can wear it next year to the Spring Dance."

"Try not to grow any taller," Aunt Mildred advised.

"I do love it, but I hope it's not too expensive." I looked at the saleswoman, afraid of what she might tell us.

"It's very impolite to ask what a gift costs," Aunt Mildred interrupted. "It's for your birthday, and there is no need to worry about the price. Now go and change while we settle up."

I threw my arms around her and hugged her tight. "Thank you. Oh, thank you." She laughed softly and hugged me back.

I hugged Aunt Eva next. "You couldn't buy me anything I'd love more."

Aunt Eva patted my back. "I must give Mildred credit. It was her idea."

Aunt Mildred waved away the comment. "You're only young once. It's a time to enjoy."

I twirled in front of the mirrors one last time, in awe of my good fortune and the generosity of my aunts. After all, Aunt Mildred certainly had reason to be unhappy with me after my part in misleading her about Mr. Dearman, but here she was treating me to the loveliest dress I might ever own.

As I went to change my clothes, I thought of the catechism lesson several weeks before on acts of grace. Sister Mary Claire had explained that "sanctifying grace" came from being in a constant state of holiness where the soul is cleansed of all sins to share God's life and love. I felt fairly certain I had a long way to go to achieve such a holy state. However, Sister went on to describe "actual grace," which occurred when God gave us strength to act according to his will. By performing acts of grace, our sins would be forgiven and our souls made pure. Perhaps I could manage this if I had a clearer idea what acts of grace might include.

I looked in the dictionary for guidance: *Grace: (1) favor or goodwill, kindness, and love; (2) a manifestation of favor, such as receiving something through someone's good graces; and (3) mercy, pardon, and reprieve.*

Mama had urged me to be kind with Aunt Mildred to soothe away the hurt we had inflicted. I began listening more carefully to what she had to say and asking questions about Lawrence and her childhood with Mama. Rather than an effort, my time with her proved enjoyable. As she reminisced, it seemed a tightly sealed door had cracked open, allowing her softer side to emerge. On our day at the Chautauqua, I had begun to feel close to her for the first time, warmed by her enthusiasm for my artistic talents. Now, here she was performing an act of grace by buying me a beautiful dress when it should have been me doing something for her.

By the time my aunts and I returned home, it was after two. Mama had arrived shortly before us after tending to an emergency at the orphanage. She seemed worn down as we sat at the dining table to eat a late lunch of sliced roast beef and deviled eggs.

"A little boy named Freddie fell on the stairs and broke his arm," she told us. "I wouldn't be surprised if one of the other boys pushed him." She shook her head. "These poor children need someone to love them. They cry out for attention."

I always felt terribly sad hearing about the poor orphans at the home. After Papa died, I had been terrified that something might happen to Mama, leaving Cole and me alone. I wondered what would become of us, and if we could end up in an orphanage. Now, I felt reassured that Aunt Eva and Aunt Mildred would look after us in a situation too awful to contemplate. I would add a prayer each night to Saint Jerome, the patron saint of orphans and abandoned children, that all children should know the love and comfort of a family such as ours.

Aunt Mildred frowned. "Do the children stand any chance of being adopted?"

"Not really," Mama said. "Occasionally a farm family takes one or two of the older ones, with the idea of putting them to work. And of course, some of the children have parents who may retrieve them if they become more financially stable. But most will be there until they reach maturity."

"At least they have somewhere to live and food to eat, and they're getting an education," Aunt Eva offered. "But it does break your heart."

254

"Of course," Mama agreed. "It's better than living on the streets or being sent to work in the coal mines or factories. We can only hope they are resilient and shall survive without loving parents."

Cole looked up. "Mama, when are we going to the library?"

"I forgot, darling. I'm a little tired today."

Cole's face clouded over. "But you promised. I need some new books to read with Aunt Mildred."

"I'll go with you both," Aunt Eva offered.

Mama smiled. "All right. It's only a short tram ride."

"I'll stay at home, if you don't mind," Aunt Mildred said.

The others left, and I asked Aunt Mildred if she wanted to keep me company sitting out back in the gazebo while I sketched. We settled with glasses of lemonade and a plate of Katherine's freshly baked shortbread cookies.

Aunt Mildred opened a letter that Katherine had handed her from the afternoon post. Her brow knitted as she read the single page once, then a second time. She sat quietly, appearing to be deep in thought.

"Is everything all right at home?" I asked.

"Yes. All is well."

Nothing made me happier than losing myself in my art, seeing the world from different perspectives, which often surprised me. My charcoal pencil flew across the paper in broad strokes as I drew the outlines of my subject. It was pleasantly warm, and the scent of roses and lilacs filled the air. A dozen tiny wrens chirped from the branches of the sprawling oak tree until two blue jays chased them away. A pesky bee hovered over me for a moment before buzzing off to gather pollen.

"I can't stop thinking about the orphans," Aunt Mildred said at last. "I know exactly what your mother means about their cries for attention and love. I see it all the time at our children's home in Lawrence." She paused a moment, heaving an enormous sigh. "It is a tragic plight for little ones to have to depend on the charity of others."

I considered whether I should say anything and decided to take a chance. "Mama told me you and Uncle Franklin couldn't have children. Did you ever consider adopting?"

Her eyes widened. "Really, Sara Jane, that is a very personal question."

"I'm sorry, but you're so good with Cole. Any child would be lucky to call you his mother."

Her face softened. "That's kind of you to say, but I'm too old now. And how people in Lawrence would talk if I did such a thing."

"I don't mean a baby. Maybe you could take in children Cole's age or older."

She smoothed the folds in her skirt. "I appreciate your thoughts, and I will think about it."

"Can I ask you something else? Something about the past?"

She lifted one eyebrow. "I suppose you will anyway. You've never learned to hold your tongue."

"What happened when we came to Lawrence years ago? What caused Mama and Grandmother to argue? I've never understood why they no longer speak to each other."

The lines around her eyes and mouth tightened. "What has your mother told you?"

"All she ever says is that she doesn't get on with her family."

"Mercy. I suppose you're old enough to hear the truth. I'll say up front I'm not proud of my part in it."

And she related the story from the beginning, how Grandmother had forbidden Mama to marry Papa because he was a Northerner and came from a family of arms manufacturers, which had supplied the Union Army. But Mama had defied her and married my papa anyway, never to be forgiven by my grandmother. It seemed no one in the family had even met Papa until our unhappy visit.

This news left me speechless for once. How could anyone not love Papa?

"Eva and I invited your family to visit thinking your grandmother would get over her resentment once you arrived. I missed your mother terribly. But your grandmother never really wanted you there and acted horrid the entire time. I was embarrassed by her behavior, but I didn't stand up for your mother. I should have. Your father was a very nice man, Sara Jane. I'm sad I never had a chance to get to know him better. We could all see how in love and happy your parents were together. Then you became embroiled in the discord as well."

I glanced up, alarmed by this revelation. "What did I do?"

"You don't remember the final day, the argument between your parents and your grandmother?" I shook my head. "Well, you were very young." She told me of my sassy retort and sticking out my tongue at Grandmother. And the harsh words exchanged afterward.

Memories flooded over me with unexpected clarity. I relived the burning heat in my cheeks, my indignation with the horrible, mean old lady I was supposed to call Grandmother. I pictured Mama and Papa packing and the silent carriage ride with Uncle Franklin to the train depot. I felt the sting of my tears as I told Mama how sorry I was for ruining everything, and Mama holding me tightly, promising it wasn't my fault.

Aunt Mildred chuckled. "Don't take it too seriously, my dear. You were protecting your baby brother and reacting to the unforgivable behavior of your grandmother."

She shifted in her chair. "My visit here this summer has awakened deep regrets. How could I have let so many years go by without having your mother and her family in my life?"

I looked up hesitantly. "I know you don't want the same thing to happen with Aunt Eva."

She pulled her lips together for a moment. "No...I don't."

"Mr. Dearman seems like a very nice man. It's clear he loves Aunt Eva a great deal."

"Time will tell." She gazed off into the yard for a moment then turned back to me. "And what are you drawing so earnestly over there?"

I turned my sketchpad around so she could see the portrait I had made of her, sitting in the wicker chair with the lilacs behind her. I thought it rather good. "I want to work on it more, but it's for you to take home to Uncle Franklin. It hardly repays you for my beautiful dress, but it's all I can offer." It was my small act of grace.

She clapped her hands together as delight suffused her cheeks. "Such a wonderful likeness, and you make me look halfway young." Her eyes grew dewy. "Thank you, dear child. I will treasure it."

The Inimitable Mrs. Brown

I wanted nothing more on Wednesday than to put up my feet and have a quiet evening at home. The busy social schedule we had kept since my sisters' arrival meant I rarely got enough sleep. I rose at dawn six days a week to face trying workdays, returning home exhausted both physically and emotionally. And I still needed to pack and get organized for our departure on Friday for Mr. Abbott's ranch. But Margaret Brown had invited us to one of her evening soirees, and I couldn't say no.

"The fresh air is reviving me," I said as we walked the five blocks to Margaret's house. I told Eva and Mildred about the gathering. "Mrs. Brown invited the planning committee for the Catholic Fair she is organizing for September. But it will be a party more than a working group. I'm sure you'll enjoy yourselves."

Mildred appeared a bit taken aback. "Will all the others be Catholics?"

"No, no. Mrs. Brown is quite persuasive at enlisting others to work on the part of the poor without regard to religious affiliations. Many guests will be members of the Denver Woman's Club who volunteer for many good causes."

"Is that how you know Mrs. Brown?" Eva asked.

"Yes, but we first met in Leadville when we were young. She was single at the time and worked as a clerk at Daniel and Fisher's. We started visiting one day when I purchased a pair of gloves. Leadville is a small town, so I ran into her often on the street. She was enchanted by Sara Jane, with her blonde curls and blue eyes."

I explained that Margaret had married James Brown, or J. J. Brown, as everyone called him. "They moved to a smaller town, where he worked in the mines. Soon after that, William and I moved to Denver, and I lost touch with her. After Mr. Brown had earned a partnership in the mining company, they struck a deep vein of gold in '93 in an old, abandoned mine. While most mine owners lost everything that year in the collapse of the silver market, Mr. Brown and his partners became very wealthy. The Browns had moved to Denver the next year. Gradually Mr. Brown expanded his interests throughout Colorado and the Southwest.

"Mrs. Brown and I met again at the newly formed Denver Woman's Club. I'm not as close to her as I am with Ellis or Minnie, but I'm quite fond of her."

I told them of the Browns' considerable donations and charitable work, which had earned them a great deal of respect in Denver. "The only people who have shunned the Browns are Mrs. Louisa Hill and her anointed 'sacred thirty-six' families. This narrow-minded group tries to dictate who is worthy of belonging to Denver high society. By Mrs. Hill's standards all non-Protestants and anyone of humble beginnings, tainted by 'new money', should be excluded. She's a ruthless snob and particularly pointed in her rejection of the Browns. But Mrs. Brown simply ignores her and continually expands her own circle of friends."

"The world is full of small minds," Mildred said. "Perhaps I've been one of them at times, but I'm striving to do better."

"I owe Mrs. Brown a debt of gratitude. She wrote a letter of recommendation for me to the medical college four years ago and was instrumental in getting my present employment. She spoke on my behalf to the nuns when I applied for the job.

"She organized the Catholic Fair two years ago," I continued, "which was a huge success. They raised enough funds for an expansion of St. Joseph's hospital. The Dioceses called upon her good nature to do another event. She recruited me for the planning committee since the funds raised this year will go to St. Vincent's Orphanage. I couldn't turn her down."

"Doesn't she realize how busy you are working six days a week?" Mildred asked.

"Yes, but I want to help. Despite her wealth and position, she's kind and thoughtful." I smiled. "She enjoys spending money and wears the latest fashions, but she's never been pretentious or forgotten her modest origins. She came from a poor Irish family in Missouri. The Brown home is surprisingly unassuming compared to some of the mansions in town.

"Ellis will be there," I added. "I don't like to gossip, but she told me Mrs. Brown and her husband are having a difficult time getting along after being apart for six months. I hope this evening won't be awkward."

"Men!" Mildred said angrily. "You can't leave them alone for two minutes if you expect them to remain loyal. They are like little children who need constant attention."

"Perhaps," I murmured, wondering what had brought on this sudden outburst. "It seems they've grown apart over time. He's older than her and not in good health after his years

261

working in the mines. They also have divergent political views. He's never approved of her suffrage work, and while she supports the temperance movement, he's known to enjoy an Irish whiskey or two."

"What a shame," Eva said. "Why can't couples put their differences aside?"

We reached the house and passed by the two enormous lion sculptures flanking the stairs leading to the front porch.

"What an unusual color," Eva remarked of the pink-toned brick and wood of the Queen Anne style house. "But it's quite nice."

"Wait until you see the inside," I whispered. "Mrs. Brown has decorated her rooms with an unusual collection of mementos from her travels. Some of them are rather ornate for my tastes, but they add character."

Mary Mulligan, the housekeeper, greet us and took our wraps.

Margaret rushed over as we entered the parlor. "Dr. Clayton, I'm so pleased you and your sisters could make it." She shook their hands enthusiastically as I introduced Eva and Mildred. "Welcome, welcome" she said.

Of medium height with dark chocolate-colored hair and lively brown eyes, Margaret presented an attractive figure. Her enthusiasm and interest in people were contagious.

Margaret put an arm through Eva's. "I've heard a great deal about you, my dear. Ellis tells me you have a delightful young man in pursuit. I met his sister Mrs. Grove at one of the national suffrage conventions a few years back. What a small world it is." And she swept Eva and Mildred to the far side of the parlor to introduce other guests.

"May I present Mrs. Kate Russell, a wonderful journalist. She's going to read us one of her new poems tonight and plans to donate a collection of works to sell at the fair," Margaret began. "And this is Mrs. Thomas Herbert, who runs a catering business with her husband. They will be providing food for the event." She turned to the older woman sitting next to Mrs. Russell. "And Mrs. Eli Ashley helped get the bill passed creating the State Home for Dependent Children. She has volunteered to help as well."

"It is such an honor to meet you all," Eva said with her usual poise.

Margaret continued, "Mrs. Bolton, I know you'll enjoy meeting Mrs. Antoinette Hawley, President of the Woman's Christian Temperance Union here in Denver. I understand you are active in the organization in Lawrence."

Mildred smiled with pleasure at this acknowledgment and shook Mrs. Hawley's hand. "I look forward to talking with you."

Margaret was a natural hostess, having done her homework on every guest to make them feel welcome and special.

"Of course, you already know Miss Meredith," Margaret concluded as they circled back to two empty chairs.

Mildred glanced at an alabaster figurine on the fireplace mantel. "How beautiful," she said.

"That's Aphrodite," Margaret said. "I picked her up on a trip a few years ago."

"Lida told me you travel a great deal. I am quite envious," Mildred said.

"I am fortunate to have the opportunity to explore this wondrous world of ours. After traveling in Europe, I decided I

263

must learn other languages and know more about art to fully appreciate the things I was seeing. I enrolled this past January at the new Carnegie Institute."

"Lida told us. I find it most admirable," Mildred said. "Our trip to Colorado has instilled in me a desire to travel. Lawrence is a very small world, I'm afraid."

I had never heard Mildred express discontent over her life. She'd been barely twenty-one when she married Franklin, and they'd never ventured far beyond the occasional trip to the Ozarks for a few days.

We settled into our seats as a maid offered us tea or lemonade. Margaret stood before the assembled group. "Now that we are all here, I thought we should get the business out of the way. Then we can enjoy the rest of the evening. First on the agenda is the price of entry to the fair. I believe fifty cents is an appropriate amount. It will bring in considerable funds but won't be out of range for those of lesser means."

A short debate followed as to whether thirty cents might be better. But Margaret held firm in her opinion and, when it was brought to a vote, the fifty cents entry fee passed.

"Next we'll discuss the booths. Mrs. Russell has already lined up twenty local businesses to donate goods at the fair, from children's toys and ladies' accessories to items for home décor." Margaret paused briefly. "I have some very exciting news, but I must give Mrs. Ashley credit for the idea. I have contacted notable women across the country to donate dolls, which they will make themselves. We've had an astonishing response from over thirty women, including the wives of President William McKinley, Vice President Teddy Roosevelt, and William Jennings Bryan. And of course the wives of Mayor Wright here in Denver and our esteemed

Colorado Governor James Orman. We should get a pretty penny for these dolls."

Ellis clapped her hands with delight. "You are a wonder, Mrs. Brown. And bravo, Mrs. Ashley."

The meeting continued for another half hour as Margaret made assignments to committee members to organize setup and cleanup crews, determine the game booths for the children, and gather more donations for prizes. I volunteered to talk to the nuns at St. Vincent's Orphanage to ask if I could lead the children in creating artworks to sell at the fair. I knew Sara Jane would love helping me.

Mrs. Russell read her poem, a lovely rhyme on the innocence of childhood. We soon gave ourselves over to lively conversations while eating strawberry chiffon cake. At ten o'clock we reluctantly headed home when Ellis offered us a ride in her carriage.

"What a perfect evening," Eva said. "Mrs. Brown is a superb hostess."

Ellis laughed. "Margaret Brown is a force to be dealt with wherever she goes. And she is one of the kindest people I know."

"I had a very stimulating talk with Mrs. Hawley," Mildred said. "I was surprised to learn she ran for mayor last year on the prohibition ticket."

"She is a tireless fighter and inspiration to all of us," I commented. "And a wonderful public speaker. I don't know where she finds the time to write magazine articles in addition to her other activities. Did you know, she wrote the famous tune 'Crusade Glory Song' for the temperance movement."

"Goodness, I had no idea," Mildred said. "These ladies put me to shame, but they've opened my eyes on many subjects,

265

Lida. I will go back to Lawrence a different and better person."

"You do many good works," Eva assured her. "And you have many years left to do more. I know I plan to make the best use of my days ahead to help others."

Ellis sighed. "If only we could convince more men to open their hearts to such sentiments."

Chapter 26   **MILDRED**

Orders from Home

Thursday, July 11, 1901

Dear Diary

Letters are flitting like humming birds across the rails from Lawrence to Denver and back again. As expected, Mother is absolutely livid that I've agreed to acquaint myself with Mr. Dearman. I thought it better to allow her time to accept the possibility that I might approve of him, but I may have misjudged the depth of her need for control. An angry letter arrived today, ranting about my ill-conceived ideas and implying I had betrayed her. Her words tear across the page full of fury, calling Mr. Dearman a charlatan and snake charmer. She claims my decision to meet with him is the utmost folly. Of course she is quick to blame Lida for compromising my good judgment. She cannot fathom that I might follow my conscience and form an independent opinion contrary to hers.

She asks if I've lost all reason and orders me to bring Eva home at once. I can only respond that the time has passed for obeying her directives. Our young filly Eva has tasted

Elaine Russell

freedom, riding down an open road to the future of her choosing. She cannot be returned to the barn so easily. My heart is at ease letting fate take its course. All the letters in the world from Mother will not change my decisions or Eva's.

I also received letters today from Franklin and Aunt Effie as Mother bullied them into writing on her behalf, urging me to bring Eva home. Imagine the nerve! Franklin mostly complained about how inconvenient it is for him with me not at home to run the household.

Franklin and Mother can stew in their own juices. I'll deal with them when I am good and ready to come home and not before. I am weary of this discord. I want only to enjoy my time here, and so I shall.

I am not sharing Mother's vitriol and bellowing with the others. The best course of action for now is to ignore her until after we return from our short holiday.

At Mother's Bidding

Tuesday, July 9, 1901

Dear Mildred,

Whatever is going on? I have not heard from you since you first arrived in Denver. Your mother is in a terrible state and carrying on. She telephoned me twice at work today, refusing to wait until I got home. Naturally, this is a great inconvenience when I'm at the bank, a completely inappropriate place for personal matters.

I understand the trouble has to do with Mr. Dearman who is pursuing Eva. I really am not interested in the details or getting involved in the debacle. He seemed a nice enough fellow to me. But you must bring Eva home right away so I may have some peace.

Jessie left for Wichita yesterday to care for her mother, who has taken ill. I couldn't deny her the time off given the situation. I am forced to take my dinners at Miller's Café.

Elaine Russell

Biscuit is hardly eating, while I spend time trying to coax her along—a terrible bother. For heaven's sake come home and relieve me of these burdens.

Franklin

Tuesday, July 9, 1901

Dearest Niece,

I imagine you continue to enjoy the lovely summer weather in Colorado, a refreshing change from Lawrence. We've been through quite a hot, muggy spell of late.

Do say hello to Lida and tell her I have missed her terribly. She was always a dear girl. The unpleasantness on her last visit was most unfortunate and hardly her fault. Let her know I would love to see her again.

Your mother asked me to write, or I would never have gotten involved in such a private affair. I'm afraid she is worried sick, quite literally. You know how worked up she gets. She did not tell me the nature of the problem at first, but this being Lawrence, I already knew the dashing Mr. Dearman has come to Denver. I only met him once, but he cut a fine figure, and I found him delightful. Eva's friend Sylvia told her sister about his visit, and her sister in turn told their cousin. The news eventually came to me through Mable Warner at the church planning committee luncheon on Monday. Really, I don't understand your mother's objections. Our sweet young Eva deserves a chance for happiness and a life of her own. She does not belong at home under your mother's thumb. There, I've said it! Being your mother's

270

sister, I have a right to express my opinion. But not a word of it to her, of course.

I am tasked with pleading for you to bring Eva home at once. So consider this my plea. In truth, I hope you stay and let Eva determine her own mind. She is a sensible girl who will make the right decision.

My love to all you girls and Lida's beautiful children. I've always thought of you girls as my children, too, ever since you lived with your uncle and me in those early years. You brought us a great deal of joy.

Love,
Aunt Effie

A Night at the Opera

Eva stepped back from her spot peeking through the parlor room curtains. For the last ten minutes, she had alternated between watching for Mr. Dearman and primping in the entry hall mirror. She turned to Mildred. "I saw you received several letters from home. Is anything amiss?"

Mildred waved a hand. "No, no. Just the usual news."

Eva pulled the curtains back once more. "Oh, here he is, at last."

"Five minutes early," Mildred said, glancing at the clock over the mantel. It was difficult to tell from her tone if this fact weighed in Mr. Dearman's favor or against him. I felt sure she was keeping a tally sheet somewhere, judging his every action. She had taken unusual care in arranging her hair in a loose bun on top of her head with a few tendrils falling down the sides, softening her face. She wore a simple gown of dark rose crepe de chine, which cast a pleasant tinge of color on her cheeks. The dress's low waist and blousy bodice allowed the skirt to drape over her full figure in a way that flattered. Teardrop rubies hung from her ears and around her neck. When she smiled at Sara Jane, I caught a trace of the vivacious young woman I had known in our youth.

We were ready to leave for the opera house. Sara Jane gave an excited shrug, seeming as nervous as Eva. I hardly recognized my beautiful daughter floating around the room in a diaphanous gown, a vision in blue. Eva had helped arrange her hair in a pompadour and added two blue plumes at becoming angles. A moment of melancholy overtook me as I thought how soon my girl would be grown and embarking on a life of her own.

Katherine answered the doorbell and led our guest into the parlor. "Mr. Dearman is here," she announced in her most dignified voice. She gave Sara Jane and me a wink as she left.

"Good evening." Mr. Dearman bowed slightly and glanced around the room. "I am a lucky man to escort four such lovely ladies tonight." His eyes fell on Eva, and a smile lit his face as he took in her gown of dark green silk, which set off her slender figure. I could not help but admire how striking he looked in perfectly tailored pants and tails, which he wore with the familiarity and confidence of a privileged upbringing.

"Dr. Clayton, what a pleasure to be in your lovely home," he said.

Cole skittered down the stairs and into the parlor. On seeing Mr. Dearman, he stopped short. He had on his pajamas, and his wet hair was slicked back after his evening bath.

"You must be Master Clayton," Mr. Dearman said, holding out his hand to shake Cole's.

Cole blinked several times and gingerly offered his hand. "No. I'm Cole Clayton."

We all laughed until Cole became cross at being made light of. Mildred pulled him to her and explained, "Master is a title for boys, like Sara Jane is called Miss Clayton."

"Is it for big boys?" Cole asked, warming to the idea.

"Absolutely," Mr. Dearman assured him. "And most appropriate, since you are the man of the house."

Cole lit up. "Thank you, sir...Mr. Dearman." He took a deep breath. "Are you going to marry Aunt Eva?"

"Mercy," Mildred muttered. "You don't ask such things."

A rush of crimson overtook Mr. Dearman's neck and face, matching the fire in Eva's cheeks. "It's quite all right, Cole. I do hope to marry your aunt if she will have me and...if it is acceptable to others."

"We really must be going if we are to make the opera," I said. "Cole, give me a hug goodnight and go find Katherine."

We gathered our evening bags, gloves, and wraps and headed outside. Mr. Dearman took special care helping Mildred into the waiting carriage and sat next to her across from the rest of us. Katherine and Cole stood on the front porch waving goodbye.

Throngs of patrons crowded into the rotunda of the Tabor Grand Opera House, with its enormous stained-glass roof, which led into the lobby. A cacophony of voices and waves of laughter echoed off the marble floors and walls as people milled about, greeting friends and hoping to be seen by anyone who mattered. The scent of perfume and stale cigar smoke hung in the warm air around the press of bodies. Society women glided past in elegant gowns as the gas lights sparkled off their diamonds. I felt nearly as elegant wearing my gold locket with a picture of William inside and the pearl earrings he had given me the Christmas before he passed.

"Remarkable," Mildred murmured as we entered the lobby. She strained her neck back to view the immense, glittering chandelier and opulent frescoes of flowers and cherubs in rich hues of rose, amber, and deep green.

I glanced at our reflections in the two huge mirrors hanging on the back wall as we moved through the crowd with expressions of delight and anticipation. How happy it made me to see us together, a family once more. I nodded to several acquaintances as we climbed the mahogany stairs covered in thick, crimson carpet and found our way to the first balcony. Our seats were split between two rows, given the last-minute purchase of an additional ticket for Mr. Dearman. Sara Jane insisted on sitting next to Mildred in the first row while Mr. Dearman, Eva, and I sat behind them.

"Oh, Lida, this is the grandest theater I've ever seen. It's so exciting," Eva said as she took in the twinkling crystal chandelier, the domed ceiling painted with puffy clouds floating in a blue sky, and three tiers of elaborately carved boxes, which framed the stage on both sides.

The orchestra tuned their instruments in the pit as people continued to take their seats. I searched the crowd for familiar faces. Mr. and Mrs. Brown occupied the middle box on the left side. They both loved the theater and attended most shows when in town. Margaret spotted us and waved.

Sara Jane spun around in her seat, her eyes wide. "Mama," she whispered, inclining her head toward me, "Mattie Silks is in the top box." Then she glanced at Mr. Dearman with a curious expression.

"The nerve," Mildred sputtered. "Disgraceful."

Mrs. Silks, dressed in a tasteful cream-colored gown, perched regally on her seat, as if challenging the people of Denver to deny her presence. She scanned the auditorium with an enigmatic smile. Undoubtedly she recognized any number

276

of men who frequented her houses of ill repute. But she was too savvy and discreet to give them away. Her companion was a handsome—though rough looking—man with longish dark hair, which he had greased back. He slouched in his seat with drooping eyes, appearing bored and unhappy. The glass of champagne in his hand tipped precariously.

I found it particularly amusing that Mr. and Mrs. Crawford Hill, the self-proclaimed leaders of Denver high society, occupied the box directly below Mattie Silks and her escort.

Mrs. Silks gazed in our direction with what appeared to be a slight nod of recognition. Could it be she remembered Sara Jane from her recent visit to the hat shop? A shiver ran down my back.

The lights flashed, and the last patrons scurried to their seats. The production of *The Mikado* proved all I had hoped for with wonderful singers and beautiful costumes and sets. It warmed my heart to watch Sara Jane and Mildred, laughing and moving their heads to the tempo of the songs.

At the intermission, Mr. Dearman raced off to purchase refreshments. We worked our way through the crowd to the upstairs lobby, while Mildred and Sara Jane softly hummed "Three Little Maids" together.

Margaret Brown appeared beside us. "Ladies, how nice to see you again. I hope you're enjoying our opera house and the production," she said.

"I'm very impressed," Mildred said.

A devious smile appeared on Margaret's lips as she glanced at me. "I wonder if Mrs. Crawford has any idea who is seated above her. Not the companions she would normally choose."

"It's beyond brazen of that woman to show up and take a box, no less," Mildred huffed.

"Denver is famous for its unique characters and irregular behavior, I'm afraid," Margaret said. "That despicable man with her is the worst. Mr. Brown has heard a tale or two about him, I promise you."

"He's not Mr. Silks?" Sara Jane asked.

"No, dear, he's simply a companion. No one knows what happened to Mr. Silks," Margaret said. "Or if he ever existed."

Mr. Dearman arrived, balancing a tray with three flutes of champagne and two ginger ales, followed by Mr. Brown with his bourbon and a soda water for Margaret. I made the introductions, explaining Mr. Dearman was visiting from Boston.

"How nice to meet you both," Mr. Dearman said as Eva and I took glasses of champagne from him. He looked at Mildred. "Mrs. Bolton, do you care for champagne on this special occasion?"

"Well, maybe just this once," Mildred murmured and took a flute, leaving Mr. Dearman with ginger ale.

Margaret held up her glass in a toast. "To Denver, where even our most unusual citizens attend the opera."

Mr. Brown turned to Mr. Dearman. "An old friend I worked with in Leadville lives in Boston now. I know it's a big city, but perhaps you've met him? Mr. Gerald McDonald."

Mr. Dearman's eyes went wide. "Why…yes. I have made his acquaintance."

"I believe he still owns a mine or two in Colorado. The last time I saw him, he was leaving for California. But I heard recently that he ended up in Boston," Mr. Brown said. "We had some good times together in our youth. I wager he's a great deal more sedate these days. As am I." He winked at Margaret. "Please give him my best regards if you run into him again."

Mr. Dearman nodded. He looked relieved when the bell rang to announce the end of the intermission.

Once more I wondered at the connections among us. It was indeed a very small world.

Two Rocks Ranch

Despite our late night at the opera, we rose early on Friday to finish last-minute packing and eat a hurried breakfast before catching our train. Katherine lamented that she wouldn't know what to do with herself while we were gone. Cole bounced from room to room asking countless questions, getting in everyone's way, and generally hampering progress, until Mama banished him to the kitchen with Katherine. At nine o'clock, we crowded into a carriage bound for the train station with our valises hanging off the back and piled under our feet. We boarded the Rio Grande nine thirty train headed south to Colorado Springs and beyond.

Once settled on the train, I tried to sketch Aunt Eva and Mr. Dearman, who sat on the seat opposite me. It was an exercise in frustration. The railcar continually bounced and swayed, sending my pencil veering out of control. With their heads bent together, they whispered back and forth, cocooned in a world of their own. She tilted her head to one side, wearing an expression of disbelief at something he said, and laughed softly. I longed to capture the joyful glow that seemed almost visible in the space around them, rather like the radiant halos encircling the saints in the paintings at St.

Mary's Cathedral. The longer I watched them together, the more confident I was of their love and Mr. Dearman's good intentions. I refused to believe he had a nefarious link to Mrs. Silks.

Aunt Mildred's decision to remain with us in Colorado and spend time with Mr. Dearman had been a huge relief to all. But the intrusion of Mr. Abbott into our lives marred this happy outcome. At least for me. I had begun to pray to Saint Paula, the patron saint of widows, to ask that Mama be content living alone as Saint Paula had been, devoting the rest of her life to study and good works.

What was Mama thinking? Mr. Abbott was far too old for her and not a thing like Papa. I was stunned when she had asked him to join our dinner with Mr. Dearman and Mrs. Grove. I became even more distraught when she accepted the invitation to visit his ranch. She hadn't even consulted me. His daughter, Bernadette, had prattled on about how much fun we would have riding horses together. Small consolation.

The day after the dinner, I confronted Mama. "Why are we going to Mr. Abbott's ranch? I've never even heard you speak of the man before this last week. And now it appears you're considering marrying him."

She blushed and waved a hand to dismiss the notion. "Darling, don't be silly. I simply thought it would be a good opportunity for Mildred to spend time with Mr. Dearman. Mr. Abbott's ranch offers a neutral setting with other people around to lighten the mood." She giggled. "Mildred won't go easy on poor Mr. Dearman, you know. We'll have to rescue him."

"We hardly know these people."

"Your aunts will get a taste of rural Colorado, and the ranch is on the way to Pikes Peak. Since we were going there, anyway..." Her voice trailed off as she took my hand. "Mr. Abbott is a kind man. And you seemed to get along well with Bernadette."

"I don't need a new father or sister."

Mama sighed, reaching up to brush a stray strand of hair from my face. "Of course not, but new friends are nice. Give them a chance."

Aunt Mildred had sensed my wariness over the trip. On Thursday, she had presented me with an expensive sketchbook and a dozen charcoal pencils. "You have a great talent, young lady. I thought you could use these on our journey." She put an arm around my shoulders in a quick, awkward embrace. "I wager we'll have a good time with the Abbotts. Don't fret."

That same day, Aunt Eva had given Cole and me Brownie cameras, the amazing new inventions that allowed anyone to take photographs. The small, rectangular boxes made with cardboard covered in leatherette cost only one dollar. All we had to do was point the camera and push a lever. A wooden roller inside held the film and turned it to each new exposure. Then we would mail the film to the Kodak Company for development, and soon six two-and-a-quarter-inch-square pictures would be returned. Cole believed it must be magic. Aunt Eva had to hold on to his camera for safekeeping, so he didn't snap all six frames immediately. She had suggested I take photographs of landscapes and things that interested me so I could draw them later. And, if need be, we could always buy another camera.

283

Now Mama and Aunt Mildred sat across the aisle while Cole played with his wooden horse on the opposite bench. They chatted easily and reminisced about their childhood. Mama laughed as Aunt Mildred reminded her of the time they hid in their Uncle Clyde's barn and jumped out at their cousin Lois, nearly scaring her to death. Mama recalled the day their father took them to Kansas City to the harness races and let them eat so much ice cream they got sick in the carriage on the way home.

Aunt Mildred gazed out the window, remarking on the simple beauty of the landscape as the train rolled along beside the Green River, the landscape sprinkled with lupine and yellow sweet clover. Off to the west, fields gave way to pine-covered hillsides and jagged rock formations. The Rocky Mountain peaks loomed far above. My aunt appeared lighter and younger somehow, as if a great burden had been lifted. Whenever she glanced at Aunt Eva and Mr. Dearman, however, her mouth still twitched involuntarily.

We planned to spend two nights at the Abbott ranch then travel to Manitou Springs on Sunday for another two days. The Abbotts would join us in Manitou to take the day long trip up Pikes Peak. Cole was beside himself with excitement about the entire adventure. He'd never been to a ranch or ridden a horse. And it would be his first time staying in a hotel, which he claimed was a place only "big boys" were allowed. My poor, unwitting brother had no idea that Mr. Abbott wanted to turn our lives upside down yet again.

We arrived in Monument, a tiny town twenty miles north of Colorado Springs, at eleven thirty. Mr. Abbott and several ranch hands met us at the train stop with two carriages and a buckboard for the luggage.

"It's a pleasure to have you visit my humble corner of the world," Mr. Abbott said, nodding to the group and shaking hands with Mr. Dearman. "It's only a short ride to the ranch, but there's a nice place to stop for lunch along the way."

Mama sat up front next to Mr. Abbott in the first carriage, with Aunt Eva and Mr. Dearman in the seat behind them. Cole and I climbed into the other carriage with Aunt Mildred. The wheels kicked up a constant cloud of dust along the rugged dirt road. Aunt Mildred held her handkerchief over her mouth and nose, grunting occasionally from the ubiquitous jolts and bumps. I watched with dismay as Mr. Abbott chatted with Mama, making her laugh with delight again and again.

After twenty minutes, we stopped in a grove of cottonwood trees by a small creek. The ranch hands unpacked hampers with chicken sandwiches and jars of lemonade and tea. Everyone was hungry.

Cole finished his sandwich and stood in front of Mr. Abbott, looking grave. "I'd like to rope a dogie, Mr. Abbott, sir. I think a baby cow will be the right size for me. But first I need to learn how to ride a horse and throw a lasso. Can you teach me?"

"Mercy," Aunt Mildred murmured.

Cole glanced at her and added, "Please, thank you, sir, if I may."

Mr. Abbott chuckled and winked at Mama. "I think that might be arranged, if your Mama agrees. You'll make a fine wrangler."

Mama appeared doubtful. "You're awfully young, Cole."

Cole's face wrinkled. "I'd be careful, Mama. And tomorrow I'll be a day older than today—and maybe a little taller." Everyone laughed, including Aunt Mildred.

Following lunch, we continued along the rutted road for another thirty minutes before coming to a simple wooden gate with Two Rocks Ranch carved in the wide beam across the top. Big herds of cattle grazed among the rolling hills and scattered oak trees, as calves lowed for their mothers. We rattled along toward a group of buildings in the distance, the sweet smell of milkweed and the pungent odor of cow dung mingling on the warm breeze. We climbed the gentle rise to the huge three-story house built of sandy pink bricks and heavy wooden beams topped with multiple gabled roofs. I hadn't expected anything so grand. Two small cottages stood to the left of the house. Down the hill on the right, a half dozen horses pranced around a corral near the barn and stables. Beyond that stretched a long, narrow bunkhouse for the ranch hands.

Bernadette stood on the front porch of the house waving as we approached, wearing a dark-green cotton skirt and white blouse. She stepped down to greet us and took my hand. The green satin ribbon tied around her blouse's high collar complemented her eyes, the color of fresh mint. Her strawberry-blonde hair fell in a braid down her back. A widow's peak and slightly pointed chin made her freckled face a perfect heart shape.

I had not seen any other ranch houses or buildings after leaving our picnic site beside the pond. I wondered what it had been like for Bernadette growing up in this remote spot without any sisters or brothers. Had she been lonely, especially after her mother passed? Surely Mama didn't think

286

this would do for Cole or me. I only had two years of school left. I couldn't bear the thought of leaving my friends and Denver to live on this desolate patch of land.

Bernadette pulled me inside the house as her father began to describe his land and cattle to the others. "You don't want to listen to Papa," she whispered. "He doesn't realize how he bores people talking about the ranch."

I gaped at the two-story-high entry hall. A wide mahogany staircase with finely carved and polished banisters curved to the upper floors. A fan-shaped stained-glass window over the front door sent arcs of rose and pale blue light rippling over the walls. The Tabor Opera House and Brown Palace Hotel were the only places I'd ever seen that were anywhere near as elegant.

To the right was a room twice the size of our parlor and library put together. A massive stone fireplace covered the far wall. French doors along the front and back led to terraces and flooded the room with light. Settees and arm chairs covered in satins and brocades of mauve, cream, and peacock blue were arranged in several seating areas by the fireplace and back of the room. Near the front were game tables and chairs next to a grand piano polished to a mirror sheen.

"Do you play?" Bernadette asked, following my gaze.

"Not really. I'm terrible," I said. "Do you?"

"My mother taught me. She was very good," she said in a wistful voice. "We played duets together." She brightened. "I learned some wonderful new songs at school this spring. I'll play them tonight."

"Do you have lots of visitors here?" I asked.

"We used to. Mama loved hosting parties. People came from the surrounding ranches, Colorado Springs, and sometimes Denver. They'd often spend a night or two." She laughed. "When I was little, I'd sit at the top of the stairs and listen to the music and laughter until Papa would discover me and bring me down."

She sighed. "Now that Mama is gone and I'm away at school, poor Papa is lost in this empty house."

Mr. Abbott led the rest of our group into the room. "What kind of stories is my girl making up about me?" He put an arm around Bernadette's shoulders. "You take the ladies and Cole to their rooms, and I'll show Mr. Dearman to the guest cottage."

He turned to Cole. "If your mother agrees, I'll take you to meet the horse I picked out for you."

"Mama, please, can I?" Cole begged.

Mama laughed and nodded. "You must do exactly as Mr. Abbott says, and I shall come along to supervise."

Mr. Abbott nodded once. "Please make yourselves at home this afternoon. If you care to ride, one of the hands will saddle a horse for you. Or the library is across the hall—read, rest. My housekeeper, Mrs. Hernandez, will provide anything you want to eat or drink. Tomorrow will be a day out on the ranch, but tonight is what my dear late wife would call a civilized evening, a formal dinner. Please join me here at seven for drinks before the meal."

Bernadette led us to the second floor, where our suitcases had been delivered. Mama and Cole settled in the front room, my aunts in the next, and I followed Bernadette to her bedroom farther down the hall.

"Your room is so pretty," I exclaimed, sinking onto the edge of the portable cot set up for me in one corner. It would have suited a fairytale princess, with its four-poster bed, dresser, vanity, and an armoire of cedar wood. Two cozy window seats provided perfect retreats for reading, sketching, or simply dreaming. The bed had a rose flowered quilt, while the curtains and window seat cushions were covered in a muted green. Life on the ranch might be more comfortable than I had imagined.

"I never fully appreciated my room until living in the women's dormitory at Pembroke. It's terribly stark, and the beds feel like wooden planks." She chuckled. "But the other girls are fun. There's so much to do and learn."

"Is it nice in Rhode Island?"

"It's very green with lots of trees and rivers. Everything is old and established, full of history. Different from here."

"Where did you go to school growing up?" I asked.

"Mama taught me at home until I was ten, then I went to school in Colorado Springs."

"You rode there every day?"

"No. I boarded at the school Monday to Friday."

"Weren't you homesick?"

"A little at first. But at least one of my parents came to visit every Wednesday, and I made wonderful friends."

Bernadette helped me lift my bag onto the bed to unpack. "And will you go away to college after you finish at St. Mary's?" she asked.

"I hope to, if we can afford it. My dream is to go to New York to study art."

She smiled. "I've heard how talented you are."

"What will you do when you finish college? Will you come back here?"

"Not to the ranch. I haven't declared a major, but I'd like to be a journalist. That will require living in a city." She sat on her bed and swung her feet up, reclining against the pillows.

"My mother has lots of friends in Denver who write for newspapers and magazines. She could introduce you," I offered.

She leaned forward. "That would be wonderful. I admire your mother a great deal for becoming a doctor. It can't have been easy." She played with the edge of the quilt. "I'm grateful she was in charge of Papa's broken leg, or he could have ended up with a terrible limp." She looked up at me and smiled. "He's been much more cheerful since he met your mother."

"You don't mind them becoming...friends?"

She scrunched up her face. "My parents loved each other very much. Losing Mama broke both our hearts, but it's been five years...I want Papa to be happy again, not so lonely."

"Of course," I murmured. I wanted Mama to be happy as well, but did it have to mean getting married again and changing our lives completely?

It was a treat to have another occasion to wear my new blue gown. Bernadette admired it at length and helped me arrange my unruly hair on top of my head. She added the tiniest touch of color to my cheeks. I stared in the mirror at the surprising image of a young woman. Surely this couldn't be me. Rose and I had spent hours dreaming about our futures after St. Mary's, what it would be like to set out in the world on our own. But now the thought of leaving home and everything familiar filled me with apprehension and sadness.

290

We gathered in the great room for drinks, the men in dinner jackets and the women in evening gowns. Mr. Abbott poured whiskey and soda for himself and Mr. Dearman while Mrs. Hernandez offered a tray filled with small glasses of sherry and tumblers of ginger ale. Once again Aunt Mildred surprised us by accepting a sherry. When I reached for one, Mama whispered discreetly in my ear that I was too young and should take a ginger ale along with Cole. I gave her a petulant toss of my head and turned away. What was the point of dressing up and acting like a lady if I couldn't be treated like one?

Cole, the little traitor, sidled up to Mr. Abbott, who was sitting in an armchair. After a moment, he asked if he might sit on his knee. Clearly there would be little resistance on Cole's part to adopting a new father. He had only been three when Papa died and remembered practically nothing about him other than the framed photos in the parlor and by Mama's bed.

At seven thirty we adjourned to the dining room across the hall. The table was set with white linens, fine china, and silver cutlery. Candles burned in tiered candelabras, casting a soft glow about the room. If all of this was meant to impress Mama and my aunts, I felt sure it succeeded. Yet none of the fine trappings could change my heart or my longing for my own papa.

Home on the Range

I woke in a large, comfortable room unsure, at first, of my surroundings. I soon remembered Mr. Abbott's ranch and the lovely evening the night before. A cool breeze soughed through the oak tree leaves and through the open window, setting the voile curtains aflutter. Cole lay sprawled across the bed next to me, lost in a deep slumber. His soft, moist breath warmed my arm. The previous afternoon in the sun at the corral had left his cheeks pink. I gently smoothed his tousled curls and pulled the sheet up under his chin. He squirmed and turned on his side, letting out a contented sigh. Did my sweet boy dream of cowboys and dogies?

I stepped out of bed and pulled back the curtain as the first inklings of dawn turned the distant horizon deep violet then russet orange. The faint line of light spread across the endless fields of grass and lifted the night as a canopy of stars twinkled a last goodbye and faded into the pale blue-gray sky.

My mind refused to rest as I contemplated the generous life Mr. Abbott could afford my family, a life free of financial worries and loneliness. Try as I might, though, I found it hard to imagine how it would settle with the children. Or myself. I knew Cole could easily adjust, but Sara Jane already had expressed her displeasure at the idea of me marrying Mr.

Abbott. She had remained sullen and quiet the night before and only reluctantly joined in the singing and games after dinner. With only two more years at home, I would not make them unhappy ones for her. Not after all we had endured.

I quietly dressed for the morning ride. It had been over four years since I'd ridden horseback in the countryside. Memories of that Sunday with William spilled into the room to haunt me. Sara Jane had been invited to a friend's house for a birthday party, and Katherine insisted she should watch Cole, just a year old, to give William and me a day alone. Our hearts were broken after losing Peter six months earlier. The pall enveloping our lives had caused us to grow distant from each other. We had retreated into the banalities of daily existence, polite and measured, unable to express our grief or find any release.

William proposed a ride to the Platte River for a picnic. We saddled our two bays and wended our way out of town on a pleasant spring day with lovely clear skies. An hour later, we settled in a meadow near the river. Bright fresh grass angled for the sun, as a trove of wildflowers competed for space. Red clover, blue flax, fairy trumpets, white yarrow, and belle flowers produced a heady mixture of scents. The air buzzed with bees, happily collecting pollen in a drunken feast, as the river raced past in a swirling rush.

We spread a quilt under a tall cottonwood tree and unpacked our sandwiches and cold tea. After eating, I laid my head in William's lap, settling into the languorous heat of the afternoon. He fed me strawberries, raising his eyebrows up and down in a provocative manner, allowing a glimpse of the mischievous man I had married. As the temperature rose, I suggested we take off our shoes and wade into the chilly waters. We carefully navigated both the rocky bottom and swift current near the banks of the river. William turned with a wide grin and dribbled the water down my neck. I giggled and returned fire. We splashed wildly, laughing hysterically and yelping at the icy cold until he called a truce. He pulled me onto the riverbank and into his arms, holding me so tightly I could barely breathe. I issued a small sob that came from out of nowhere.

"I love you more than anything in the world," he whispered in my ear. "We will survive this, no matter how hard it seems." And he kissed me as he hadn't kissed me since before Peter became ill.

We fell onto our blanket and made passionate love, overwhelmed by the exquisite pleasure of once again sharing our bodies. William was right. We did survive and slowly recaptured our happiness. But it only lasted a few more years until I lost him as well.

Cole murmured something in his sleep, rousing me from my memories. I hurried to finish dressing and headed downstairs for breakfast. Eva and Mr. Abbott were already at the table, and Mr. Dearman arrived soon after me. Mildred had volunteered to entertain Cole while we rode, while Sara Jane and Bernadette opted to sleep in.

Eva and I did not have formal riding clothes, but I assured her we could manage wearing my bicycle pants, which flared out and fell midcalf over long stockings. In Colorado, we accepted more informal and practical choices. As always Eva looked lovely in a crisp white blouse and my charcoal bicycle pants.

Mr. Dearman was clad in newly purchased denim pants and a brown checked cowboy shirt, still bearing the fold lines from their store packaging. His shiny boots and dark brown belt smelled of newly tanned leather. The costume created a comical and incongruent image on his slender, elegant figure. Surely, he was more accustomed to well-tailored riding attire intended for fox hunts in the New England countryside. I feared if I met Eva's eyes, we might start giggling. Mr. Dearman displayed a good-natured enthusiasm about our outing as Mr. Abbott slapped him on the back.

I had been encouraged the night before to see Mr. Dearman and Mildred sitting at the side of the room, carrying on a cordial conversation. Mildred actually appeared interested and friendly.

The ranch hands had the horses ready when we reached the corral. Mr. Dearman assisted Eva in climbing astride the Western saddle.

"Are you sure you wouldn't rather ride sidesaddle?" he asked, seeming a touch embarrassed as he stood next to her stockinged leg.

"I'm much more comfortable and secure this way," she said. "It's how I learned to ride at home."

"I worry you might fall," Mr. Dearman persisted.

"Mr. Dearman, you forget our father raised thoroughbreds," I interjected. "We rode horses from the time we could walk."

Mr. Abbott winked at me. "I have every confidence in you ladies."

Mr. Dearman stared up at Eva. "And you feel strong enough for such a long ride after your illness?"

"We already discussed this." Eva stretched her hand toward me. "Trust my doctor. She assures me I am fine."

Mr. Dearman let out a long sigh. "I shall be right next to you…in case."

"You mustn't fuss over me, Bertram," Eva said, her voice a bit sharp. "Or I shall feel as if I'm riding with Mildred." It was the first time I'd heard her call him by his first name in front of others.

He looked up, chastened. "My apologies. Your well-being is my primary concern."

"Shall we go?" Mr. Abbott said. "We'll likely see eagles circling this early. By ten o'clock the sun begins to grow hot, and we'll want to head back."

We ventured along dirt paths, trotting and cantering through pastures. As promised, two enormous bald eagles soared aloft. Their vast wings effortlessly caught the wind's currents as they arced through the faultless blue sky, impervious to gravity. A dozen or more hawks claimed the lower air space over the fields, competing for mice and other prey. In an instant, one of the eagles dove straight down, swooping along the ground and ensnaring a baby rabbit in its talons. It ascended into the sky once more with minimal movement from its powerful wings. Poor little rabbit, I thought with a pang of sadness. Life can end so unexpectedly.

The cows chewed their cuds contentedly, barely looking up as we passed. They swished their tails every few minutes, sending up dark clouds of flies. The sun rose higher and higher as light played across tall stalks of grass. Ever-shifting shades of lavender, purple, and slate crept over the vast peaks and crevices of the Rocky Mountains, which loomed in the distance.

Without warning, Eva dug her heels into her horse and took off at a gallop. She flung one arm out and let go a wild whoop. Her braid flew out behind her. We all took off after her but couldn't come close until she finally slowed down.

Mr. Dearman grabbed onto her horse's bridle. "Are you all right? Did your horse get away from you?"

Eva laughed. "No. After all those months of being ill and confined to my bed, I needed to break loose and feel free again."

"You might have warned us," Mr. Dearman said, sounding a touch miffed.

"I'm sorry if I scared you," she said and turned to Mr. Abbott. "I hope you don't mind."

"Not in the least," he said. "These are working horses, used to long days racing around herding cattle."

A half hour on, we reached Cherry Creek and followed the banks of the stream through stands of cottonwoods and aspens. The cool shade offered welcome relief.

We stopped to rest, and Mr. Abbott took a rolled-up blanket from the back of his saddle and spread it on the ground, then he brought out a flask of tea and a packet of cookies from his saddle bag. Mr. Dearman helped Eva off her horse, grasping her waist to steady her as she landed on the ground and stumbled. They smiled with shy pleasure. A twinge of envy nipped at me for the delight these young lovers shared. I realized Mr. Abbott and I would never capture the wondrous feelings I had so happily felt for William.

We stepped to the creek's edge to wash our hands and splash cool water on our faces and necks before settling on the blanket for refreshments. Mr. Dearman held Eva's arm as she bent to sit down.

"Thank you, Bertram, but I am not an invalid," she said, her voice light but firm.

He cleared his throat. "Of course. I only wanted to help."

"You don't see Mr. Abbott assisting Lida, do you?" she persisted.

"Ah, but I must learn to be more considerate like Mr. Dearman," Mr. Abbott countered. "Living away from civilization, I've forgotten the finer niceties, Miss Delacroix. Mr. Dearman is a true gentleman."

Eva blushed slightly and patted Mr. Dearman's arm. "You're right; he is always most solicitous. I'm sorry to be testy, but I grew so tired of Mother and Mildred treating me like a small child after my illness. I need some space to breathe on my own."

"Lucky you are to have a thoughtful friend like Mr. Dearman, Eva" I said, feeling a bit sorry for her devoted suitor.

"It's alright. I understand how hard it has been for her," Mr. Dearman said.

We nibbled on cookies amid the deep shade of the trees as the gurgle of water splashing over and around stones created a tranquil mood. I closed my eyes for a moment, enjoying the dappled sunlight on my cheeks, listening to bluebirds and larks cheerfully calling out.

Mr. Abbott told a story about riding with Bernadette when she was ten. "She had just started at the school in Colorado Springs," he said. "She invited her new friend, Elisa, home for the weekend. She wanted to impress Elisa with her skills as a horsewoman. But when we arrived at Cherry Creek, Bernadette's ornery old horse decided to sit down and cool off in the middle of the creek. She slid right off as if sitting on a greased pig. She stood up soaking wet with her hair dripping down her face. Elisa and I couldn't stop laughing. She didn't speak to me for two days, and it took her all afternoon to get over her wounded pride with Elisa. In the end they became best friends."

"Poor Bernadette," Eva said, chuckling. "I sympathize with the indignities of youth when we want so much to be accepted by others."

"As a young woman, does it no longer matter to you what others think?" Mr. Abbott asked, a smile playing at his lips.

"Not in the least," she responded, lifting her chin. "I've adopted a new philosophy about life since my illness. I will choose to do what suits me and not what others want."

Mr. Dearman raised his eyebrows. "Within certain confines of society, I assume."

Eva shrugged. "I would never do anything morally wrong or inappropriate, but I won't be dictated to by others as to what is right for me or what a *woman* should or shouldn't do."

"Here, here," I added, grinning. "The Delacroix women are an independent lot, Mr. Dearman. You shall have to get used to it."

He smiled ruefully. "My mother and sisters are the same."

"I'll have to consider that," Mr. Abbott said, laughing. "But for now, we should head back before the heat grows too uncomfortable."

After lunch, our group headed to the corral to watch Cole ride Star, a seasoned old mare with a calm temperament. Mr. Abbott took the lead and walked the horse around the ring a few times before picking up the clip to a slow trot. Finally, he allowed Cole to venture forth on his own, while he stayed close by to assist, if needed. Cole grinned from ear to ear as he clung to the reins and saddle horn with one hand. His head bobbed like a woodpecker drilling into bark.

I still worried about Cole falling and hurting himself, but he looked comfortable and more confident with each pass around the ring. It gladdened my heart to see him so thrilled. There had not been enough joy in his young life.

"Mama, Aunt Mildred, I'm riding all by myself," he called, waving his hat at us.

Mildred chuckled. "Look at the little rascal. He's a natural in the saddle. It comes from his Delacroix heritage, of course. Think how Father would have loved to see his grandson ride."

"As would have William," I said softly.

Sara Jane and Bernadette had decided to venture out on a ride of their own, despite the hot afternoon. They mounted the saddled horses, a gray-and-white appaloosa and a pretty chestnut mare, and headed off in a cloud of dust. They had vowed to be back by four o'clock to get ready for the surprise evening Mr. Abbott had promised.

Cole came to a halt and watched in awe as one of the hands demonstrated his roping abilities, throwing a lasso around the neck of another horse.

Mr. Abbott winked at me. "You ready to practice your roping again, little wrangler?" Cole nodded enthusiastically, and Mr. Abbott helped him down.

I glanced over at Eva and Mr. Dearman. They were strolling along the pasture fence. Eva had brought a bunch of carrots to feed the horses and was attracting a loyal following. She giggled as a black steed grabbed a carrot, nearly consuming her hand with it. Mr. Dearman gently pulled Eva's arm from harm's way, holding on to it a little longer than needed. He stared with wonder at the beautiful creature next to him, leaning in to nuzzle Eva's cheek.

"You must admit, Mr. Dearman appears to adore Eva," I said, noticing Mildred was watching them as well.

"Yes. I believe he is sincere in his affections," she allowed. "I had a nice conversation with him last night after dinner. He seems an agreeable young man."

"I remember that heady period when William and I were newly in love. You must recall what it was like with Franklin."

"I assure you, we were never that enamored, but I do remember our early happiness. The question is will it last? Or will he grow tired of her and break her heart?"

"There are no guarantees in life, but he strikes me as loyal and honest. Of course, love changes over time to something more comfortable and familiar."

Mildred suddenly leaned her head down on her arms where they rested on the fence rail. A small sob shook her back.

"Mildred, dear, whatever is the matter?" I put an arm around her shoulders.

She lifted her head and dug a handkerchief from her pocket, dabbing her eyes. "It's Franklin. I fear I've lost him."

"But how?"

She took a letter from her other pocket and handed it to me. "Mother sent this last week."

I read it through, stunned by the implication of Franklin's infidelity. "It's a rumor. Some unfounded gossip." I squeezed her shoulder. "Franklin is a good and true man. I refuse to believe he would betray you this way."

"I've never doubted him before, but we've grown so distant over the years. He works all the time and is hardly at

302

home. I have no idea what he's capable of anymore." She heaved a deep sigh. "As Mother says, if we had been blessed with children, things might have been different."

"I know that was a terrible disappointment. But you mustn't despair until you have a chance to talk with him and uncover the truth. I'm sure it's a misunderstanding."

She placed the letter in her pocket. "I hope so. If it's true, I don't know what I shall do. I'd like another chance to rekindle our marriage."

"I feel sure this will resolve itself. When you return home, you can discuss things at length and find a way to be close once more." My words sounded feeble. What did I know of their relationship?

"Don't tell Eva. I wouldn't want her to worry."

"Have you written to Mother about Mr. Dearman?"

"Yes, and of course she's fit to be tied." She snickered softly. "She ordered me to bring Eva home at once. Ha! She thinks she can snap her fingers and control everything."

"You mustn't fret."

"I'm ignoring Mother, for the time being. And Franklin." She stood quite straight, her eyes filled with sorrow. "You do know I only want Eva to be happy. She deserves a life of her own, not tied to Mother out of guilt or duty. Yet, I'd like to feel confident that Mr. Dearman is the right man."

The Glory of Pikes Peak

Monday, July 15, 1901

Dear Aunt Effie,

I received your nice note on Thursday. I'm sorry I haven't written before, but Lida has kept us busy every moment of our stay with teas, dinners, and meetings among her admirable set of friends. I can say without hesitation that the trip has brought us all a great deal of happiness. After a tentative start, Lida and I have reconciled many times over from the estrangement Mother created eleven years ago. I find Sara Jane and Cole the dearest children and have become quite close to both. I promise to tell you everything once I return to Lawrence. For now, I must limit this letter to our delightful trip over the past four days.

Lawrence has never felt farther away than at this moment. I am sitting on the porch of the Grand View Hotel in Manitou Springs. And oh, what a view! Manitou is south of Denver and a little east of Colorado Springs, perched at the base of Pikes Peak. It is a resort town that developed initially around the healthful mineral springs in the area. People come to take the waters, which are credited with curing all manner of ailments from tuberculosis to the palsy. The town has been dubbed the Saratoga of the West. According to the hotel clerk, once the Manitou and Pikes Peak Railway was built ten years ago, the town rapidly expanded. There are no less than seven grand hotels, while many smaller hotels and private cottages are springing up.

But I should begin at the start of our adventure. On Friday we took the train from Denver south to visit the ranch of Lida's friend Mr. Abbott (Mother may have told you about him). As you know, I agreed to spend time with Mr. Dearman to determine his true nature and suitability for marrying Eva. Mr. Abbott invited him to come along to the ranch and Manitou; thus, we are all together now.

We spent two delightful days at Mr. Abbott's "Two Rocks Ranch," which sprawls across the Colorado plains. The others enjoyed horseback riding, and little Cole learned to ride a tame old horse and throw a lasso. He actually succeeded in throwing a rope around an unsuspecting barn cat, which led to a wild, screeching melee. Now he has announced that he will be a cowboy and ride the range when he grows up. Adorable!

The second night we had a delicious dinner served from a chuck wagon as we gathered around a bonfire under the stars. One of the ranch hands played guitar and serenaded us with cowboy songs, while coyotes howled in the distance. Can you imagine me of all people in this setting? I thoroughly enjoyed myself.

Yesterday, we left the ranch midmorning in carriages bound for Manitou. We stopped along the way at the Garden of the Gods for a walk and picnic lunch. We wandered among the most unique landscape one can envision of weathered red (Mr. Abbott says this is due to the presence of iron) and white sandstone canyons in strange layered formations. Some looked like upside-down pyramids, wide at the top and narrow at the base, threatening to topple over at any minute. Several enormous ridges form an arch, which looks exactly like the outline of two camels kissing.

I had a shock when we rounded a large rock and came upon a group of Ute Indians with their horses, wearing deer skin clothes and beads with their hair in long braids. They were selling silver and turquoise jewelry and other wares. Cole approached an elderly man and said in his most solemn voice, "I like your horses, sir. I've heard you are very good riders and hunters." The Indian gave him a wrinkled smile, revealing several missing teeth, and greeted him back. The two of them proceeded to have a long conversation as Cole explained how he had learned to ride a horse and lasso dogies and would appreciate any tips the man could share. The elderly man seemed quite charmed by our boy. He gave Cole a beaded necklace with a carved bear on it, explaining this would give Cole courage and protect him when riding. I bought Cole a small deerskin drum, which he proceeded to pound on for the rest of the ride to Manitou (what was I thinking?). I also purchased some pretty silver earrings for Sara Jane and Bernadette.

We arrived in Manitou a little after two, walking about town and trying the renowned natural spring water. Perhaps I have found the fountain of youth. Ha, ha! We had a lovely dinner at the hotel. I fell into bed and slept more soundly than I have slept in many years.

307

Elaine Russell

We boarded the Manitou-Pikes Peak Railway, or "cog train," at eight o'clock this morning. It is a thrilling ride I assure you. We were blessed with a perfectly clear, sunny day. The sky here is the most dazzling sapphire blue. The cog train is an ingenious invention. To assist the steam engine in pulling the single passenger car, there is a third rail down the middle of the track with slotted teeth. As the train progresses, the cog wheels under the engine catch the metal teeth of the rail, pulling the car up the hill. Given the steep climb of almost eight thousand feet, the steam engine alone is inadequate.

The trip cost five dollars each—a small fortune! It was well worth the price for the spectacular vistas along the way and at the top. (Of course, Mr. Abbott and Mr. Dearman insisted on treating). It took over four hours to travel a little under nine miles up the mountain. On the way we passed through verdant meadows awash with wildflowers, deep canyons, and forests dense with all manner of pine trees and quaking aspen. Every new turn along the route revealed a river or creek tumbling over enormous weathered boulders. There were several dramatic waterfalls sending clouds of mist into the air, which the sun transformed into beautiful rainbows. Twice we spotted Big Horn Sheep perched along the rocky precipices.

About two-thirds of the way up the mountain we passed through a forest of gnarled spruce trees until we emerged at the timberline into a barren rocky terrain. It appears much as I would expect the moon's surface to look. Once we finally reached the station at the peak, a glorious panorama spanned before us. I could see along the Continental Divide and across the great plains east and west as far as the eye can travel.

Breathtaking. The only negative was the difficulty I had breathing in the high altitude, and I developed a severe headache. Lida made me sit down and take some aspirin with lots of water. I felt better once we headed down the hill. We stopped for a nice luncheon at the halfway house, a large wooden lodge.

Despite the long day on the train, the others are out at the moment riding burros. I refused to stoop to such a lowly tourist stunt. (Do you remember the goat cart my father made for Lida and me when we were children?) Once the others return we will dine at the grand Miramont Castle Hotel, which looks exactly like a Medieval stone castle from Europe.

I have never considered myself much of a naturalist, but the wild and rich landscapes of Colorado have captured my heart. You cannot imagine the splendor of seeing the Rocky Mountain peaks rise like fierce giants. Many remain snow-capped year-round, glistening in the sunshine as if touched by God. The rolling foothills and forests contain a profusion of wildflowers, birds, and tiny creatures. Small, rural towns like Manitou maintain the ambiance of the Western frontier, while Denver is surprisingly cosmopolitan. Certainly, you can hear my enthusiasm. Part of this is my contentment of once again having the presence of dear Lida. I wish you could be here to share all these marvels.

I have not formed a final opinion of Mr. Dearman, but he and Eva seem truly in love. His manners are impeccable, and he is most solicitous toward me, despite all the distress I fear my past behavior has caused him. He comes from a well-to-do and respected family in Boston. My only worry is the constancy of such a handsome man. But Eva must have a life of her own away from Mother. So I am leaning in favor of the match unless something unforeseen occurs.

Eva and I do not plan to return home early. Mother will have to adjust to the idea that she cannot dictate Eva's future, or mine, for that matter. I'm a bit long in the tooth to turn rebellious, but it's never too late to stand up for yourself.

I look forward to spending time with you on our return home. In the meantime, good luck calming Mother down, and give my love to all the family.

Your niece, Mildred

The Second Time Around

I woke to find Cole's face bending over mine with his nose a few inches away. "What in the world are you doing?" I asked, struggling to keep my eyes open.

"I wanted to know if you were awake. Your eyelids were moving."

I laughed and pulled him down into a hug. "I was dreaming of riding a horse at Mr. Abbott's ranch, and you were on Star beside me."

"I want to go back to the ranch. Can I keep Star for my own? Mr. Abbott says I can ride anytime we want to come."

"We'll see about that." I glanced over to find the bed on the other side of the room empty. "Sara Jane must have gone downstairs. Did you see her?"

"No. I just woke up." He pulled away from my embrace and sat up. "Are you going to marry Mr. Abbott?"

I blinked several times, thinking how to answer such a momentous question at this early hour of the morning. "Mr. Abbott and I are good friends, but I'm not planning on marrying anyone right now. I miss your papa."

Cole frowned. "I miss Papa, too, but you said he's in heaven with Peter, and we won't see them until we go there."

"That's true. But I'm still not ready to marry again. I like Mr. Abbott, and sometime soon we'll go back to visit him at the ranch." I made the promise to appease him without any idea if it was true. Was I a terrible mother to give him false hopes?

"I'd like to live on the ranch and ride Star every day. I want to be a cowboy and rope cattle."

I chuckled again. "That would be fun. But first you must go to school and grow up to be an educated young man. Then you can decide what you want to do."

I grabbed William's pocket watch from the bedside table and checked the time. "Goodness, it's already nine. I can't remember when I last slept so late. We must get dressed. The others will be down at breakfast."

"I don't want to go home," he grumbled. "I like being on holiday and staying in a hotel."

"We've had a wonderful time, but Sara Jane and I must both go to work tomorrow, and you and Mildred can get back to learning your letters and numbers." I ruffled his hair. "It's always hard to end a holiday.

"And, Cole, do not repeat our conversation about Mr. Abbott to anyone. Is that clear?" He nodded reluctantly and climbed out of bed.

He dawdled over his pancakes at breakfast and was anything but helpful as Sara Jane and I finished packing. We took a last stroll around Manitou before Mr. Abbott's men loaded our cases in the carriages. Cole had to be called three times to get in for the ride to the train station. I'm sure he hoped to keep us from making the train. Our bags were loaded onto the twelve forty-five train bound for Colorado Springs and Denver. It was time for goodbyes.

Bernadette hugged Sara Jane and offered a solemn handshake for Cole. "We shall miss you. It will be very quiet at the ranch without you, Cole."

Mr. Abbott slapped Mr. Dearman on the back and offered his best wishes. "You're all welcome anytime," he said, shaking hands with Eva, Mildred, and Sara Jane. I was relieved when Sara Jane smiled and thanked him politely for the nice time.

Cole gave Mr. Abbott a big hug. "I'll be visiting the ranch very soon, sir," Cole reassured him. "Maybe I can stay awhile."

Mr. Abbott laughed. "That would be wonderful."

"Cole, what shall I do with you?" I shook my head, embarrassed. It made me ache to see how desperately my young boy wanted a man in his life.

Mr. Abbott held onto my hand, staring into my eyes. "Dr. Clayton, I hope we can see each other soon. Bernadette and I are coming to Denver for a few days two weeks from now, as I have a business matter. And I'll come again when she heads back to school in September. Perhaps you would allow me to take your family to dinner."

"That would be nice. Or you could come to our house for dinner." I smiled. "I've promised Bernadette I'll introduce her to my journalist friends. We can make a party of it." I caught Sara Jane watching us with a pensive expression.

The train was filling up fast. I pulled my hand away from Mr. Abbott. "Thank you for a lovely time and for bringing us to Manitou. It was a special treat."

We settled in our seats as the cars began to move. Bernadette and Mr. Abbott waved from the platform. I gazed at Mr. Abbott's solid, reassuring figure, thinking how attractive a marriage to him sounded. I puzzled over my emotions as the train chugged through the pine forests of the foothills into the valley knolls of grass and oak trees. I was drawn to him. The relationship offered an easy companionship, like a well-worn pair of slippers that are cozy and reliable. A deep, enduring passion like I'd shared with William would never come again. Yet I could be happy with this kind man. Much depended on how the children felt. We would need to find a way to meld the conflicting aspects of our lives. I could not abandon my work at the Catholic homes. Perhaps he would be willing to live in Denver part of the week. If it was meant to be, solutions would reveal themselves. I would not rush into anything.

Sara Jane smiled at me from across the aisle, her sketchpad and charcoal pencil in hand. She turned the paper to show me a drawing of Cole leaning into Mildred, his mouth half-open in concentration, as she read him a book. Oh, my lovely daughter, what complicated thoughts filled her mind? Only time would tell.

The train arrived in Denver at three forty-five. Mr. Dearman found us a carriage and loaded our bags.

"I must go on to the hotel," he said. "I need to prepare for a meeting tomorrow morning. Would it be acceptable if I called on you ladies tomorrow afternoon?"

"You're more than welcome," Mildred said with a warm smile. "And I'm sure we would enjoy having you stay for dinner."

I think my mouth must have fallen open, but I recovered quickly. "It would be a pleasure to have you, Mr. Dearman."

When we finally arrived home, Katherine was waiting with tea and a chocolate layer cake, which she served us in the parlor. She fussed over Cole, and he followed her through to the kitchen, spilling forth with tales of his adventures on the ranch.

"Then Star started to trot, and I rode her all by myself," he reported. "I've become a cowboy, Katherine. You can say 'howdy' to me from now on." They disappeared into the kitchen as the rest of us burst into laughter.

"That boy is as cute as a button, Lida," Mildred said, wiping away a tear at the corner of her eye. "He certainly keeps us entertained."

Eva held up a letter she had found waiting for her on the silver tray in the hall. "I have exciting news. Bryn Mawr has accepted me to return to school in September."

Mildred smiled. "Wonderful news, and a very sensible move. You will be well served by completing your education." She paused a moment. "And Mr. Dearman is in agreement?"

Eva pulled her mouth to one side, hesitating. "I haven't told him yet. He's always professed to be supportive of women having careers, but we'll see how he reacts when the woman is me."

"He's an enlightened man. I'm sure he'll understand," I said.

Eva looked at the two unopened envelopes in Mildred's lap. "Are those both from Mother?"

"Yes," Mildred said, gazing down as if they might belong to someone else. "At the moment, I'm not really interested in what she has to say." She tossed the letters onto the side table. "Perhaps I'll read them after dinner."

Eva slid closer to Mildred and took her hand. "How can I thank you enough for going on this trip and giving Mr. Dearman a chance? Did you write to Mother about it?"

Mildred patted the top of Eva's hand. "Yes, I thought it best to prepare her."

Eva cringed. "I can guess her reaction."

"As you might imagine, she's beside herself and floundering to regain control." Mildred gave a short laugh. "But I'm not paying any attention to her."

Eva took a deep breath. "And what are your thoughts on Mr. Dearman?"

Mildred smiled gently. "I find him a lovely young man. Clearly he is most in love with you, my dear. If he makes you happy, you have my blessing."

Eva threw her arms around Mildred as Sara Jane and I looked on with delight, and tears prickled at my eyes.

Chapter 33 **FRANKLIN**

Across the Wires

WESTERN UNION JULY 16, 1901

TO: MILDRED BOLTON

ARE YOU BACK FROM EXCURSION? STILL WAITING
TO HEAR OF YOUR ARRIVAL IN LAWRENCE.

FRANKLIN

WESTERN UNION JULY 17, 1901

TO: FRANKLIN BOLTON

ENJOYING COLORADO. RETURNING AUG 3 AS
PLANNED.

MILDRED

Elaine Russell

WESTERN UNION   JULY 17, 1901

TO: MILDRED BOLTON

WHAT ABOUT EVA? YOUR MOTHER? BISCUIT? AND
ME?
PLEASE RETURN NOW.

FRANKLIN

WESTERN UNION   JULY 18, 1901

TO: FRANKLIN BOLTON

EVA IS HAPPIEST I'VE EVER SEEN.
MOTHER CAN MANAGE.
ASK MRS. BECKER FOR HELP WITH BISCUIT.

MILDRED

A Troubling Encounter

As we finished lunch on Friday, Cole was excused to go play with his friend Bobby. Once he departed, Mama announced to my aunts and me, "I'm taking you on an adventure to Chinatown."

"Mercy," Aunt Mildred gasped. "Why would we want to go there?"

"I read an article last night on the treatment of scarlet fever and its lingering effects in the May issue of the *American Institute of Homeopathy Journal*. It recommends a number of herbs for rebuilding the constitution by strengthening kidney function," Mama said. "I know a Chinese doctor, a very nice man, who will have the ingredients or will be able to order them for me. He's extremely knowledgeable."

Aunt Mildred frowned. "I thought you said Eva had fully recovered."

Mama folded her napkin and placed it on the table. "She has made a remarkable recuperation, but it can't hurt to give her an extra shot at good health."

Aunt Eva startled. "It involves shots?"

"No, no. The herbs are brewed to make a tea," Mama reassured her.

"And you're sure it's safe for ladies to go there alone?" Aunt Mildred asked.

Mama smiled. "Perfectly. I've been there numerous times by myself."

This surprised me, as only the summer before, she had warned me never to go near Chinatown. "It's not a proper place for a young woman," she had insisted, explaining there were still illegal opium dens and gambling clubs in some of the buildings. Wazee Street, the back alley between Market and Blake streets, was better known as "Hop Alley." Hop was slang for opium. The Chinese section also bordered the Market Street brothels, giving the area an even more unsavory reputation.

"The description in the Denver *Visitor's Pocket Guide* makes it sound intriguing," Aunt Eva enthused. "I read an article in the *Denver Post* last week detailing how much the area has changed since that terrible riot in 1880."

Mama frowned. "It was a dreadful incident. Some three thousand white men, most of them drunk, ransacked and burned down most of Chinatown. One young Chinese man was killed." She sighed. "It happened several years before we moved to Denver, but Ellis said yellow journalism was to blame. The newspapers wrote exaggerated stories about illegal activities in Chinatown and claimed the Chinese were taking all the jobs. I'll never understand what possesses men to promote hate and carry out such evil acts."

"I think we should wait and ask Mr. Dearman to accompany us," Aunt Mildred said. "You know he'd be happy to chaperone."

"He's busy concluding his business," Aunt Eva said. "I hate to bother him."

Mama nodded. "He told me it's been a difficult negotiation, and he's anxious to be done with the case."

Mr. Dearman had come to dinner on Wednesday and again the night before. He was gaining confidence and appeared more relaxed around the family, even Aunt Mildred. He told us funny stories about his first cases as a lawyer representing clients in court and his childhood with four older sisters who teased him incessantly. Cole asked him a million questions, of course.

Since Aunt Mildred had given her vote of approval, I anxiously awaited news of Aunt Eva's engagement. But nothing had transpired as yet. I prayed to Saint Expeditus, the patron saint of prompt solutions, that an announcement would soon follow.

We walked to the corner and hailed a carriage for the trip to Chinatown.

"Where to, ma'am?" the driver asked.

"Market and Fifteenth Streets, please" Mama said.

The driver looked mildly surprised. "Yes, ma'am."

"Are there really still opium dens?" Aunt Eva whispered to Mama.

"A few, even though the city outlawed them three years ago." Mama's voice sounded indignant. "The police look the other way, as they do with most illegal activities in this city. It's scandalous."

We descended from the carriage and walked a half block to Wazee Street. The Chinese immigrants had built the fronts of their stores and homes to open onto the narrow alleys rather than the main streets. Perhaps they felt safer in smaller quarters, given the hostility of the white citizens. My eyes darted back and forth taking in the strange sights. One- and two-story wood and brick buildings housed all manner of shops, from grocers and restaurants to dry goods establishments. Red signs and gold banners were written in bold Chinese characters, sometimes alongside English translations. We passed an open door and saw a large gold Buddha on an altar. It was surrounded by candles, plates of food, and burning sticks, which Mama said were incense. Their odd, sweet smoke drifted into the alley. The sound of Chinese music filtered down from an open window on the second floor of a building, along with the strong smell of garlic and onions cooking. We passed one of the numerous Chinese laundries where many of Denver's households brought their washing. Men were steaming and ironing piles of clothes.

Most of the Chinese men we passed wore loose cotton trousers and jackets with Mandarin collars. Older men had shaved heads, except for a long braid hanging from the napes of their necks down their backs. A store across the alley sold Western-style clothing. Two young men, dressed in dark suits with white shirts and ties, smoked cigarettes out front and eyed us as we passed.

Lee Wong's Herbal Shop was located on the first floor of a ramshackle wooden building on the corner of Sixteenth Street and Hop Alley. Strange plants hung upside down in the windows above pots filled with mysterious contents. When we opened the door, a wind chime tinkled a greeting and a mixture of pungent odors—acrid, woodsy, sweet, spicy, peppery, and smoky—assaulted our senses. Behind the counter, jars of herbs in a rainbow of colors filled the floor-to-ceiling shelves. I saw crates with dried mushrooms and green powdery fungi. Other containers held crushed leaves and twigs, dried flower blossoms, and finely ground powders. Low tables lined the wall under the front windows, covered with glass vials of strange-looking oils and other liquids.

A tiny man with a deeply wrinkled face stepped through a curtain of hanging beads into the room. He wore a long robe of embroidered black silk. When he recognized Mama, he broke into a smile. He put his hands together under his chin and bowed his head.

"Dr. Clayton, what a pleasure to see you again."

"It's very nice to see you, Dr. Wong." Mama gave a small nod. "I've brought my daughter, Sara Jane, and my sisters, Miss Delacroix and Mrs. Bolton." Mama took a paper from her reticule with the list of herbs she hoped to buy. "I'm looking for a number of roots: goldenrod, celery, dandelion, and marshmallow."

"I see. Perhaps you are treating someone for weakness of the kidneys?" Dr. Wong asked.

Mama handed him the list and took Aunt Eva's arm. "Yes. My sister had scarlet fever last fall. While she appears to be fine, I read an article recommending this mixture for restoring full functioning of the kidneys."

Aunt Mildred wandered about peering into containers as Dr. Wong donned a pair of gold wire-rim spectacles. He walked in front of the counter, standing close to Aunt Eva. "If you don't mind, I will study your color." He looked closely at her eyes, the sides of her face, her neck, and her ears.

Aunt Eva shifted uncomfortably but allowed the inspection. "This is important?" she asked.

Dr. Wong stepped back. "Yes. One can learn a great deal this way. Your eyes are clear, and I don't see any swelling.

Your skin is a bit dry, but that is not unusual in this climate. Does it itch?"

"Only a little," Aunt Eva said, flushing slightly. "I feel fine."

He spoke to Mama, "This mixture will be very good for your sister. I recommend adding ginger as well. I'll prepare a bag for you and explain how to use it."

He began taking down jars. With a small scoop, he took a little from each container and weighed it on a copper scale, then poured the herbs into a paper bag, mixing everything together.

Out the side window I noticed two well-dressed white men climb out of a carriage. They slipped down the alley, glancing back as if they expected someone might be following them.

Dr. Wong gave the bag of herbs to Aunt Eva. "Put one teaspoon of herbs into three cups of boiling water. Let it steep overnight. Drink one cup of tea at room temperature in the morning, at noon, and after dinner. Do this for a month."

Mama insisted on paying for the potion. "I hope this makes you feel even stronger."

We said goodbye to Dr. Wong and stepped into the alley. "Shall we peek in the store windows before we find a carriage?" Mama asked.

"Oh yes. I must have a souvenir," Aunt Eva said.

We set off down the alley toward Seventeenth Street. The afternoon sunlight scattered ineffectively between the shadows of the narrow lane. We passed another laundry, then a tobacco store. A delivery cart, pulled by a donkey, stood out in front of a grocery store as several young men unloaded enormous bags of rice and other goods in wooden boxes stamped with Chinese writing.

324

Next to the grocery, a beautiful young woman stood in the doorway of a curio shop, which offered delicate porcelain dishes, statues, and vases. She wore a purple brocade dress that wrapped around her slender figure and fastened with clasps made of coiled silk cord. She smiled shyly and invited us to come inside. We browsed among the shelves of hand-painted china plates and cups and porcelain figures of beautiful birds, women in elaborate traditional dress, and a fat, happy Buddha. Aunt Eva bought two small glass vials decorated with delicate pink peonies. The woman explained in broken English that the flowers had been painted on the inside of the glass. This seemed an impossible feat. Aunt Mildred selected a pretty platter with a scene of a temple next to a lake. Mama let me get a small figurine of a yellow cat that had a passing resemblance to Buttercup.

"This has all been very interesting," Mildred said as we exited the store. "Not what I expected at all. And your Dr. Wong seems most knowledgeable."

Mama smiled. "I thought you might enjoy the visit."

As we neared Seventeenth Street, the door of the last building swung open. A white man stumbled out, blinking as if he had come from darkness and was blinded by the sunlight. He wore a disheveled shirt, and his jacket was slung over his shoulder. He staggered past us, reeking of a powerful, sweet odor. A Chinese man peeked out. When he saw us watching, he quickly slammed the door shut.

"Goodness, do you think...?" Aunt Eva said, sounding dismayed and slightly thrilled at the same time.

"Most likely," Mama said. "Many people in Denver, including well-to-do women, experiment with opium, but if they become addicted, it's a terrible habit to break."

325

"Mercy," Aunt Mildred said. "We best go home."

"You wouldn't guess from the front of the buildings what's inside," I said.

"The back rooms often hold something quite different from the fronts. You never really know," Mama said as she took my elbow. "Let's find a cab before we discover something else we shouldn't."

We turned down Seventeenth Street and reached bustling Market. Mama hailed a carriage and helped Aunt Mildred inside.

As I waited my turn, I glanced in the window of a Chinese tea shop directly in front of us. My mouth fell open on seeing a man deep in conversation with the famous Mattie Silks. "Mr. Dearman," I uttered.

Aunt Eva pivoted on the step of the carriage and followed my gaze. "What is he doing here? Who is that woman?"

Mama leaned out of the carriage window. "Good Lord. It's Mattie Silks."

Aunt Eva gave a sharp cry. "We must go. Right now!" She dove into the carriage.

I stood there frozen, unable to take my eyes off the scene. How could he be consorting with this woman yet again? Mr. Dearman turned and caught sight of me. His face filled with horror as he sprang up, knocking over his chair.

"Sara Jane, get in," Mama called. I hopped into the cab. Mr. Dearman emerged from the tea shop, calling to Aunt Eva as the carriage swept away.

A Scented Note

Sara Jane sank into the seat next to me, looking devastated. She undoubtedly regretted calling Mr. Dearman's presence to our attention. But, poor dear, she could not be blamed. We sat in silence, too shocked to speak for some time. Sara Jane began to weep, and I gave her my handkerchief.

"Why would he be with that…that creature?" Eva's voice quivered.

"It's all my fault," Sara Jane cried out. "I should have told you before." We stared at her, puzzled by the outburst. "I saw Mr. Dearman talking to Mattie Silks and an older man by the ice cream store right after he arrived in Denver. I was sure there was an explanation, so I kept it to myself."

A small sob escaped Eva's lips. "I've been such a fool." She pulled her handkerchief from her pocket and covered her eyes.

Mildred put an arm around Eva's shoulders. "Dear, you must pull yourself together. I'm sure it's not what it seems." Her words surprised me, as I expected her to conclude the worst.

Eva wore an expression of total bewilderment. "How could he proclaim his love for me and talk of marriage while he is taking up company with a person of her nature?"

I reached across to grasp her hand. "Have faith in his love and wait to hear the purpose of the meetings. Surely there is more than meets the eye."

It was nearly four by the time we entered the house. Eva retreated to her room without a word, her sobs echoing down the stairs. Sara Jane looked almost worse than Eva, dropping onto a chair and putting her face in her hands. "I'm so sorry, Mama. It was stupid of me not to tell you."

"Let's wait to see what happens," I answered. "Can you please ask Katherine to make us some tea?"

Mildred collapsed on the settee. "What could he have been discussing with that wretched woman?"

I still expected Mildred to condemn Mr. Dearman, perhaps to gloat that she and Mother had been right all along. But she simply sighed with an expression of great sadness.

"After spending time with him over the past weeks," she said. "I can't imagine he could deceive us so convincingly. I have come to admire his sincerity and devotion to Eva." Her eyes met mine. "How do we ever truly know anyone? I never fathomed that Franklin could betray me."

Sara Jane emerged from the kitchen with a tea tray and poured us steaming cups. We sipped our tea, nervously waiting for something to transpire—anything to resolve the terrible knot of disappointment and sadness shrouding the room.

Thirty minutes later, the front doorbell rang. Katherine answered it and came into the parlor holding a pale pink envelope. "A delivery boy brought a note for Miss Delacroix." She wrinkled her nose. "Quite a lot of perfume."

I wanted to grab the envelope and rip it open, but instead I turned to Sara Jane. "Would you take it up to Eva? And please give her privacy to read it."

Sara Jane bounded up the stairs and rapped on Eva's door. We heard the murmurs of their exchange before she returned to the parlor. "It's definitely from a woman," she said. "Could it be Mattie Silks?"

"We'll see if Eva wishes to share it," I said.

We had our answer a few minutes later as Eva pattered down the stairs and into the parlor, holding a note in her hand. A rush of color filled her tear-streaked cheeks. She perched on the edge of the green armchair. "Let me read it to you."

Dear Miss Delacroix,

I write to dispel any misunderstanding you may have regarding my consultation this afternoon with Mr. Dearman. I have met with my attorney and the honorable Mr. Dearman four times over the last few weeks on a legal matter between myself and Mr. Dearman's client in Boston. I was acquainted with the Boston gentleman many years ago, and we have a dispute over property and mutual interests going back twelve years.

I asked Mr. Dearman to meet with me alone today, as my attorney has done nothing but muddle the settlement. I felt I would do better negotiating on my own. I provided Mr. Dearman with information, which I didn't want my attorney or anyone else to see. You should know that Mr. Dearman refused to come to my home, given the nature of my business, but agreed to meet in an out-of-the-way café. And, thus, you came across us in Chinatown.

I can assure you Mr. Dearman is above reproach and there has never been anything untoward between your gallant young friend and myself or the ladies in my employment. I hope this will not cause a problem between you. He has not informed you of our business in order to comply with the strict code of ethics on attorney-client privilege.

I read about you and Mr. Dearman in Polly Pry *a few weeks ago and saw you at the opera one night. You make a lovely couple. I do hope you will not let this sully your relationship. I wish you both all the happiness possible.*

> *Sincerely,*
> *Mrs. Mattie Silks*

Sara Jane had been listening with rapt attention, and now her expression turned to visible relief. "Oh, I knew there must be a reason. Mr. Dearman is too honorable to do anything immoral." She paused a moment, cocking her head to one side. "Mrs. Silks sounds like a normal person. I mean, a nice person." We all laughed, releasing the tension holding us captive.

"She has a heart, I suppose," Mildred said. "Now we can relax. There is no need for concern."

Eva took a deep breath. "I should not have believed the worst so easily." Once more, tears filled her eyes. "And I was so unkind about Mrs. Silks. I'm unworthy of Bertram's love."

"Nonsense," Mildred said. "Mother and I filled you with doubts from the moment you met him. We tainted your view." She rose from her seat and came to Eva, hugging her tightly. "I'm so sorry. So very sorry."

Cole scampered into the room as Mildred turned to him, wiping tears from her eyes. "Why are you crying, Aunt Mildred?"

Mildred chuckled. "I'm happy, Cole, happy because I have such a wonderful family."

Cole thought about this for a moment. "And that includes me?"

Mildred pulled him into a hug. "Most certainly you."

The doorbell rang again, and Cole raced to answer it. We heard Mr. Dearman asking for Eva.

Eva blotted away the last of her tears. "I look a terrible fright."

"You are as beautiful as ever," I assured her.

Eva rose and met him in the doorway to the hall. He stood before her, twisting his hat round and round in his hands. He glanced into the parlor and took a deep breath. "Good afternoon, ladies. I hope you will excuse the intrusion, but it is most urgent that I speak with Miss Delacroix and explain myself."

"It's quite all right," I said. "Eva, why don't you go out to the gazebo so you can talk in private?"

Sara Jane sighed with disappointment as they headed outside.

The Announcement

I led Bertram out back, filled with remorse. I could hardly look him in the face, ashamed that I had placed so little faith in him. When we reached the gazebo, he took my arm and turned me to face him.

His forehead was beaded in sweat, and he licked his lips several times before speaking. "Please forgive me, my darling. I understand you could only think the worst when you found me with such a person. I assure you it was not as it appeared."

I put a hand on his cheek. "I received a note from Mrs. Silks not ten minutes ago. She explained the nature of your meeting."

"I know it must have shocked you to see me with her. I can't apologize enough for any pain this misunderstanding caused."

"Oh, Bertram, it's I who must apologize. I doubted your honor when I should have trusted you. Mrs. Silks's note showed me what a fool I am."

"She offered to write you immediately. I am grateful for that." He let out a long sigh. "She is a rough and unseemly woman but not unkind. I must say, she drives a hard bargain in her business dealings. I feel some sympathy for her and the difficult life she has led."

We sat down in the gazebo chairs next to each other. "Why didn't you tell me your client's business was with her? You didn't have to reveal the nature of their relationship, but I should have known to prevent this kind of situation."

Bertram ran a hand through the top of his hair, making it as mussed as I had ever seen it. "My client instructed me to keep the matter secret. He's a well-known member of Boston society now, but he had a wild youth and fathered a child with Mrs. Silks. He is at least honorable enough to take responsibility for the girl's rearing and education. I didn't want to offend your sensibilities by relaying the story."

"Goodness." I chuckled. "You must not think of me as a delicate flower. I have not been so sheltered from the realities of life. If we are to be together, you need to take me into your confidence. I would never betray it."

He ducked his head. "Of course not. You are an intelligent woman of the world, and I have not treated you as such." He gave me a rueful smile. "You are my first true love, dear Eva. I fear I have many lessons to learn. Please be patient and guide me."

His words evoked the most tender feelings possible. How could I not love this man who intended only the best for me?

Bertram bent down on one knee in front of my chair. He took both my hands in his. "I've declared my feelings for you many times, and we've talked of a future together. At last we have Mildred's approval. I love you completely and cannot live without you. Please agree to marry me, Eva Delacroix."

"I *will* marry you. I love you with all my heart."

"What about your mother?"

"She will have to accept my choice. I cannot worry about her."

"I had planned to ask you this evening." He pulled a box from his coat pocket and opened it, revealing a gold and sapphire ring. "This was my grandmother's." He slipped it onto my finger. It was slightly large, but that could be fixed.

"It's beautiful and perfect. Just as you are."

He stood and pulled me up into his arms. We had never stolen more than a few chaste kisses in brief moments alone. Now we kissed with all the pent-up emotions and uncertainty that had clouded our courtship, the passion held in restraint these many months.

I pulled away, trying to catch my breath, knowing this was the moment to speak my truth. It had been a tumultuous time, from the moment we met, through the months of my illness, culminating in this remarkable day. The drama with Mother and Mildred had only strengthened my resolve. I must be free to pursue happiness in every aspect of my life and not bend to the will of others. Not even Bertram's.

"A friend recently told me that before marrying I must clearly explain my expectations, so there are no disappointments. I have several conditions to present to you."

Bertram blinked several times. "Of course. Whatever can they be?"

I took a deep breath. "I wrote to Bryn Mawr four weeks ago. I plan to complete my final year of college and earn my degree before we marry. They wrote back to say I am welcome to return this September."

He pondered the proposal and smiled. "Yes, of course. As much as I'd like the wedding to be tomorrow, I suppose it will take until next June to plan one, anyway." He laughed. "At

335

least from what I observed when my sisters married." He raised an eyebrow. "Is there anything else?"

"After we marry and I move to Boston, I would like to apply to Boston University to earn a master's degree. I wish to teach at a college."

"I hope you realize you have no need to work. I am quite comfortably fixed."

"I understand. While your love brings me great happiness and strength, I need to follow my dreams as well. I could not be content otherwise. I need your support to pursue a career, as I will support your career."

"I do hope we'll have children one day," he said, his voice tentative.

"Of course. We'll make it work, as Lida did with William." I kissed him gently. "And one more thing."

He grinned. "This is quite a list you've been preparing."

"I plan to be active in the women's suffrage movement until we have gained the vote for every woman in this country."

"I wouldn't have it any other way." He put his forehead against mine. "We shall each have our lives while being husband and wife, a family. I cannot imagine a happier circumstance."

I glanced up and caught Sara Jane and Katherine peering out the kitchen window. They jumped back, and the curtain fell in place.

I laughed. "We best tell my family."

We walked hand in hand to the parlor and found Sara Jane back in her chair, sitting primly with my sisters. Cole was sprawled on the floor, adding a brown moth to his bug collection. Everyone looked up with expectant eyes.

Bertram cleared his throat. "Eva and I have an announcement to make."

Chapter 37 **AUNT EFFIE & FRANKLIN**

Regrets

Thursday, July 18, 1901

Dearest Niece,

I am full of regret over a dreadful mistake that is of my making. I write to put your mind at ease. As you know, your mother is quite perturbed with you and won't write at the moment. She'll get over it and, in fact, is no longer staying in bed, since that failed to bring you scurrying home.

I know she wrote you about Miss Henrietta Hamilton's visit to her cousin in Eudora the week before last, where she claimed to have seen Franklin enter the home of her cousin's neighbor. Miss Hamilton was only too delighted to report the alleged transgression to me, being a terrible gossip. At the time I could not believe a man as stalwart as Franklin could be so foolish and thoughtless.

I began to question Miss Hamilton's story after running into her at the church social yesterday. She mentioned seeing me at Taylor's Dry Goods on Saturday and wondered why I hadn't spoken to her. I told her I have not shopped at Taylor's in several weeks. She admitted her eyesight is not as sharp as it once was.

I decided to do a bit of sleuthing regarding her story. I felt like a regular Sherlock Holmes! Miss Hamilton called on her cousin in Eudora on a Monday and saw the man (supposedly Franklin) enter the neighbor's home at three o'clock. Why would Franklin leave the bank in the middle of the afternoon on a Monday to travel to Eudora? I visited his bank during the noon hour today, when I knew he would be at lunch. I spoke with the assistant manager, Mr. Lennox, and asked if he recalled Franklin being gone that day. He assured me Franklin remains at the bank all day, every day, from nine o'clock to at least six. The only time he leaves is during the lunch hour to dine at Miller's Café. Thus, we can now conclude Miss Hamilton is a nearsighted old fool and no more saw Franklin in Eudora than she saw me at Taylor's Dry Goods.

Franklin may be a serious, quiet man who isn't as demonstrative as some husbands, but he is unquestionably loyal and trustworthy. I can only apologize for Miss Hamilton and the fact that I entertained the possibility of truth in her accusations. It has undoubtedly caused you a great deal of worry.

I received your lovely letter from Manitou. What a thrilling excursion. I look forward to your return and want a full accounting of everything you have done in Colorado. I'm delighted to hear your enthusiasm for Mr. Dearman. I do hope we shall hear wedding bells before long. And please convince Lida to visit Lawrence again soon. She can stay with me, and we need not even tell your mother. Even I am getting rebellious at my advanced age!

340

With love, Aunt Effie

Thursday, July 18, 1901

Dear Mildred,

Your second wire arrived today. I cannot understand what is going through your mind. I've never known you to be so unconcerned about your mother. Or me. I share your sympathies toward Eva and Mr. Dearman. I feel he is most likely an acceptable young man, and Eva should be allowed to make her own decision regarding her future. Your mother's dissatisfaction with him is based on her needs, not Eva's. She demands too much of her daughters. I appreciate that you are enjoying your visit and do not wish to return home early. Please stay. I will make do and work with Aunt Effie to calm your mother.

I sense you are unhappy with me for some reason, but I have no idea what I've done wrong. Perhaps I should have written more, but work has been particularly demanding of late. I am sorry if I complained about your mother and Biscuit and Jessie being gone. The house feels empty without you here, and nothing runs properly. Please forgive me.

Who is Mrs. Becker? Is this someone Jessie will know? Speaking of which, I received a note from Jessie today that she is returning tomorrow. The house will be clean again, and I'll be able take meals in my own home.

On another note, I read a most informative article last night in the July issue of the Delineator Magazine *about the Pan-American Exposition in Buffalo, New York. I must say,*

341

the descriptions of grand buildings, such as the Electric Tower and Temple of Music, sparked my interest. The vast grounds include gardens with fountains and exhibits from all over the world. Let me quote to you, "...the latest inventions in wireless telegraphy, the newest things in electric lighting and the telephone, electricity applied to vehicles, and lastly the X-ray." Perhaps more appealing to you might be the network of canals and bridges, which allow visitors to ride in gondolas as if in Venice, Italy. At night over three hundred thousand lights turn the grounds into a veritable fairyland. It sounds intriguing.

It set me to thinking that we are due a nice vacation together. You mentioned the Chautauqua in New York before, but I think we might enjoy a visit to the Buffalo Exposition with a side trip to Niagara Falls. It would be pleasant to spend time together, away from work and Lawrence. The audit of the bank will be completed in early September. If you have recovered from your trip to Denver, we could go soon after when the weather will still be temperate. Give it some thought.

As you know, I am not good at expressing my sentiments, but your absence has made me realize how much I value you. I miss you and look forward to your return on August third.

Your devoted husband,
Franklin

Chapter 38   **MILDRED**

Thankful

Sunday, July 21, 1901

Dear Aunt Effie,

I received your letter Saturday with the greatest relief. In my heart I found it unfathomable that Franklin would betray me. But the possibility hurt me deeply, and for the past few weeks I've been filled with doubts. Thank heavens you were clever enough to recognize Miss Hamilton's poor eyesight and how unlikely it would be for Franklin to take off from the bank for an illicit assignation. Sherlock Holmes would be most impressed!

Indeed, wedding bells will ring next summer. Eva and Mr. Dearman are officially engaged, and we are celebrating the occasion at every turn. I admit I've had more than a few glasses of champagne of late. (Don't tell the ladies at the Temperance Union.) Mr. Dearman leaves for Boston this coming Sunday, and we return home the following Saturday. Lida is throwing a small party next Saturday for the happy couple.

Eva and I will inform Mother of the engagement once we arrive home. I wager she'll throw one of her fits and take to her bed again. But once she realizes her tactics will not have the slightest influence on Eva or any of us, she'll accept the inevitable. I can no longer be estranged from the people I love and care about because of her.

Lida sends you her best and looks forward to seeing you when she comes for Eva's wedding. It has been wonderful getting to know my dear sister once more after all the missed years. We will never allow anything to come between us again.

With love from all your girls,
Mildred

Sunday, July 21, 1901

Dear Franklin,

I cannot begin to tell you how your last letter has cheered me. I apologize for not being more forthright in my correspondence, which has led us to several misunderstandings. The time spent in Colorado with Lida, her children, and her friends, not to mention Mr. Dearman, has changed my perspective on life. It is difficult to explain in a letter the satisfaction and happiness I now feel, but I look forward to sharing my discoveries with you on returning home.

Eva and Mr. Dearman are engaged, and I have given my full blessing. He is a stellar soul and and completely devoted to Eva. The wedding will take place next summer.

I miss being home with you. More than that, I miss the closeness we shared in earlier years. Growing older, along with the disappointment of not having children, has worn away our happiness. I yearn to reestablish that connection.

Some years ago, you suggested adoption. I was not willing to accept the idea at the time, to have all of Lawrence know of my failure to become a mother. Now I'd like to reconsider. Although we are in middle age, we could adopt several older children. There is certainly an ever-present need for families to love and care for orphans. I'm sorry to write all this in a letter, but it will give you time to think about my idea before I come home.

I enthusiastically accept your proposal for a trip to Buffalo and the Exposition. It sounds delightful. I relish the thought of time away from Lawrence together. More than anything else, I want you to have a nice vacation. You work too hard.

I am most thankful to have you awaiting my return. Please give Biscuit a pat on the head for me and say hello to Jessie.

With love,
Mildred

P.S. Forget I mentioned Mrs. Becker. I will explain when I get home.

Chapter 39   **BISCUIT**

Awaiting Your Arrival

WESTERN UNION   JULY 24, 1901

TO: MILDRED BOLTON

FRANKLIN AND I ARE GOOD FRIENDS NOW. WE
MISS YOU AND LOOK FORWARD TO YOUR RETURN.
WE WILL BE A FAMILY ONCE MORE.

LOVE, BISCUIT

An Independent Woman

M r. Abbott refilled champagne glasses while Katherine made the rounds with a pitcher of lemonade for temperance supporters. Cole followed, looking very proud of himself as he passed out napkins and gave advice on where bowls of sugared almonds could be found.

Mrs. Bradford offered yet another toast to Aunt Eva and Mr. Dearman. "I wish this charming couple a very happy marriage. And success in your career, Miss Delacroix."

Mr. Dearman gazed at Aunt Eva with adoring eyes. "It will be my greatest joy to see my soon-to-be bride pursue her many talents."

"With Mr. Dearman at my side, everything is possible," Aunt Eva joined in. "The only other thing I can ask for to complete my happiness is the speedy approval of women's suffrage for the whole nation."

"Here, here! I second that and join the campaign," Aunt Mildred called out.

Mama smiled and took a sip from her glass. We had but a week to plan the engagement party for this Saturday evening. Mr. Dearman's work requires him to return to Boston the next morning. Happily, almost everyone invited was able to attend, despite the short notice.

The guests mingled on the backyard lawn next to flowerbeds bursting with coral tea roses and bright-pink dahlias. A long table covered in a white linen cloth proffered an array of dainty sandwiches, hot cheese and mushroom cups, potato salad, and tomatoes and cucumber compote. Katherine's famous lemon chiffon cake sat at the far end, tempting even those who cared nothing for sweets.

I stood next to Aunt Mildred as she allowed Mr. Abbott to refill her champagne glass for the second time. "Just this once, as it's a special occasion." She appeared a bit tipsy as she entertained Mr. and Mrs. Brown with a story about Aunt Effie. "She's a delight and has proved a clever sleuth. Just recently she investigated the rumors of a wayward husband, reported to her by a nearsighted friend. Luckily the story proved unfounded." No names were mentioned as the tale unfolded. "It's the epitome of life in a small town like Lawrence. Gossip is a full-time occupation," she concluded, chuckling.

Aunt Mildred had finally shared the story of Uncle Franklin's mistaken identity with Aunt Eva and me, which clearly had given her a turn. Over the past week letters and wires had been scuttling back and forth between them. She seemed extremely happy. I envied their plans to travel to New York for the Pan-American Exposition.

I joined Bernadette as she told Miss Meredith about her journalism classes and writing for the Pembroke College paper. "I'm afraid the articles are a bit boring, really," Bernadette said. "Nothing exciting happens on campus."

"It's the experience that counts, Miss Abbott. It's invaluable," Miss Meredith assured her. "I look forward to our meeting on Monday. I will impart what pearls of wisdom I can muster on a career in journalism and show you around the paper. There are several writers you must meet. And we'll plant the seed with my father to give you a job next summer."

Bernadette's eyes sparkled. "I can't thank you enough. It's so exciting."

Miss Meredith turned to me and raised her glass. "And a toast to the newest member of the *Denver Post*. Father was very impressed with your drawings, Sara Jane. I hear you have an assignment this next week."

I let out a happy sigh. "I'm going to sketch Senator Blakely when he speaks to the Knights of Columbus on Wednesday evening. I hope I can capture it properly." I had never been as nervous as when I interviewed with Mr. Meredith, the paper's editor, and Mr. Martin, the head of the design department. They told me my drawings, including recent sketches from our trip to Pikes Peak, showed a great deal of promise. Technically, I wasn't an employee, but would be paid a flat rate for each sketch they published. Mama told me I couldn't commit to more than one assignment each week, and my schoolwork had to take priority.

Rose appeared at my side and took my arm, leading me toward the food table. As we passed by Aunt Mildred put a hand on Rose's arm. "Rose, dear, did Sara Jane tell you she is going to help me pick out a new traveling suit on Monday? She has a wonderful eye for color and style. You're welcome to accompany us. And please tell your mother we shall come by her shop so I can purchase a new hat. I'd like something

Elaine Russell

with a bit of flair this time." Then Aunt Mildred turned back to her conversation with Mrs. Brown.

"Do you think we could steal a piece of cake?" Rose asked with a mischievous smile. "It looks so delicious. Or maybe we could sneak a glass of champagne."

"Oh Rose, I can't do that. I make my first confession tomorrow."

"Oh, that," Rose scoffed. "I bet you can't even think of anything you've done wrong."

Ever since my talk with Mama about our new religion, my fears and confusion had subsided. I interpreted the tenets of the Catholic church as they felt true and comfortable to me. Talking to the priest in confession didn't really worry me, but I wanted to keep it simple. I planned to say I had sinned by being impatient with Cole, a minor infraction. I saw no need to mention my sins of omission as everything had turned out well in the end. I chose to focus on my new faith by emulating the saints—that is, by being a good person and showing kindness to others.

"I don't want to start by confessing I stole champagne."

She waved a hand of dismissal. "Nothing will happen."

"Anyway, Mama says I can try a small glass on my sixteenth birthday in two weeks. You can come for dinner and have some, too."

"Okay." Her face brightened. "I put aside my romance novel for now and I've written ten pages of a new story based on your aunt Eva and Mr. Dearman. Of course, the names are different, and I've changed a few details. I think it's my best work ever. I can't wait for you to read it."

I laughed and put an arm over Rose's shoulders. "I hope I have a starring role."

352

Just then I caught sight of Mama, standing next to Mr. Abbott, as they visited with Mr. and Mrs. Forest. Everyone laughed at something Mr. Abbott said. He fit in easily with Mama's friends, and I liked the way his presence lightened Mama's mood.

After Aunt Eva and Mr. Dearman announced their engagement, I lay in bed that night reflecting on Mama's life. I thought of the many difficult choices and sacrifices she'd faced, from following her heart to marry Papa to earning her medical degree, while keeping Cole and me whole after the loss of Peter and Papa. She was one of the most courageous and independent women I could ever hope to meet.

The next afternoon, I asked her to come out back to talk. "Seeing Aunt Eva so happy has made me think that you deserve to be happy, too. If you want to marry Mr. Abbott, you should. I approve."

Her eyes welled with tears. "Dear girl, you don't know what that means to me. I have given the situation a great deal of thought." She brushed a tear from her cheek. "You know I'll never love anyone as I did your father, but I'm very fond of Mr. Abbott and enjoy his companionship. Perhaps down the road we will marry. But not quite yet."

I admit I felt a tremendous relief that her decision was not imminent. "I'd like to finish school at St. Mary's with Rose."

"Of course. And I'm not about to give up practicing medicine. I'm not sure how we will manage to integrate our lives in Denver and on his ranch. Time will tell."

"Have you told him?"

"I wrote to say I'd like to build our friendship and spend more time together." She smiled. "He thinks that's an excellent idea."

353

"I do like him, Mama. And Bernadette is wonderful."

"We'll take it slow."

As the sun drew lower in the sky, the air turned cooler, and shadows stretched across the yard. Katherine cut pieces of cake, and everyone lined up to take one. Cole took Mr. Abbott's hand, leading him to the table, chattering away. Mama put an arm around Aunt Mildred's shoulders and whispered in her ear. They laughed.

When my aunts had arrived in Denver at the end of June, I'd sensed the summer might bring surprises, but I never imagined the events that had transpired. Mama and her sisters, three independent women of strong convictions, had weathered their differences (and the long reach of my grandmother) to embrace the bonds of family. Love and respect brought us all together, a kinship of the heart. I admired each for choosing her path in life—Mama and Aunt Eva for pursuing an education and career and choosing the men they loved despite opposition, and Aunt Mildred for reexamining her past and opening her mind to new ideas and a renewal of her marriage. These brave women would continue to lead the fight for the women's vote and equality. I planned to follow in their footsteps to help other women find their rightful place.

For the time being, I savored this happy moment, surrounded by family and friends, because I knew how capricious life could be. I wasn't sure if my prayers to a host of saints had helped bring about this joyful outcome. Or perhaps it was simply the strength and love of like-minded women supporting one another and working for a better world.

Acknowledgements

I want to thank editor Jennifer Pooley, who gave me excellent suggestions on an early version of this story. A big thank you to my writing pals, Susanne Sommer and Mary Euretig, for listening to drafts of chapters and offering comments. I appreciate my friend, Jackie Pope, who read the manuscript as well. And finally thanks to my husband Roy McDonald who is excellent at checking historical facts. I don't know what I would do without him always cheering me on.

ABOUT THE AUTHOR

Elaine Russell is an award winning author of the novel *Across the Mekong River* and a number of children's books, including the young adult novel *Montana in A Minor,* the *Martin McMillan* middle grade mystery series, and the middle grade picture book, *All About Thailand.* Elaine lives with her husband in Northern California and part time on the Island of Kauai.

To contact Elaine:
www.elainerussell.info

Made in the USA
Monee, IL
25 June 2021